THE BUTTERFLIES ARE FREE

THE BUTTERFLIES ARE FREE

Anne-Marie Vukelic

CHIVERS

British Library Cataloguing in Publication Data available

This Large Print edition published by AudioGO Ltd, Bath, 2012.
Published by arrangement with Robert Hale Ltd.

U.K. Hardcover   ISBN   978 1 4458 2588 5
U.K. Softcover   ISBN   978 1 4458 2589 2

Printed and bound in Great Britain by
MPG Books Group Limited

Author's Note

To suit the purpose and flow of a novel some facts and dates in the lives of Dickens and his contemporaries have been adapted. An appendix is included to clarify where this may have occurred.

Acknowledgements

I would like to thank Mr Roger Flavell (Oxon) for unlimited access to his library and for ever sharpening my knowledge and use of the English Language.

For George and Eleanor

'I only ask to be free: the butterflies are free . . . '

BLEAK HOUSE— CHARLES DICKENS

Chapter 1

July 1856

Tavistock House, London

The Narrative of Charles Dickens Junior

My mother approached the pavilion carefully carrying a tray of tea for Mr Collins, who was seated at a wicker table engaged in conversation with himself, just the same as if there had been someone sitting right next to him.

'He wants me to tell her the secret of the hidden letter, but I will not—No!'

Mr Collins raised his voice in vehement objection and Mama almost dropped the tray in alarm as she entered the pavilion.

'It is in the Myrtle Room and has been hidden there since the death of Rosamund,' he continued, in a state of agitation.

'Mr Collins, are you quite well, sir? I have your tea here.'

Wilkie Collins blinked at my mother behind his thick-lensed glasses, looked at his pen and then at the paper.

'Ah, yes, Mrs Dickens, I was just – er – well, he has gone again now, but yes, tea would be very good, madam; so good of you to bring it out to me yourself.'

Mama wondered if she would ever become used to Mr Collins strange behaviour: it had no doubt been my father's idea of a joke to send her out with the tea, she told me crossly upon returning to the house.

Mr Collins was much addicted to laudanum, which he took for his rheumatism, but it produced in him the most bizarre of symptoms. He believed that he had a double, who accompanied him wherever he went. Of course, one could never address this subject with him, for if you asked him to whom he had been speaking he would look at you askance as if *you* were the one who was quite mad.

From the house I looked out of the dining-room window to the garden. Mama was heading hurriedly back indoors and I could see Mr Collins in the pavilion, taking out his tincture bottle again and tapping the contents into his drink. He had been sitting there all morning, working on a new play that he and my father proposed to put on later in the year, but I wondered how he had such patience when my father re-wrote almost everything that Mr Collins put down on paper. He changed phrases, altered lines, rewrote parts, so that the thing might as well have been written by Papa himself.

The inspiration behind the play was the loss of Sir John Franklyn's men during the Arctic expedition of 1845. My father had taken a great interest in the idea that there may have been survivors who had never been found, and thus he began to conceive the idea of a story which would form the basis of a performance. But as he was so busy with the production of his current novel and the oversight of his periodical, *Household Words,* he had charged Mr Collins with the actual task of putting the plot down on paper.

I could see it now: Papa would play a principal character—if he could induce the audience to tears, all the better—he would drill the actors, organize the costumes, direct the staging. I pitied the poor fellows who would be employed to paint the scenery as he would surely stand over them watching for the smallest mistake. Nothing could ever be good enough for Papa unless he put his own hand to it last.

*   *   *

I had returned from Germany for the summer. I had been sent there with the purpose of learning the language, but on my return I sensed that all was not well at Tavistock House. I asked Katie if she could feel it too.

My sister was attired in gingham, and seated at the table where she had arranged a vase of flowers, and was now absorbed in painting a watercolour of them.

'Does Mama always stay in her room so much these days, Katie?' I asked.

She did not look up but simply nodded her head in response to my question.

'Yesterday I did not see her until dinner, and today she came out only at Papa's request that she take tea to Mr Collins. Now she has returned immediately to her room again. What on earth is wrong with her?'

Katie sighed, exasperated that I was disturbing her in her artistic endeavours and dashed her brush into the jar of water on the table, before wiping her hands on a paint-stained cloth.

'Charley, you know that Mama has not been quite herself since little Edward was born. Papa is very busy these days, and I think that Mama still dwells on the death of baby Dora and how things might have been.'

It had been five years since my sister had died.

'But they hardly address one another, Katie. Papa consults with Aunt Georgina about almost everything, whether it is in the house or connected with his work. It is as if Mama were invisible.'

The conversation was making Katie uncomfortable. She loved our father dearly and did not like to hear a word said against him; her cheeks coloured a little with temper.

'You are not here to see how difficult Mama can be sometimes, Charley. I am convinced that she does not appreciate everything that Aunt Georgina does for us. I think that she—'

Katie stopped as she realized that my mother had entered the room, but Mama was not at all perturbed by Katie's words, for she seemed preoccupied with looking for something which she appeared to have lost.

'Have you seen my embroidery, dear?' she said abstractedly. 'I am certain that I left it here when I came down a little while earlier, and now it has disappeared.'

I noticed that Mama had mis-buttoned her dress, and that her hair was coming unpinned a little, and I went to her aid immediately. 'Do not fret, Mama. I am sure that it will be here somewhere. Why don't you sit with us a little while and I will ask Alice to fetch some tea for you. Katie and I can look for your sewing.'

Mama looked anxious, and twisted her string of pearls around her fingers, glancing nervously out of the window at the pavilion.

'I feel so uneasy when Mr Collins is here. Your papa insists that I come down for dinner lest the man think me rude, but otherwise, I am much happier in my room, dear.'

At the sound of my father's study door opening out in the hallway, Mama did not know whether to sit down or remain standing and appeared quite flustered.

'Is there no end to the jumping on and off of stairs, and the stamping up and down of them? Why is it that my children seem to have as many feet as a millipede?'

The door flew open and Papa entered the

room. He did not look at Mama but addressed Katie instead.

'Do you know where your aunt is to be found, Lucifer-box?' *Lucifer-box* was Papa's pet-name for Katie, for as much as they loved one another, they both shared the same short temper.

'I last saw her talking to Cook about tonight's supper, Papa. She will no doubt still be in the kitchen.'

Papa took his pocket-watch from his waistcoat and examined the time.

'I want her to accompany me on my afternoon walk. No point asking Collins, he's too busy talking gibberish again.' My father backed out of the room, closing the door upon himself and then, almost as an afterthought, he pushed it open again slowly, peeped around it, and addressed Mama.

'All right, are we?' He did not wait for an answer, but before she could respond, nodded, 'Good, good', and then closed the door again.

I looked at Katie as if to make my point. All was not well at Tavistock House.

*   *   *

I had finished my schooling at Eton now, and Papa never let me forget what a debt of gratitude we owed to Miss Angela Burdett-Coutts. My father had first become acquainted with the heiress when he was in the early days of his fame, and together they had heightened awareness for social reform and carried out many acts of charity. I, however, did not want to be indebted to anyone but remain free to establish my own identity and to make my own way in life.

How many times had I been reminded that my father's name was my best possession in life? Now, I not only bore the same name as the most famous man in England, but found myself beholden to the richest heiress in England who, out of friendship for my father, had paid for my education at Eton.

She was also, my father reminded me, one of the most industrious of women who not only assisted with the running of the family bank, but involved herself actively in a wide range of philanthropic projects, and I should learn from her purposefulness.

One of these causes was Urania Cottage in Shepherd's Bush, a home for fallen women, which my father had set up with Miss Burdett-Coutts's assistance. I was very curious about the young women who had repented of their past, and were now engaged in learning skills which might enable them to start out on a new life. I was curious also how my father seemed so ready to forgive the defective path that these flawed young woman had chosen to take, but was so exacting and unforgiving about any weakness on the part of his own children.

He continued, 'Yes, without the patronage

of that dear lady, Charley, you would not have had such a privileged education. You have much to thank her for.'

Papa was now standing in the hallway putting on his jacket in readiness for his outing.

'Yes, Father, I know. You tell me every time I come home.'

He was not listening. 'I have asked her to enquire at Barings Bank about a position there for you.'

'But Papa, I have not yet decided upon what path I mean to take . . .'

'And that is precisely the reason why someone must decide it for you, Charley. You cannot let the world pass you by without taking a firm grip on the rudder of life and steering your course with a clear end in sight.'

I had absolutely no desire to join the bank at all. I had once mentioned to Papa that perhaps I, too, would like to write, but he immediately stamped upon the embers of that idea.

'One needs stamina and determination to succeed as a writer, my boy. You have a little too much of your mother in you to make a success in that quarter.'

My aunt descended the stairs, and my father's face lit up.

'Ah, Georgie, there you are! Ready for our perambulation? I thought that we might go out as far as Holborn today, I feel as if I need to blow off a little steam.'

8

'Of course, dear, whatever you wish,' my aunt replied, pulling on her gloves.

In contrast to Mama, her sister was a vision of neatness. The buttons of her dress did not dare to be misaligned, and her hair was firmly fixed in its place.

Papa took her hand and patted it fondly, 'Then let me fetch my hat, and we'll be off.'

As he bounded up the staircase, my aunt turned and addressed me coolly.

'I hope that you appreciate everything that your father is endeavouring to do for you, Charley. You must never disappoint him: you do understand that, don't you?'

I gritted my teeth. Inside I was churning with anger. I wanted to tell her to go to hell, tell my father to go to hell; but instead I smiled and nodded.

'Yes, Aunt, I understand perfectly.'

Chapter 2

October 1856

Folkestone

My Dear Collins
I cannot tell you how grateful I am for all that you have done with regard to 'The Play', and, without the least objection, you

have readily accepted all of my suggestions and alterations. I am confident that the end result will be worthy of your good name and set you further along the path as an established writer.

With all my other commitments, I find myself to be in a constant state of restlessness, so that I can hardly put my mind upon any one thing without feeling that my thoughts should be elsewhere. In a bid to enjoy a moment's respite, I wandered back again in my imagination to those days we spent in Paris together over the summer, when we amused ourselves in the city.

Do you remember how my attention was engaged by a striking young woman wearing an Indian fringed shawl about her shoulders? I told you then that I meant to search her out and follow her, but I never did find her again.

Well, the night before I left for Folkestone, I had the most curious of experiences that has left me in a state of wonder and with a great deal to ponder upon, and I sense that my life is about to change in a way that I could never have believed possible . . .

The rattle of carriage and cartwheels had stopped for the night, and darkness enveloped the great spire of St James's. The thoroughfares were empty, but this particular strip of road is always a nefarious place to pass whatever the time of day. At night, however, it holds all that is offensive: for this is not respectable Belgravia, Bloomsbury or Bedford Square, this is the corner of The Haymarket and Piccadilly and, as Dickens's footsteps approached, a face emerged from the darkness and a hand grasped at his coat-tails.

'It is a little late to be out alone, *monsieur*, will you not keep me company?'

Dickens stopped and slowly took in her features, and then his face broke out in to a smile.

'Well, well, well, upon my soul! If it's not the little lady who inhabited my dreams in Paris!'

The wind rippled through the fringes of the Indian shawl draped around her shoulders. She loosened it a little and smiled. 'And why would that be, *monsieur?*'

'I saw your face in that great French city during the summer months and I could not get you out of my mind. I tried to look for you again, but you had disappeared.'

She smiled her beguiling smile again. 'Well, here I am, *monsieur.*'

Dickens decided, once again, just as he had in Paris, that she could only be described as 'handsome, regardless'. He offered her his arm, 'Would you care to accompany me to Le Café de l'Europe? Their lobster is excellent and I would be most grateful if you would keep me company.'

11

She hesitated, curious about his manner for a moment. She had grown used to rough speech and harsh treatment; it was part of the life that she had come to know since leaving Paris, but his gentleness intrigued her. It had been a long time since someone had been gentle, and she thought how lonely he looked. It was the kind of loneliness that comes to a man of a certain age, the kind of loneliness that she had seen many times before.

She took hold of his arm decisively and nodded. As they walked, the sound of singing could be heard in a tavern. She had not eaten since a breakfast of cold mutton pie and the smell of roast beef roused her hunger.

Midnight was approaching and the streets, which boasted a large number of gin-palaces, were now beginning to fill with people again. The carriages that had been idle at the roadside were now in demand by the patrons of the theatres and gaming houses who tumbled out onto the pavements.

She noticed that Dickens had turned up the collar of his coat as if he were suddenly afraid of being recognized, but it was not an unusual response from a man who was keeping company with a woman such as herself and she thought nothing more of it.

Upon arriving at the Café de l'Europe, they entered the establishment and were greeted by a waiter who was heavily laden with supper-trays, and he led them to a quiet corner behind a screen. They passed whiskered gentlemen in their black-velvet evening-jackets, seated opposite ladies whose crinolines slowed the progress of those who wished to pass.

Lest the waiter should disappear among the multitude, Dickens ordered lobster for himself and his companion. He then drew back a chair and, once she was seated, took his place opposite her. He thought that her features in the candlelight were more beautiful than he had remembered. She was so like someone else that he had known in his youth, and just for a moment he forgot all the cares that came with being the man that he was.

'My dear, I have to confess that my purpose in bringing you here is not entirely what you might have expected, that is to say that my purpose is to speak to you of a proposition that is dear to my heart.'

She was quite used to unusual propositions, but true to his word what followed next was unexpected.

'I run a charitable home which would offer you some respite from this life you are leading, which I sense has not come about as a result of your own wickedness. I would like to help you.'

Her face took on a look of amusement and she poured herself a glass of wine from a jug on the table, took a large gulp, which she held in her mouth for a moment, before swallowing and speaking.

'*Monsieur,* you know nothing about me or

my wickedness. If your intention in bringing me here has been to "save" me then you are wasting your time and mine.'

She picked up her purse from the table and got to her feet. 'Good evening, *monsieur*.'

Dickens reached out a hand and clasped her gently around the wrist.

'I am sorry, I appear to have offended you when my intention was to help. Please, *mademoiselle,* don't leave.'

She looked at his hair and thought how luxuriant it must have been at one time and wondered how his face would look if it was a little less lined. There was something about him that she could not put words to. She acknowledged that, despite his middle years, he was still a handsome man.

'Forgive me?'

His hand, which had remained clasped around her wrist, loosened again as she sat down and he smiled.

'Very well, *monsieur, I* will tell you my history, and then you will know that I can never be saved from my wickedness, as you call it. But first you must tell me about your own history, for looking at you I conceive that it must be a very interesting one.'

She was surprised that an expression of sadness crossed his face, and he appeared reluctant to speak.

'*Monsieur?* What is it that has made you sad?'

He poured himself a glass of wine.

'When I was a very young man, I was deeply in love with a young woman named Maria Beadnell, who was every bit as beautiful and wilful as you are. I gave her my heart completely, unreservedly, in the foolish belief that she had given her heart to me. After exchanging secret letters for three years, her father—who was a very wealthy man—found out about our friendship and sent her away. I was convinced that she would write, but although I wrote to her daily and waited with my heart in torture, I received not one word in reply. When she finally returned to England, she refused to see me and I had to accept that her feelings for me had never been as mine had been for her.'

The waiter approached with two plates of lobster and placed them on the table. Dickens nodded that all was satisfactory and the man left.

'I see,' said the woman. 'And you have never forgotten her?'

'I have never forgotten the *memory* of her, or how she made me feel. And since that day I have never experienced the intensity of such feelings again.'

She hesitated for a moment as if she were about to suggest something, but instead she asked, 'So you are not married, *monsieur?*' He looked sad again.

'I am married, but . . .'

'You no longer love your wife?'

'If I say that her presence irritates me, it would not be too far from the truth, but I can only suppose that she must be unhappy too.'

Dickens noticed how hungry his companion was, as she ate large bites of her dinner in rapid succession.

'And now you find yourself trapped, no?'

'I could not have described my feelings more accurately, *mademoiselle*. It is always yesterday with me, or else tomorrow, and never today. I feel so restless that I believe that I shall combust and perish.'

She put down her knife and fork for a moment, and ran her tongue over her lips, her initial hunger satisfied.

'I understand something of restlessness, myself. I once belonged to the aristocratic circles of French society, but I never truly felt at home. I married a man of title but quickly found that I did not love him at all, and knew that I had made a match that would only cause me unhappiness. I took up with his *grand-ami* and we left Paris together, but he abandoned me as soon as we came to London, and I began the life that I have now chosen. I emphasize the word *chosen* for that is what it is, *monsieur*, a choice. I feel more at home in this strange, unpredictable life, than I ever felt within the constraints placed upon me by my birth. You labour under a misapprehension if you believe that a woman could never choose this life.'

16

Dickens was confused: it did not make sense. This was not his ideal of a woman at all. He was both upset and, yet, strangely intrigued.

'But you are at risk of harm—death even, every night that you continue such a life in this violent city.'

'And you, sir, I suspect, have achieved everything that you ever hoped to achieve, and yet you are at risk from unhappiness and death from overwork. Perhaps, you should take a risk yourself.'

She took a final bite of her meal, threw back her head to drain the remainder of her wine, picked up her purse and, leaving Dickens deep in thought, she disappeared into the night.

Chapter 3

November 1856
Tavistock House, London

The Narrative of Charles Dickens Junior

My father had returned from Folkestone where he had taken a short break to avoid callers and to make progress with his current novel, but since his return he had been more mercurial than ever, as if something were preoccupying his thoughts. He had not spoken to me this morning, much beyond asking me to pass him the salt for his eggs, but when he got up from the breakfast table, he wiped his mouth with a napkin, threw it down on the table and said, 'I wish you well this morning, Charley, but remember, as I have told you before, don't disappoint me.'

A neckcloth was wrapped several times around my throat and tied in a bow at the front, and a satin waistcoat was buttoned almost up to my chin. My glovess were leather, purchased especially for this day by my father—'*a sure* sign of a gentleman, my boy'—and today I had no other end in view but the bank.

I had visited the bank on a number of occasions with my father and observed the clerks, seated behind their narrow sloping desks, struggling to add up ledgers, balances and cash books by the light of a gas lamp, and I had always reflected upon the painful monotony of their task.

As far as I knew, the affairs of the bank were overseen by the governor, a deputy governor and a board of directors, but in order to gain experience I was to start my career as nothing more than an apprenticed clerk—of which it is estimated there are eleven hundred in London. I could see it now, someone was bound to ask my name and when I replied, '*Charles Dickens, sir*', I was sure that they would throw their heads back and roar with laughter.

I examined my reflection in the cheval-mirror and poked a finger inside my collar in an attempt to ease my sense of constriction. A tap upon the door was followed by Mama's voice.

'Can I come in, Charley?'

'Yes, Mama.'

She entered the room and I noticed how pretty she looked today: she was wearing a tartan dress and her hair was tied up in a becoming fashion. I was pleased to see her looking better. As she took in my own appearance, her eyes moistened.

'My goodness, Charley, you look the proper gentleman. It doesn't seem a moment since I held you in my arms and—well, you don't want to hear your mama talking of such things on such an important day as this, your first day at the bank.'

Before Mama could say another word, my aunt breezed into the room without so much as a knock on the door.

'Come along, Charley, you must not dawdle about your business. You do not want to be late on your first day, do you? It wouldn't reflect well upon your papa at all.'

I caught a sympathetic glance from Mama, who understood completely.

*　　　*　　　*

19

Later that morning Dickens sat at his desk. His pens were laid out on a tray in order of size, his silver inkwell—a gift from his beloved Mary—was newly topped up with ink, and a clean sheet of blotting paper was close at hand.

He still thought of Mary daily. Small things would remind him of her: the silver inkwell, the sound of Katie's laughter, the smell of Catherine's hair. His wife's sister had been gone for almost twenty years and yet he knew that he would never forget her. He still wore upon his little finger the small ring which he had taken from her hand the night that she had died.

He had been in his study since shortly after eight, but had struggled to put anything of substance down on paper. He had much upon his mind and no matter how he tried to focus on his work, disquieting thoughts intruded persistently. When Alice knocked the door and entered with the morning post, he was glad of the interruption for he simply could not concentrate at all.

'I've y' letters, here, sir.'

'Thank you, Alice,' Dickens acknowledged with a nod, as she left the room.

Alice, who had been with the family for many years, observed everything but passed comment upon nothing, as was befitting a loyal servant.

Dickens noticed that there was a letter from Urania Cottage and, upon opening it, his lips moved as he read it, his eyebrows alternating between an arch and a frown. The matron had written to inform him that one of the girls wanted to leave and return to her old life. He pocketed the letter quickly, and put on his coat with the intention of taking a cab across town to see what could be done.

He encountered his wife as he closed the study door behind him and jumped with surprise.

'Good God, Catherine, don't you know not to creep up on me like that? You nearly scared me half to death!'

'I'm sorry my love, it was not intended. Are you going out, dear?'

'Yes, my dear, when I put on my hat and my coat, it usually signifies that I am going out.'

He had been particularly irritable since his return from Folkestone and she did not attempt to question him further, for she knew that it was pointless. She watched as he pulled on his gloves and hurried out of the house.

He stepped out onto Tavistock Square and signalled to a driver parked across the road.

'Momin', guvnor.' The man tugged his cap as he approached, seated on top of his vehicle.

Dickens nodded but did not engage in conversation, for he wished to return to the problem which perplexed him more than any other and had occupied his mind all morning, indeed, since his return from Folkestone. He climbed into the cab and became engrossed in

21

his own thoughts again, his lips still working silently.

He was thinking about the Frenchwoman, for a different reason now, but nonetheless, he could not get her words out of his head.

'And you, sir, I suspect, have achieved everything that you ever hoped to achieve, and yet you are at risk from unhappiness and death from overwork. Perhaps, you should take a risk yourself.'

In part she was wrong: his unhappiness did not stem from overwork. He worked to *escape* his unhappiness. He knew exactly what the cause of that unhappiness was, and the risk that he had to take, but had he the courage to take it? It could mean the loss of his readers' good-will, the loss of his good name.

But it was not his fault, he reasoned. How long had he endured Catherine's failings as a wife? She was indolent, she was clumsy, and of late she seemed as if her mind was anywhere but upon the children or upon him. He had asked her to answer some correspondence: nothing complicated, just simple letters of acceptance, but could she manage that without smudging the ink? Of course not!

What could he do about it though? He could not make her disappear. He had taken an interest in the recent trial of William Palmer who had poisoned his wife, Ann. This he understood only too well — wives could be an encumbrance, but *he* was a civilized

22

man, who could not even entertain such an idea. Then what if he sent her away? He could find another property, somewhere in the countryside, and they could just appear together on social occasions. This was something to which he would have to give more thought.

Dickens's reverie was broken by the driver's voice alerting him to their arrival at Shepherd's Bush.

'Here we are then, sir.'

Dickens said that he hoped that he would not keep the man waiting long, stepped down onto the pavement and knocked upon the door of Urania Cottage.

The home was overseen by a matron, Mrs White, a chaplain, the Reverend Potter, and a tutor who instructed the girls in both their education and household duties. It was hoped that in time, the girls would learn how to become efficient maidservants who could emigrate and start a new life overseas. But today there appeared to be a defector.

Dickens was met at the door by both the matron and the Reverend Potter, who talked over one another, agreeing and disagreeing, and Dickens did his utmost to pay little heed to either of them.

'I have tried speaking to her myself, sir,' the reverend lisped, following close on Dickens's heels, 'but she would not listen to reason. The girl seems determined to go.'

Dickens led the way into the kitchen, took off his hat and gloves and dropped them onto a table which was in the centre of the well-ordered room.

'Where is the girl now, Mrs White?' He smoothed down his hair and straightened his cravat.

'She is in her room, packing up what few belongings she first arrived with. I will have her brought to you, sir, if you wish.' The matron's tone was anxious; she did not want the master to hold her responsible.

Dickens nodded and drew out a chair to sit down at the table.

A few minutes later, a slightly built girl of about eighteen stood before him with a look that alternated between awe toward himself and defiance of the matron. He inwardly remarked that she had the daintiest pair of feet.

'So, Sarah, I hear that you want to leave me?' His voice was kind. She looked a little embarrassed, 'Well, not you exactly, sir.'

'Then the matron is lying?'

'No, sir, she don't lie, but it ain't you I wants to leave, sir, it's 'er.' She nodded in the direction of Mrs White.

The matron took out a handkerchief from her apron, but quickly pocketed it again when the master shot her a sharp look.

'She has us up at six, a-saying our prayers at seven, and alearnin' at eight.'

'Just as you instructed, sir,' Mrs White interposed.

Dickens raised a calming hand.

'Yes, Mrs White is correct, Sarah, those are my instructions; but I can see that in your case my efforts appear to be in vain. If you really want your old life back, if you really *are* determined to leave me, then take her at her word, Matron; she can go after dinner, although I fear that the workhouse will be closed by then.' Dickens affected an air of sadness and sighed deeply.

He opened the household accounts which were on the table in front of him, and busied himself with looking over them. He knew precisely what he was doing and the reaction that it would effect, if he waited.

The girl remained, shuffling from one foot to another.

'Sir?'

Dickens did not look up or reply. The bird was almost in the trap and he wanted to make sure that it did not fly away.

'Sir, I think I've a-changed my mind. That is to say, I don't want to leave you.'

Dickens put down the accounts, and looked up slowly.

'I see, then you must continue to do exactly as Mrs White instructs, and remember that when she speaks, it is just as if *I* were speaking.'

'Yes, sir.' She turned to leave.

'And, Sarah?'

'Yes, sir?'

'If there is trouble, I shall hear of it.'

'There won't be no trouble, sir.'

'Very well, then off you go.' He smiled.

Dickens watched as her tiny figure disappeared out of the room, and then he turned to address the matron.

'I hope you will remember, Mrs White, that here we instruct with kindness. We must never forget kindness.'

The matron nodded, 'Yes, sir, I will remember.'

*   *   *

On the journey back to Tavistock House, Dickens thought no more about his problem. Instead he smiled and hummed to himself. He was satisfied with his morning's work after all. The world was in order again, just as he liked it.

Chapter 4

November 1856
Gad's Hill Place, Kent

The Narrative of Charles Dickens Junior

As a very young boy, my father would walk hand in hand with his own father, from Rochester to Gad's Hill, whereupon they would pass a grand old house that sat back from the road. They would stop, look over the gate, and my grandfather would say that if his son were to work very hard, and apply himself, then one day he could own a house as fine as that.

Many years have passed and my father is about to fulfil this paternal prophecy. The old house at Gad's Hill is for sale and Papa has purchased it from the daughter of a recently deceased clergyman. It is sad that Grandfather is not here to see this day, for he was the greatest of optimists and would surely have said, *'I 'ad no doubts that the guvnor would make his way in this world, I always said as much to his dear mother.'*

Gad's Hill Place was a handsome house with a bay window at either side of a wooden portico, and when my father invited me to view the property with him he advised me of his plans for minor improvements.

'I intend to have the builder raise the garret-roof to allow for extra rooms. You and the girls will enjoy the views from up there. The bell turret is in need of some repair, but a lick of paint on some new wooden boards should fix that.'

At the back of the property were open fields on which sheep would graze in warmer months. And my father joked that if he could make no further success of being a writer, then he would take up farming instead.

'What do you think of it, my boy?'

'It is just as you described it, Papa, a very handsome house, indeed.' And I braced myself lest he repeated to me what his own father had said to him.

I could not tell him how much I hated my new work at the bank. Each day so far had been a torture, and I wondered how much more I could bear without going insane from boredom. Papa had hinted, however, that there might be opportunity for me to move into brokerage if I worked hard, so for now I knew that I must endure my current post in the hope of a promotion with Miss Burdett-Coutts's assistance.

When we returned, Mr William Thackeray had called by with his daughters, Ann and Harriett, who were friendly with my sisters. The Thackeray girls had grown to become sensible, well-educated young ladies, despite their mother's absence. Ann favoured her father both in looks and temperament. She had an air of gentleness about her and an easy temper, and she was a little protective of her younger sister, Harriet, who appeared to be prone to nervousness.

Mrs Thackeray remained at Brompton Asylum, where my mother continued to visit her from time to time. Ann and Harriet had not seen their mama since she was sent away, for their father felt that it might distress them and he had been warned by the doctors, according to my mother, that it would do their mama no good.

'And how did you find Gad's Hill, my love? Was it all that you remembered?' Mama enquired, as my father and I entered the sitting-room.

Papa gave scant response, grunting.

Mama persevered. 'I think my mother would enjoy a ride out into the countryside to view it. She always did like Rochester.'

At this, Papa's face turned purple with rage and he spluttered at the suggestion.

'Don't even mention it, Catherine. After the state of disorder your parents left this house in while we were away in Boulogne, I would not have a moment's peace as long as your mother were present. Give her five minutes at Gad's Hill and she would be bound to break something. I suppose it is where your own clumsiness comes from.'

Mr Thackeray winced at my father's apparent cruelty and attempted to change the subject by suggesting a game of cards.

It was further proof to me that the tension that I had first sensed upon my return, was not imagined and was not improving. Now visitors were becoming aware of it too.

Since mentioning it to Katie, I had not spoken upon the subject again. I was unsure as to what thoughts my sister, Mary—whom we called Mamie—had upon the matter, and my six brothers, who were aged from five up to fifteen, centred their cares only upon tomfoolery or school. They acted as if all were in order.

Francis, however, who was twelve, was of a sensitive nature and had developed a stammer of late. When Papa upbraided him for his impediment, I understood his hurt and disappointment: it was not easy being the son of such an accomplished man.

Papa and Mr Thackeray went to my father's study so that Papa could show him some new leather-bound books which he had just purchased for the study at Gad's Hill, Mama returned to her own room, and Katie, Mamie, Ann and Harriet moved to play cards in the morning room. As I approached across the hall, I heard them talking and laughing.

'And how is your brother faring at the bank, Katie?'

Katie laughed. 'He hates it with a passion

and says that he is miserably bad at it. He wants to be a writer, but Papa has said that he has not the stamina for it.'

'I think that he would make a very fine writer. He has the noble features of an author, don't you think, Harriet?'

Mamie giggled. 'There is no point you setting your intentions upon my brother, Ann, for he is in love with Bessie Evans, the daughter of my father's publisher.'

Katie interposed sharply, 'Mamie, you have no business saying such things. What evidence do you have for such a supposition?'

'Then why does he stammer so, whenever she visits with her Papa?'

And they all laughed again.

I turned about quickly on my heels: the company of young women can be quite alarming at times!

Chapter 5

November 1856

Tavistock House
My Dear Collins
I have read over the final draft of the play, and it is more that I could have hoped for. You have certainly excelled yourself, and I think that the title, The Frozen Deep,

is splendid.

As for me, my restlessness continues, and i f I can absorb some of it in the production of this play, all the better. I have asked Clarkson Stanfield who has painted scenery at Drury Lane, if he will come and view the school room at Tavistock House and I think that, with some minor alterations, it will serve as an admirable theatre for the performance.

I have also engaged the services of a young musician, Francis Berger, who is composing some incidental music, which, I am certain will add the atmosphere that I am seeking to create. As for the prologue, my old friend, Forster, has agreed to deliver it; Katie, Mamie, and Georgina have already begun practising their parts, and I hope that with all these arrangements in hand, we will manage our first performance in January.

The purchase of the house at Gad's Hill is going ahead at last, and I have begun to think that it might offer me a temporary solution to my difficulties at home, which I have hinted to you of. With a house in town and a house in the countryside, I may be able to put a little more distance between myself and 'my problem'.

I only wish I had a little more of your own unconventionality about me, but I fear that I have too much at stake. However, for now, just to speak of my feelings to someone is a relief.

In the meantime, I press on with my work.

Your sincere friend
Charles Dickens.

*   *   *

April 1857

Tavistock House

Dickens sat at his desk, drinking a glass of brandy, his fingers lodged in his hair. *The Frozen Deep* had been a tremendous success, with more that one hundred people squeezed into the school room at Tavistock House. His own performance had been so powerful, that he had moved both the audience and his fellow actors to tears, and he had found it a release to pour some of his unspoken emotions into such a dramatic part. But after the final performance he realized that nothing had changed: his troubles were still there and he was completely depressed. The scenery was dismantled, the costumes were folded away and life, in all its weariness, resumed.

He did not usually drink to drown his sorrows, but he felt terrible. Strangely, he found that when he was a little drunk he could think more freely, and in that moment, he was struck by an idea. He would take the family to Italy: a change would do them good.

Maybe his view on matters was all wrong. Perhaps he should give his marriage another chance: after all, Catherine was amiable and compliant, and were these not among the reasons why he had chosen her after the end of his ill-fated relationship with Maria Beadnell? His youthful heart had faced such uncertainty in the hands of that passionate young creature. Hadn't he decided then that if he were to make any sort of success as a writer, then he must marry a reliable and placid woman? Catherine had more than fulfilled her part in this respect, so could he really hold her to account for his unhappiness?

But he had not known then, that as the years passed, there would be no meeting of minds. Oh, how he missed Mary. He realized now, that before he had even married Catherine, he must have sensed that something was missing. Wasn't this why he had asked her sister to live with them? For the first three years of his married life, Mary's presence had filled the house with gaiety, but then she had left him and nothing had ever been the same without her. Even now he could not visit her grave without reliving the terrible day when she had died in his arms. He sighed deeply, picked up the decanter and refilled his glass.

He had thought that in bringing Catherine's youngest sister, Georgina, into the home he might recapture some of Mary's spirit, that she would fill the void that had been left in his life, and he acknowledged that he did not know what he would do without Georgina now. Georgina practically ran the home, and he knew that without her capable hands, he would have gone insane at Catherine's ineptitude with regard to household matters.

But what would he do if Georgina left him too? She had already turned down one offer of marriage, and had vowed that she would never leave him. But he could not hold her to such a promise: she deserved a life of her own. However, the thought of a life with Catherine, the children fully grown and left home, and Georgina finally wed, was too much to think upon. Oh, what torture!

He would go to Italy, he could think more clearly there, among those winding streets which he loved so well. And he would look up his old friends, Emile and Augusta de la Rue, in Genoa. Yes, now his idea was becoming more attractive by the minute. He took another mouthful of brandy, held up his glass to the light of his desk-lamp and, turning it back and forth, he thought how the russet liquid reminded him of Augusta's fiery hair. And he smiled.

*   *   *

Catherine stared out of the carriage window,

looking past the whitewashed houses, the fields and the church towers. Her husband's suggestion to visit Italy had both confused and surprised her. Since his return from Folkestone she had noticed his increasing remoteness towards her and, although she acknowledged that this had characterized the nature of their relationship in more recent years, she sensed that this time there was something more.

She called to mind the day, only weeks into their courtship, when she had found the letters that he had written to Maria Beadnell at the height of their passion, and that she had hardly recognized the composed young man that she knew, in the wild emotion of words recorded within them. In their own courtship, Charles had written to her too, but the tone had been simply playful. She had been over this in her mind so many times before in the years that had passed, she had even questioned her husband's feelings for her sister, Mary, but it had only ever ended in disagreements and tears, so she had learned to speak of these things no more.

Since leaving England, she had noticed that Charles was endeavouring to be kinder to her. They had toured the old harbour in Genoa, viewed the beautiful Palazzo Reale, and inspected the Cattedrale di San Lorenzo. Today, however, a visit was to take place that she could hardly bear to think upon and it was about to change the mood between them completely.

Dickens's voice broke into her thoughts. 'It's so good to be back here in Genoa again, isn't it, my love?'

She managed to nod politely: what was she supposed to say when they were journeying to the house of Augusta de la Rue, a woman who, twelve years before, had bewitched her husband to the point that she had become almost mad with jealousy? Charles was either utterly thoughtless or completely cruel.

Madame de la Rue was married to a wealthy banker of Swiss descent, who adored his beautiful wife. Upon meeting Dickens at a party during their previous visit all those years ago, Emile had confided that his wife was beset by anxieties and strange imaginings.

You would think to look at her now, that she is as sane as you or I, but, when we are alone she imagines that we are being watched everywhere we go. By day she falls into the most terrible fits and by night she endures the most terrifying nightmares. I have consulted the best physicians in Europe, but as yet no one can find the cause of her anxiety.'

Madame de la Rue had been so taken with Dickens's conjuring tricks at the party, that she had teasingly suggested that she believed that such a talented magician could certainly cure her of her troubles. Completely flattered, Dickens became caught up with the

37

idea of his own power and in the weeks and months that followed he spent hour upon hour in the company of Augusta de la Rue. Emile, who wanted nothing more than his wife's happiness, was delighted when she appeared to prosper from Dickens's visits; but when Catherine could tolerate his actions no longer she issued him with an ultimatum and, resentfully, Dickens saw Madame de la Rue no more.

'I hope that you will greet Augusta with warmth and generosity, Catherine, and set right any feelings of mistaken jealousy that you directed toward her all those years ago,' Dickens said as they drew near to the de la Rue residence.

'I do not believe that I was mistaken, Charles. If you remember, there were many hours that you spent alone in her company. Should a wife not be bound to feel resentful?'

Dickens sighed. 'I don't want to argue with you, my dear. I had hoped that in our coming away together, we might enjoy one another's company, not quarrel.'

Catherine felt guilty. She *was* glad that he had invited her to accompany him and she did not want them to bicker either.

'I am sorry, my love. I will try my best to be cordial to Augusta, I promise.'

The carriage pulled up outside a large villa, set amongst luxuriant grounds, and Emile de la Rue was instantly on the steps, running out to greet them with his arms outstretched.

'Signore Charles! Signora Catherine! How good to see you both again. It has been too long.'

Catherine stepped down from the carriage and was kissed warmly upon both cheeks by the genial host. Charles, meanwhile, strolled on ahead and his wife watched him closely as he ran up the steps and disappeared into the villa. Emile asked her about the children and she vaguely recognized the sound of her own voice responding that Katie, Mamie and the younger boys were with their governess at the apartment; her eyes, however were scrutinizing the villa, wondering what sort of greeting was being exchanged between her husband and the woman inside.

*   *   *

Augusta de la Rue stood on the back steps of the villa looking out at the gardens. Her russet hair had faded in the years since Dickens had last seen her, but, when she turned, her face was as beautiful as he remembered, and her figure was that of a woman half her age.

'I thought that you would never return,' she said softly.

Dickens walked towards her, put his hand to her face and stroked it, 'Are you quite well, now, dear Augusta?'

'Alas, no, my love, I am just as I was,' she

39

replied sadly. 'And you?'

'If melancholy is a disease, then I suffer intensely.' He sighed.

'Ah, look at these two old friends!' Emile enthused as he walked across the tiled hallway with Catherine, 'Glad to be reunited, again, I'll be bound.'

Catherine did not know whether the man was blind, insane or stupid, and witnessing the caresses that had been exchanged, she knew then that her husband's motives in bringing her to Italy had not been about the good of their marriage at all, and she was not about to be humiliated for a second time. She took a step forward and narrowed her eyes.

'You must think me some kind of a fool, madam.'

Augusta took a step back and began to blink rapidly.

'You must think that I don't know . . . '

She began to hum strangely.

'. . . what went on all those years ago.'

Augusta's eyes rolled backwards, and she began to jerk uncontrollably. As she fell, Dickens caught her in his arms.

'Quick! Emile, fetch a chair!'

Augusta's husband ran and put his hand upon one of a pair of gilt chairs, which were placed either side of a hall table.

'No, man, something softer. The *chaise*, there!' Dickens barked.

Emile took no offence at being spoken to

like a servant, and dragged the *chaise* across the hallway to where Dickens held Augusta in his arms. Dickens laid her shaking body upon the sofa and Emile placed a cushion beneath her.

Catherine stood and watched in horror. She had never seen anything so frightening in all her life before. Augusta's head thrashed violently from side to side and a dribble of saliva ran from the corner of her mouth.

'Augusta, Augusta, shh . . . ' Dickens knelt at her side, stroked her forehead with his fingers and whispered softly, 'I am here now, all will be well again. I will not leave you.'

The tension in her body began to slowly dissipate and her breathing, although laboured, was becoming calmer.

Emile, who had hovered over them both, clasped his hands together. 'Oh, my dear friend, Signore Charles, *grazie, grazie.* You have not lost any of your power, at all.'

The relief on his face was clear to see.

'One touch of your hand, and she is restored instantly. It is just like old times. I insist that you vacate your apartment and move in here with us. A few weeks of your treatment and Augusta will recover again. I will not take no for an answer, *signore.'*

Dickens did not smile, but requested, 'Leave me here with her for a while, that she may recover, and we will talk about arrangements later, Emile.'

41

'Of course, of course,' and he put out his hand to Catherine. 'Shall we leave them, *signora?*'

Realizing that she was beaten, Catherine took Emile's arm and made to leave.

Dickens lifted his face, fixed his eyes upon his wife and whispered, 'That was a fine performance from you, my dear. I hope that you are happy now.'

*   *   *

Dickens sat on a *chaise* on the patio overlooking the picturesque gardens. Augusta lay with her head in his lap and he stroked her russet hair absently.

She sensed him sigh deeply and she asked, 'What are you thinking, my love?'

'Oh, I was just looking at the butterflies and thinking how free they are. Wouldn't you love to be able to drift from place to place like they do, completely unhindered?'

'Yes, I suppose I would, but sadly such freedom cannot be ours. For now, you and I have only the few days while Emile is out of town. We must be content with that, my love.'

'Why did you marry him, Augusta? Did you love him?'

'It was the plan of our two families. Our fathers were old friends and they made the match for us. Papa knew that as Emile's wife I

42

would not want for anything materially, and I can only say that he has been a most attentive husband. I must not complain.'

'Ah, for when we complain, we say what is really in our hearts, do we not, my love?' Dickens said with a hint of irony.

'And what about you? Did you ever truly love Catherine?' Augusta was most curious about the plump and amiable woman who was wife to such a dynamic man. She had been completely shocked when Catherine had found the voice to challenge her. Dickens began to recount the time when he had first met Catherine at her father's home, and had been drawn to her shy nature and placid temperament.

'I suppose at the time I believed myself to have been in love with her. I am certain that I believed that she was the *sort* of woman I should be in love with, and, yes, there are times when I did love her, but never as a man should love his wife.'

Augusta had become very quiet and Dickens sensed that his voice had been going unheard.

'Augusta?'

He looked down at her face: her eyelids had begun to flicker, a tremor had commenced in her hands and her beautiful lips were grotesquely contorted. He looked sadly at the butterflies flitting from flower to flower, and began to stroke Augusta's hair again, his eyes brimming with tears.

Chapter 6

April 1857
Genoa, Italy

Katie sat at the apartment window with an easel, sketching the view of villas and trees dotted over a hilly landscape and set against a clear blue sky. She had adored Italy since her first visit as a child, had become fluent in the language and felt completely at home whenever she was surrounded by the sights and sounds of the Mediterranean culture.

As she used her pencil, her expressions changed from moment to moment and in this, she followed her father: when she was drawing she was lost in her own world and did not like to be disturbed at her art, any more than her papa tolerated being disturbed at his writing. For the last four years she had received instruction in drawing and painting at Bedford College, just off the Tottenham Court Road and was eager to perfect her art in all its forms.

Although she was more than twelve months younger than her sister, she had always been viewed by Mamie and her brothers as the eldest, for she was every bit as determined and spirited as her papa, and would voice her thoughts to him in a way that her siblings never dared. As a small child she had once been stung by an insect in the garden but refused to be comforted by her mama; and even though she was reminded that her father was trying to work she screamed and wailed for him until he came. He took her up in his arms immediately and had not the heart to scold her for the disturbance.

Mamie, who was more like her mother in looks, shared one thing in common with her sister: they both adored their father. Mamie recognized that she possessed many of the traits of her mother's family, and wished that this was not so, for she sensed that her papa had little admiration for his in-laws. But no matter how she tried, she could not emulate Katie's energy for life and was destined to continue in her own placid way. She could not imagine how her father cherished her, for she had been named after her Aunt Mary whom he had idolized.

While Katie sketched, Mamie, who was feeling hot, held up her skirts and walked about the marble floor in bare feet, endeavouring to cool down. Last night she had hardly slept and had twisted and turned in every direction seeking a cool place in the bed.

The heat had not been the only reason for Mamie's restlessness last night. Her mother had returned in the carriage alone, and Mamie

45

had heard her crying. She had crept out of bed and tried to listen at the door to what was being said, but could only hear the muffled sound of her mother's sobs and her aunt's flat responses. She was unsure whether her sister had heard it too, as she had mentioned nothing of it this morning.

'Did you know that Mama had returned alone, last night?' Mamie whispered, looking at the door for fear she might be overheard.

'Yes,' Katie replied indifferently, 'I asked Aunt Georgina about it after breakfast this morning.'

Mamie was shocked that her sister had been so bold, and yet had told her nothing of it. 'You did? And what did she say?'

'She said that Papa was visiting a sick friend, and that Mama had returned to the apartment because she was feeling unwell herself.'

Mamie threw up her hands in the air and sat down on an armchair in the corner of the room, with a sigh of exasperation.

'Why is it that we are treated like children, as if we see and hear nothing and as if everything were in order? At our age, I think that we are old enough to be given some sort of explanation as to why our parents behave so oddly at times.' She wriggled her toes in an attempt to feel the air between them.

'What is there that is odd?' Katie answered irritably. 'Papa is visiting a sick friend and Mama is unwell. There is nothing strange in

46

that at all.'

'It is strange that our mother has returned in tears, wouldn't you say?'

Katie stopped sketching for a moment and turned her head this way and that, trying to decide whether her shading was satisfactory or not.

'Mamie, Mama is always crying. If she is happy she cries, if she is sad she cries. So who can tell what she thinks and feels? It is a wonder that Papa is as patient with her as he is.' Katie took a small knife from the ledge of the easel and began to sharpen her pencil.

'Do you think that they still love one another, Katie?'

She realized that, of late, she had not seen her father kiss her mother affectionately, or even pat her hand.

'One doesn't have to be in love to be married, Mamie.'

A look of horror crept over Mamie's face, 'Katie, of course one has to be in love to be married, or else what is the point?'

Katie ceased sharpening her pencil and looked at her sister as if she had no brains at all. 'The point, Mamie, is to find someone who will be able to keep you in the manner to which you have become accustomed. Love has nothing to do with it at all.'

'But what if he was old, and fat!' Mamie was serious. 'Do you remember when Mama's niece, Lucy, married Captain Lane? He must

47

have been old enough to be her father. His whiskers were quite grey in places.'

'No matter. If one's husband is older, then you can hope to learn things from him.'

'Oh, how dull, Katie, I shall marry only for love, even if he hasn't a penny to his name.'

'I think you will find, dear Sister, that without pretty gowns and fine jewels life *would* be very dull. And as for love, it won't keep you out of the workhouse.'

Mamie called to mind her peach ball-gown and her favourite oriental fan, and inwardly acknowledged that she would miss those things a good deal.

'I know that Mama loves Papa very much,' Mamie said thoughtfully, 'And I think that she tries very hard to make him happy, but maybe she doesn't know how to. Perhaps that is why she is always crying.'

'I hope you girls have remembered that your father has arranged for a tutor to come and instruct you in Italian this afternoon?' Their aunt had entered the room carrying a jug of iced water and two glasses upon a tray.

The girls nodded, and Mamie threw her sister a look which signalled that she wished her to ask about their mama, but Katie had resumed her sketching and had become quickly absorbed in it again.

Mamie cleared her throat, 'Aunt Georgina, Katie thinks that we are old enough to know where Papa has gone, and why Mama is upset.'

Katie glared wildly at her sister, 'I never said—'

'As long as you are under your father's roof,' Georgina replied sharply, 'he is not obligated to tell you of his whereabouts. *He* will decide what you are old enough to know and when you are old enough to know it. Now, as you have been told, your papa is visiting a sick friend, and as for your mama, she has returned alone because she is feeling unwell herself.'

Georgina poured the water into the glasses, and handed one to each of the girls.

'There'll be no more talk of this matter now, it is closed, and, Mamie—put some slippers on.'

Chapter 7

June 1857
Tavistock House

Catherine sat on the end of her bed deep in thought and she twisted at her necklace, wondering what the future held.

Charles had stayed with Augusta de la Rue for several days in Genoa and, when he had returned to the apartment, he had acted as if there had been no disagreement between the two of them at all.

49

Catherine had continued as if nothing untoward had taken place, her daughters had eyed her curiously from time to time as if watching her closely, but said nothing; and the atmosphere on the journey back to England was, on the surface, as jovial as the atmosphere had been on the journey to Italy. This strange charade was completely unnerving.

In her mind she could hear the beginnings of music: the melody of the flute hovering above the strings, and she recalled a time when she was young and had loved to dance. She had never been able to dance quite as nimbly as her sister Mary or with Georgina's stamina, but she *had* been able to dance.

Now she wondered if she would ever dance again. She pictured herself waltzing round and round, the music in her head grew louder and unable to block it out, she put her hands to her ears and shouted, 'Make it stop, make it stop!'

The bedroom door opened and her husband's face appeared wearing a frown, 'Catherine, will you keep your voice down. Whatever is wrong with you?'

*   *   *

Dickens walked at his usual brisk pace and, by now, Tavistock Square had been left behind some streets away, but already Wilkie Collins was complaining.

'Hold up there one moment, my energetic

friend, this rheumatic gout is playing the devil with my feet, you know.'

Dickens had begun to notice that of late his young companion, who was twelve years his junior, was becoming something of a hypochondriac and if it was not his feet that he was grumbling about, then it was neuralgia.

When they had first met, an instant friendship was formed and it was not long before Wilkie Collins found himself invited to contribute regularly to *Household Words*. The two men dined together, travelled to France and Italy together, and frequented late-night dance-halls, and Collins had fast supplanted Dickens's friends of much longer standing.

The fraternal relationship that Dickens had enjoyed with his old friend John Forster over many years had waned since Forster's marriage to a widowed heiress, and in Dickens's view, Forster was settling down to precisely the sort of life from which he was seeking to disentangle himself.

Other friends had also become set in their ways and Dickens did not want to be held back by them. It was too much of a reminder that he was also in his middle years and it was for this reason that he had sought friendship with young Collins. They had travelled to Naples together, even climbing Mount Vesuvius, but now it almost seemed as if Collins were becoming an old man himself.

'I thought that you were only planning a

stroll,' Collins panted, wiping his top lip with the back of his hand.

'Not flagging already are we, Wilkie?' Dickens laughed. 'It has only been a mile that we have gone, so far.'

'Are you sure?'

Collins was disappointed. He realized that he should have known better than to join his friend on one of his 'strolls', but he was mindful that he was fast running out of laudanum, and that an excursion into town would allow him to call in at the chemist, and replenish his supply.

Dickens, however, had decided upon an entirely different route to the one that Collins had anticipated, and was heading for the stationers in Tottenham Court Road. They had passed a tobacconist, a cobbler and two milliner's shops, but as yet no sign of a chemist or stationer's. The pain that throbbed in Collins's feet was not the only kind of ache which was troubling him. By now the need for his routine dose was becoming overwhelming, and he could see nothing more than those enticing bottles which lined the shelves of the apothecary, and their colours began to sparkle before his eyes.

'Charles, I really do need to find—'

'Oh, Lord. No! It can't be true.'

Dickens had stopped to purchase a newspaper from a street vendor and was stunned by the headlines.

'Douglas Jerrold is dead.'

Douglas William Jerrold had combined many careers: actor, author, playwright and journalist, and having met him in the early years of his fame, Dickens had sought to emulate him, recognizing versatility as a key to his own longevity. Jerrold, who equally admired his young imitator, had always been the first one to seek a place at the private readings of Dickens's latest novels.

'His poor, poor, wife.' Dickens was shaking his head. 'Something must be done for her in the way of financial assistance.'

At that precise moment Wilkie Collins did not care one jot about Douglas William Jerrold, and was only thinking about his own slow death from lack of laudanum. He was grateful to see a chemist's sign hanging above a shop door on the opposite side of the road and, forgetting all about his pain, dashed across the street to get to it.

Dickens leaned against a shop window in disbelief and called to mind his friend of old and thought of all his wonderful accomplishments: plays at Drury Lane, satirical and humorous contributions to *Punch,* and the editing of a variety of newspapers and magazines. He could hardly believe that he would never see the sparkle in those intelligent blue eyes again.

He sighed and realized that life was all too short and in that moment he knew, with the greatest certainty, that he could not and would not grow old with Catherine. Whatever span of years lay before him now, he determined then that he must find in them the one true companion that he had missed in life. How he would tell her, where their lives would go from here on, he did not know; but there was no other way forward for him now.

Collins, meanwhile, was haggling about doses with the chemist and endeavouring to keep his double under control.

'The apothecary in Marleybone sees no difficulties in supplying me with such a quantity—*take your hand off my shoulder!*'

Seeing his customer slapping at his arm, the chemist quickly decided that the man was completely delusional and the sooner he gave him what he wanted the better. He wanted this short, squat, bulbous-headed individual out of his shop, lest he scare away his more respectable customers.

Dickens was still musing over the brevity of life when his friend rejoined him and furtively drained the last drops of his potion from a tincture bottle, in the confidence that he now had more in his pocket.

'*The Frozen Deep* is the answer, Collins.'

Dickens's voice sounded strange in Collins's ears, as if he was speaking under water, and he had absolutely no idea what *The Frozen Deep* was, or what it was the answer to.

Dickens could see that his friend's mind

was elsewhere and suggested that they go into Black's Coffee-House for coffee and toast. He needed to sit down; he had had quite a shock.

The waitress bought their strong-smelling coffee and two plates of toast and placed them on the table. Dickens noticed that Collins's hand trembled as he brought the coffee cup to his lips.

'I've been thinking, my friend. What if we were to revive *The Frozen Deep* and perform it in a theatre? We could give the money raised to the Jerrold family?'

Collins nodded with abstraction, not at all comprehending, and fixed his gaze upon his toast, wondering whether it was poisoned or not. His eyes narrowed and he looked with suspicion upon the waitress, who was serving at another table.

Dickens had not noticed, he was working out the details of when and where a performance could be held. Who would take the parts? Certainly Mamie, Katie and Georgina would not have the training to act in a large theatre setting. He had other ideas too: he could revive a reading of *A Christmas Carol* and ask Thackeray and Forster to deliver lectures. His mouth was working all of the time, relaying ideas to Collins, answering his own questions, and completely oblivious to his friend who was carrying on his own quiet conversation with a slice of toast.

'And as for my domestic "problem", Wilkie,

I have decided. I will start by separating our sleeping arrangements, and thereafter, when Catherine has become accustomed to the idea, I shall take up permanent residence at Gad's Hill.'

Collins picked up his toast, closed his eyes hard and bit into it. If he had to die, he would rather it be from poisoning than starvation.

Chapter 8

June 1857
Gad's Hill Place

Catherine Dickens and Ellen Ternan slept, each one in her own room, in her own accommodation, neither aware that their lives were about to change at the hand of the same man.

*   *   *

Catherine awoke, her dark hair streaked with grey, spread across her pillow; turning her head she found that she was alone in her bed at Gad's Hill Place. Her husband had retired to another room last night, citing his old kidney trouble as an excuse: he was getting up frequently at night. But she had also noticed that, with increasing frequency, he had also been retiring to another room when they were residing at Tavistock House.

On these occasions he had said that he did not wish to disturb her when he had been working late at his desk. The fact that he had worked late at his desk many nights since they were wed, appeared to have momentarily escaped him, and in Catherine's eyes the excuse was a weak one.

His pocket book of Shakespeare, a gift from Forster, which was always on the bedside table at Tavistock House, was no longer in its usual place, and his hairbrush and comb which were routinely laid out on the dressing-table were also missing. Catherine had begun to wonder whether his intention to sleep elsewhere had been entirely planned.

Dickens had been spending more time at Gad's Hill Place since the repairs had been completed but had experienced some difficulty deciding upon which room would be his study. Initially he had tried the room which overlooked the back garden, but it was, he felt, better suited to being a billiard room. Then he had experimented with the room off the hall to the left, but had found that the natural light was not good. Finally he had decided upon the room overlooking the front garden, and he had set up his desk under the window, arranged his books in order and hung a mirror above the fireplace to reflect the light.

Catherine had been upset on the night of

her first visit to the house some weeks ago. She had called upon their new neighbours and left her husband's calling card, only to find that he was furious with her, saying that he had neither the time to visit or be visited. With Georgina increasingly in charge of household matters, Catherine wondered exactly what her role as the wife of Charles Dickens was meant to be. It was a role that appeared to be diminishing daily.

As a family they were playing host to the author Hans Christian Anderson at Gad's Hill Place, and Catherine realized that she must hurry herself to get up and be at the breakfast table to greet their guest. She did not want to give Charles any excuse to label her a poor hostess.

She pushed herself upright wearily and moved her legs over to the edge of the bed. She placed her feet very carefully upon the floor, always mindful of the weakness in her left ankle, which had been injured in the carriage accident she had had all those years ago in Scotland. Catherine paused for a moment and reflected how her husband, terrified by the thought that he had almost lost her, had reassured her then of his love for her.

'If I ever struggle to tell you how I feel about you, know now that I love you more than words can say.'

She wondered if she were to have such an accident again, whether her husband would repeat those words to her now. The feeling of unhappiness that washed over her in that moment forced her to put such thoughts from her mind immediately; the answer was too painful to reflect upon.

After dressing and going downstairs, Catherine was pleased to find that although her husband, Georgina, Mamie and Katie were already at the breakfast table, she had still arrived before their guest.

'Good morning, my dear, so good of you to join us.' Dickens looked at his watch.

As Catherine pulled out her chair to sit down, Mr Anderson came into the room, trying to adjust his cravat which was badly tied and subsequently almost tripped over his own feet.

'Oh, mijn goedheid!' Oh my goodness!

Catherine, who was prone to a little clumsiness herself, felt his position keenly and went to his aid immediately.

'Come, Mr Anderson, take my seat. Are you all right, sir?'

'Ja, ja mevrouw, alles is goed.'

Mr Anderson's grasp upon the English language was poor. On a previous visit, Charley had endeavoured to speak some German to him, and found that he could not understand Mr Anderson's German any better than his broken English. So the family continued to communicate via a series of facial expressions, gestures and a raised voice.

'DID YOU SLEEP WELL, ANDERSON? SLEEP WELL?'

Dickens fashioned his hands together in the manner of a pillow, and put his head upon them with his eyes closed.

'*Ja*, Mister Dickens, I sleep well.'

'I HOPE THAT THE DOGS DID NOT DISTURB YOU, THIS MORNING?' Dickens began to bark and pant.

'Ah, very good. En hund!' Anderson barked and laughed in response.

Dickens shot a comical look at his daughter, Katie, who always appreciated her father's humour, and both tried to suppress their amusement.

Alice's young niece was waiting upon them that morning as her aunt had severely scalded her hand the week before. Not wanting to cause any inconvenience to her employers Alice had requested of her mistress if she might send her relative in her place until she recovered.

The young girl was experiencing some difficulty operating the dumb waiter and quite suddenly the strange conversation that had been going on over the breakfast table was interrupted by a loud crash.

Dickens leapt to his feet.

'Are you hurt, miss?'

'I think that I have bruised my arm, sir.'

He gently took her arm and asked if he might examine it, and then pushed up her

60

sleeve.

'A little arnica will help, my dear. If you will accompany me to my study I think I have some there. Here, lean on me, young lady.'

Catherine's face began to redden, and Mr Anderson patted her hand fondly.

'*Din mand er meget venlig.* Your husband . . . very kind man.'

Georgina, who had left the room to go down to the kitchen and examine the broken crockery, returned promptly with the morning post, and handed a letter to Mr Anderson.

'*Ah, et brev* . . . thanks to you, Miss Georgina.'

He turned to Catherine and seeing that she still seemed a little out of sorts asked her, in his own strange way, to accompany him for a walk in the gardens.

Catherine was grateful for his kind attention and took his arm, accompanying him out through the French doors at the back of the house.

'You know Mr Anderson, my children always enjoy your story about the ugly duckling.'

He hesitated for a moment and then smiled and nodded, '*Ah, ja, Den Grimme Aelling.* This is the story about me, madam.' And he pointed to his own face.

It was true that Mr Anderson was not in the least bit handsome, and Catherine was unsure as to whether he was joking or in earnest. But his large nose and awkward physique made her suspect that he was quite serious, and she felt sorry for him.

He excused himself for a moment and began to open his letter, reading it carefully. Quite unexpectedly he threw himself to the ground and began to cry inconsolably.

'Oh, my dear Mr Anderson, whatever is wrong?' But she could elicit no answer that she could understand and ran in the house for her husband.

She hesitated outside the door of his study, always a little nervous to enter without knocking, but the thought that he had taken a servant into his hallowed room was enough to embolden her to enter unannounced.

Dickens was perched on the edge of his desk and the young servant was sitting in his chair pulling down her sleeve. At the sight of Catherine entering the room, his face flashed with annoyance.

'Catherine, have I not told you before, to always knock before coming in to my study?'

Catherine quelled her natural inclination to apologize and instead concentrated her efforts upon recounting the unusual behaviour of their guest.

'But Mr Anderson is crying like a child upon the lawn, my dear. You must come at once.'

'You look after yourself, my dear, no more mishaps, eh?' Dickens winked at the young lady, who blushed.

Upon going out to the garden, Dickens managed to piece together that Mr Anderson's letter had borne the news that his latest story had received a very poor review, and understanding completely how painful such things could be, endeavoured to comfort him.

He crouched down next to the distressed author and put his finger in the dirt of the adjacent flowerbed.

'Look, my dear Hans, this is criticism.'

He wrote the word *criticism* in the dirt with his index finger.

Mr Anderson looked at it without comprehension, his face expressionless, his eyes blinking. Dickens brushed over it again with the palm of his hand.

'And thus, it is gone my friend.'

Mr Anderson began to smile, sat up and looked at Catherine. 'Your husband . . . very kind man, yes?'

*   *   *

Ellen Ternan sat in front of her dressing-table mirror, brushing her thick hair, flecked with blonde streaks. In the looking-glass, she tried out expressions of surprise, alarm, sorrow and delight, and in contrast to Catherine Dickens, her young features bore no trace of the lines that had come with time.

She had been invited to understudy the part to be played by her sister, Maria, in the performance of *Atlanta,* at the Haymarket. She had played the part of little girls on many occasions, but this would be her first role in the part of a woman. At eighteen years of age, the only desire that Ellen Ternan had more than being an accomplished actress, was to become a *famous* actress. She called to mind what she had overheard Frank Talfourd, a playwright and producer, say to his assistant.

'That girl has a pretty face and a well-developed figure. If she could learn to act a little more convincingly, then we might make more use of her talents.'

Ellen stood in front of the mirror with her hands on her hips, turning this way and that, admiring her shape. She smiled to herself: yes, Frank Talfourd was right, she had a well-developed figure.

Her father had died when she was just seven, and Ellen, her two sisters and her mama had moved from town to town, theatre to theatre. She was grateful, however, that her mama had always taken rooms in respectable lodgings, and employed a tutor whenever they were in town for a stretch of time.

She had studied the other actresses carefully, observing their facial expressions and their manner of delivery, and was convinced that no matter what she lacked in the way of experience as an actress, she could make up for with her looks and intelligence. She was not a feather-headed fool.

Ellen knew that somehow she had to do more to capture Frank Talfourd's attention; she was not simply content with being just the understudy. If he could not help her then she was certain that he would know someone who would. It was just a matter of time before she would be playing a lead role.

Chapter 9

June 1857
Regent's Park, London

On a warm summer's evening, the moon lit up the narrow leafy lane along which Wilkie Collins and his brother, Charles, strolled in the direction of Hanover Terrace, where they both resided in great comfort with their mother. They had been to view the latest panoramic landscape at the Diorama in Regent's Park.

The Diorama, which had originated in Paris, was a theatrical experience viewed by an audience in a highly specialized theatre. The huge transparent painting would change its appearance both subtly and dramatically, and with the aid of lighting and sound effects, the result was so spectacular that the audience believed themselves to be looking at a natural scene.

'Quite a show tonight, wasn't it, Charlie?'

Wilkie said, looking up at the moon and recalling the drama.

'Yes, it was truly awe-inspiring.'

Charles Collins noticed that his brother was limping. 'Is your pain still as severe?' he asked.

'Alas, Charlie, it is no better, but I endure it with a little help.' And he patted the jacket pocket which held his tincture bottle.

A look of disapproval crossed Charles Collins's face.

'You would be better served praying to aid your endurance than relying on that cursed potion, Wilkie.'

Wilkie Collins suppressed a good-natured smile. The serious-minded Charles, who was a rather pale-looking young man with a shock of red hair and blue eyes, often found himself to be the cause of wry amusement amongst his brother's friends with regard to his piety and asceticism.

'You have your religion and I have mine. Let's leave it at that, shall we?'

'Yes, Wilkie, but I—'

Charles Collins was interrupted in his moralizing, by a piercing scream that came from a nearby villa. His faith momentarily abandoned, he gripped the arm of his older brother in fear.

'What in heaven's name . . . ?'

Running through the garden towards the wrought-iron gate of the villa, was a beautiful woman in flowing white robes. She looked over her shoulder in fear, and then turned a face filled with supplication towards the brothers.

Charles closed his eyes and began to pray, and Wilkie—who was quite used to surreal hallucinations—blinked rapidly, but only found that the woman was still there. He admitted to himself that although the sound of her screams had been most alarming, the woman was indeed very beautiful and that he wished that all of his visions were so lovely.

'Please, sirs, you must help me,' she implored. 'I have been shut up in that house a prisoner some three months at the hand of a madman.' She pointed with a trembling finger towards the house from which she had run.

At that moment a man wielding a poker, dashed out of the villa.

'Caroline?' he snarled. 'Damn my eyes, where are you?'

Wilkie, not usually given to displays of physical agility, pulled his brother and the woman into the hedging and indicated with a finger to his lips that they should remain silent. The man was obviously drunk as he stumbled through the gate on to the lane.

'Caroline! There is no used trying to leave me.' He thrashed about in the bushes trying to locate her. 'I will hunt you down and find you, upon my word.'

He gave the poker a final wave in the air and, calling her name once more, keeled over backwards, collapsing in a drunken stupor upon the ground.

Wilkie saw their chance and, taking the woman's hand, began to run along the lane forgetting his customary pain in the excitement of the moment; Charles followed close behind.

When they arrived at Hanover Terrace, the woman was breathless and shaking, not sure if she had escaped from one captor only to fall into the hands of another.

'This is our mother's house,' Wilkie panted. 'You will be quite safe here.' He bent over double with his hands on his legs, trying to catch his breath.

The woman in white shook her head and began to back away slowly.

'Really, madam, you will be quite safe, I will call my mother to the door and you can see for yourself. Charles, go and fetch Mama,' Wilkie urged, not wanting to let this beautiful creature out of his sight.

Charles Collins, who, having recovered from his alarm, was beginning to wonder about the propriety of the proceedings, decided that his mother would know exactly what to do and hastened into the house to fetch her.

Harriett Collins, a youthful-looking woman in her fifties, was well liked by the assorted and numerous friends her sons brought to her door. The widow of a landscape artist who had left her well provided for, she delighted in the animated discussions about art and literature that took place in her front room. She did all that she could to develop the different talents that her sons possessed: Wilkie, an accomplished writer, and Charles, an artist with a practised eye for botanical detail.

Her younger son was attempting to breach the inner circle of the members of the Royal Academy, but his strict religious views were proving a barrier to acceptance. Although some of his views could be jested about, depriving himself of food was a step too far in the eyes of his fellow artists. Harriett Collins felt that her two sons could do with a little mix of each other: Wilkie, a little more self-discipline and Charles, a little more liberalism.

Upon being told of the visitor at the door, she came immediately and found Wilkie endeavouring to reassure the young woman.

'Come in, my dear,' Mrs Collins welcomed. 'Don't stand out there, you'll catch your death. Look how you are trembling.'

The woman in white was offered a place by the fireside and a glass of warm brandy. She was in no hurry to reveal her history and Mrs Collins did not press her for she had learned to develop an open mind towards the variety of unorthodox characters who frequented her house at the invitation of her sons.

Wilkie could not take his eyes off her. He had never seen anyone so beautiful in his life before and, when she lifted her eyes and managed to smile, he thought that she looked just like an angel.

'You have been very kind, sir, I thank you for that.'

'Not at all, madam, not at all. You are most welcome to stay the night, isn't she, Mother?'

Mrs Collins smiled. 'Of course, my dear, there is always a spare bed made up for guests.'

There was so much that Wilkie wanted to ask her. Where was she from? How had she come to fall into the hands of her captor? Where were her family?

As if she sensed his curiosity, she said, 'I feel that I must repay your hospitality by at least telling you a little of myself. I cannot expect you to open your home to someone of whom you know nothing.'

'Only if you wish it,' Wilkie replied kindly.

She nodded. 'My name is Caroline Courtney Graves. My late husband was a captain in the army, and had substantial independent means; but upon his death some months ago, I found that he had made no will and that I was forced to seek assistance from his brother here in London. It was he who kept me captive.' She lifted her glass of brandy to her lips, her hand trembling again.

'Really, madam, there is no need for you to continue. Do not distress yourself,' Wilkie soothed.

In an act of practicality, Mrs Collins said that she would ask the cook to prepare a light supper for them and a short while later they sat down to a meal of potted meats, beetroot, salad, bread and butter which Charlie toyed with, eating very little. The maid, Lucy, tried not to stare at the celestial attire of the unexpected visitor and acknowledged that by now she should be well used to the exotic appearance of Mrs Collins's visitors: Mr Dickens, who sported colourful waistcoats, Holman Hunt with his red bushy beard, and Dante Rossetti with his array of spectacular hats.

'Do you not have any family who you could turn to?' Harriet Collins asked the woman in white. 'Someone whom we could advise of your position, Mrs Graves?'

'My family are in Ireland, and as yet do not know that I am a widow. I hoped to make contact with them once I had been given some aid from my brother-in-law. Upon first receiving me, he was most kind and promised each day that he would write to them on my behalf, but as the days passed he changed, and when he was drunk he became so violent towards me that . . .'

Seeing her distress, Wilkie felt as if he wanted to return to that leafy lane and dash out the brains of that man with his own poker.

'Please don't feel that you have to say anymore. You must stay here with us, and we will contact your relatives first thing tomorrow. You will be quite safe here, madam, you can be sure of that.'

She lifted those same eyes that had first entranced him and settled them upon his own. 'You are very kind, sir, thank you.'

Wilkie Collins smiled in return, and had absolutely no idea that the mysterious woman in white was not Caroline Courtney Graves at all.

Chapter 10

July 1857
Tavistock House

Ellen Ternan sat in the drawing room of Tavistock House, wearing a deep-green silk day dress, and the sun, which streamed through the window, caught the threads of the ribbon which trimmed her sleeves, shimmering in the light. Her eyes scanned the room. She had never seen such beautiful mahogany doors, such large gilt mirrors or such delicate glass chandeliers.

Dickens had lived at Tavistock House for six years: a plain brick house, surrounded by mature trees, standing behind wrought-iron gates. It was an accommodating, if not handsome house, with eighteen rooms which well served a large family. The property had been in dire need of redecoration when

Dickens had bought it, but, after many alterations — changing doors, extending passageways and installing bathroom fittings — it finally met his exacting standards.

'I see you are admiring the room, Miss Ellen,' Dickens said. 'I am utterly drawn to the light myself and inspired by it, for I could never live in a house where the lighting was poor.'

'It is a very impressive room, indeed, sir,' Ellen replied.

She could hardly believe that she was in the same room as Charles Dickens, and although she trembled slightly with a mixture of awe and excitement, she employed all her skill as an actress to hide it. After all, she did not want him to think her immature.

'It is very good of you to find the time to rehearse with us, Mr Dickens. You must have so many other commitments, sir.'

'It is my pleasure, Miss Ellen. I am happy to give of my time, as you, your mother and sister have taken up these roles at such short notice.'

The Ternan ladies could hardly believe their good fortune. Only a few weeks before, they had been recommended by Frank Talfourd and Alfred Wigan of the Olympic theatre, who had heard that Charles Dickens was seeking actresses to take the parts which had been played by his daughters and sister-in-law.

There had been some whispers of disapproval about the propriety of Katie and Mamie's appearance on the stage in public, and although not usually directed by the opinion of others, Dickens did not want to jeopardize his daughters' reputation in society and conceded that their parts must be taken up by professional actresses, hence the appointment of the Ternan ladies.

'And you say that you remember my husband, Mr Dickens?' Mrs Ternan sipped her tea.

'Yes, madam, I remember seeing him at the Theatre Royal in Rochester, when I was a young man and, of course, I remember your own performance in *Hamlet* alongside William Macready at Drury Lane.'

'You remember my father, sir?' Ellen said with interest.

'Yes, but as I said to your mother, Miss Ellen, I was no more than a boy.' Dickens smoothed down his hair.

Mrs Frances Ternan tried not to look dismayed that their host appeared to be passing himself off as so much younger than herself.

Her late husband, Thomas Ternan had originated from Ireland and, upon marrying Frances, had sought fame in America with a travelling theatre company. When he met with little success the couple returned to London, but bitter with disappointment, Thomas began to suffer with bouts of depression. When his wife became the more successful of the two, his health deteriorated and he died in an asylum. All that Ellen could remember about her father was the image of a hazy figure slumped over a table, his hand clutching an empty glass.

Maria Ternan, who had had some success as a child actress, was interested to learn more about Mr Dickens's daughters who were near to her in age.

'And I understand that Her Majesty was most taken with the Royal Gala Performance which featured your daughters, sir.'

'Yes, it was a wonderful privilege, Miss Maria. We performed at the Gallery of Illustration in Regent Street, and accompanying the Queen were the Prince of Prussia, the King of Belgium and our own Prince Albert. Her Majesty's patronage garnered further support for the Jerrold fund, for which I was most grateful.'

Dickens and the Queen had long enjoyed a mutual admiration for each other. Although Lord Melbourne had advised her against reading Dickens's work because, in his opinion, it dealt with unpleasant matters, she became an avid reader of his novels.

In 1838, the young Charles Dickens had been among the crowds of well-wishers when Queen Victoria's coronation procession made its way through London; and when she had become engaged to Prince Albert a year later, Dickens had found himself strangely filled with jealousy and declared to his wife and friends that he was in love with her.

When he first began to act in amateur theatricals, the Queen often accompanied by a distinguished entourage, frequently requested to be a part of the audience.

Maria imagined how delighted she would be if she were presented to the Queen after a performance. 'How lucky your daughters were, sir.'

Dickens began to laugh, 'You cannot imagine how embarrassed we all felt at the idea of being presented to Her Majesty in our costumes. You see, after the performance of *The Frozen Deep*, we put on a short farce, and there I was being called before the Queen dressed in a false nose, a huge wig and an oversized coat.'

The ladies laughed.

'Oh, you must have felt quite foolish, sir,' Maria smiled.

Dickens expression abruptly changed to one of earnestness. 'Oh, no, miss. I refused her completely, on the grounds that I was not properly attired and, of course, Her Majesty understood entirely.'

The Ternan ladies were taken aback by Mr Dickens's boldness, and the Queen's apparent acceptance of it.

'Do you know, ladies, although I never imagined that anything could call me away from my desk for any length of time, I have to confess that I am completely addicted to the stage.'

Since boyhood, Dickens had found that whenever he was in a theatre he saw and heard nothing else beyond what happened in the performance; and when he himself had his own audience there was nothing that could compare with it. When the applause finally came, he drank it in, willing it to go on and on, and what an addiction it was. For those few short hours Dickens lived another life, he was transported to another world.

Ellen was caught up in his passion. 'I have to admit, Mr Dickens, that I completely fell in love with the character of Richard Wardour. He is so noble, intelligent and self-sacrificing. No wonder you have had the audience in tears, sir.'

'*Always seeking, but never finding true love . . .* ' Dickens whispered, lost in his own thoughts for a moment.

Ellen nodded, thinking of the hero, who travels to the Arctic to forget the painful rejection by the woman he loves.

'May I ask what inspired you, sir?'

'Yes, of course. When Sir John Franklyn did not return from his Polar expedition, and his wife, Lady Franklyn, hired a ship to search for him, I was moved to write a story of love, devotion and courage, set in hostile conditions.'

'It is certainly a moving story, Mr Dickens.'

'Please, call me Charles.'

'Oh, no I couldn't . . .'

'Please, you must . . . Ellen.'

Talk of the performance continued, and she leaned forward as Dickens talked, not wanting to miss one word.

Catherine was not at home, and had gone into town with her daughters; however, if she had been present she would have noticed that as much as her husband tried to direct his attention to Mrs Frances Ternan, and then Miss Maria Ternan, that it was to Miss Ellen Ternan that his eyes returned again and again.

She would also have noticed how he was enchanted with the way in which Ellen Ternan put her head on one side and listened as he was talking, the way that he was mesmerized as the sunlight caught the trimmings on her sleeves and, if she could have read his thoughts, then she would have known that the years were falling away from him and in that moment he was feeling like a youth in the first flush of romance.

Mrs Ternan, who with length of years was very perceptive, had noticed his attentiveness too, and ideas in her mind began to form around the opportunities that such interest could bring. Year upon year she had worked tirelessly to provide for her girls to maintain a degree of respectability and a certain standard of living. She reflected upon the long hours that she had spent training and rehearsing and then delivering performance upon performance.

Life on the stage was hard work, but she could never have imagined a life sitting at home, politely receiving callers. Being an actress had given her the power to voice her emotion in a way that women were not usually allowed. But she acknowledged how often she had packed up trunks, only to unpack them again a few days later, and that she and her daughters had seen one shabby dressing-room too many. Yes, an influential patron could change their lives for ever.

Chapter 11

August 1857
Gad's Hill Place

My Dear Wilkie
I have not known a moment's peace since the last night of The Frozen Deep. Miss Ternan's performance was electrifying, and now all that I can see, all that I can hear and all that I can think of is her. I feel the sun on my face and I think of the warmth of her smile, I walk in my garden and I hear the rustle of her gown. She is everywhere and everything to me and knowing that the

object of my affection is just out of reach at a theatre in Doncaster, is complete torture.

Last night I dreamt that my hands and feet were bound, and before me was a series of barriers. I woke up struggling to untie myself and climb over them and, when I could not return to my slumber, I got up at two in the morning, left Tavistock House and walked the thirty miles to Gad's Hill. Mile after mile I walked, unaware of my exertion, dreaming and falling asleep to the sound of my own feet, seeing her before me still.

You cannot conceive how I feel, Wilkie. I can only describe myself as being in a daze, unable to write or think clearly and, as I cannot discipline myself to work at anything here in London, the only way forward is to go to her in Doncaster, and you must come with me. We could attend the races together on the premise that we are writing an article for Household Words. Please say you will accompany me.

I have only one person and one destination in mind, and can think of nothing else.

Your Friend
Charles Dickens

Dickens drummed his fingers on the door of the carriage, and Wilkie Collins sighed for the third time.

'We will be there shortly, Dickens. Try to relax, you are making me uneasy.'

'I'm sorry, Wilkie, I am in such a state of agitation, it is unbearable. I just want to see her again, to talk to her, and to see that sweet, young face and then I will be able to know some contentment.' He sighed and then had an idea. 'I say, Wilkie, why don't you tell me something more of your unusual visitor to distract my mind?'

Since her arrival, the woman in white had remained almost as much of a mystery to Wilkie Collins as she had been on that first night. She had spoken nothing more of her past or her family and Wilkie had not pressed her, for he felt that she must have suffered a good deal of distress at the hands of her captor. At the suggestion that he send the police to the home of her brother-in-law, she had become distressed and made him promise not to speak upon the matter again; and Wilkie promised her immediately for, such was the depth of his feeling, that he did not believe he could refuse her anything.

'For now, she is staying with us at Hanover Terrace, and she has written word to her family in Ireland. I have mailed the letter for her, but everyday I dread the arrival of the post and find that I am tempted to throw the damned reply on the fire when it arrives. You see, I have to admit, Dickens, that I find myself

81

much in the same predicament as yourself.'

Dickens interest was now aroused. 'Really? In what way, my friend?'

'I find that I cannot think of anything except for Caroline, and the idea of her going to her relatives is unbearable. When I think that I might not look upon that angelic countenance again . . .'

'Well, my friend, there is nothing for it, you must make her an offer.'

'That is just the problem: I can't.' Collins's voice was becoming thin and reed-like with anxiety, and he began to perspire slightly.

'Why ever not?'

'I have a horror of marriage, Dickens. You above all people should understand that. I yearn to be with her, but to find myself in a permanent state of matrimony would somehow change how I feel about her, how I think of her.'

'I see,' said Dickens, not really seeing at all.

'I'm afraid that if I get married I will start a chain of events that will ultimately lead to me having offspring, having grandchildren and growing old. I will always imagine that every man who is unattached is happier and enjoying more freedom that I am.'

This, however, Dickens *could* see, and nodded with understanding.

'Perhaps you are right, my friend, maybe you are as well to stay in your current state as a bachelor.'

The carriage arrived outside the Angel Hotel in Regent Square about a mile from the Doncaster Racecourse. The driver helped with the luggage and while Wilkie Collins took a discreet sip of his tincture, and insisted that he needed an early night to get over the journey, Dickens had already determined to pay a visit to the Princess Theatre in town.

A short while later, he had rearranged the furniture in his room, moving the bureau to the window so that the light fell upon it, and had also taken from his carpet-bag several sheets of writing paper, two cut-quill pens, a pot of ink, and blotting paper. He arranged these items with meticulous order on the carefully positioned bureau. He then unpacked his case and folded everything away with the utmost precision, leaving only a burnt-orange waistcoat with brass buttons lying upon the bed.

After refreshing himself with a wash, Dickens dressed, donned the waistcoat and pondered his appearance in the looking-glass. He realized that, on reflection, he did not want to draw attention to himself this evening, and he reached for a more sober replacement from the wardrobe.

The Princess Theatre was situated just off Station Road and, although the performance was due to commence at 7.00 p.m., for his own purposes Dickens wished to arrive a little late. He took a cab and, caught up in his own thoughts, he recalled the last night of *The Frozen Deep*. He could see the object of his affection now, the tears running down her cheeks.

'I will always stay as I am, because the man I love is married. I don't think that he will ever know how I adore him with all of my heart.'

They were only words in a script and yet, to Dickens, they could not have felt more real. Ellen Ternan had stirred within him the most dangerous of emotions and he knew that after that night, there was no turning back.

*   *   *

The lights had already dimmed when he slipped into a side-box at the theatre, and situated himself behind the curtain, lest he be seen by the audience. Immediately he felt nervous, but he told himself that he had no need. After all, what was he doing wrong? He was there to watch the performance, the same as anyone else. In his heart, however, he knew that it was false reasoning; he was not there for the same reason as anyone else, for there was not another man in the audience who was falling in love with Ellen Ternan as he was.

He looked down at the stage and she was there, just as he remembered her. Everything about her was perfect: her voice, her poise. She addressed the audience, her arms outstretched, her eyes moving amongst them. Suddenly she lifted her gaze to the box where Dickens sat, and she stopped speaking — only momentarily—but to him it seemed like an eternity.

She had caught a glimpse of him and forgotten the script. It was his fault entirely. The audience would look up at the box and suspect something. Someone might see him leaving. Everyone would link his name with hers . . .

She dropped her eyes again, smiled discreetly and resumed her lines. No one had noticed, but she sensed that he was there, and he in turn, with his heart thudding in his chest, knew that she had sensed it and, consequently, loved her all the more.

After the performance he left an envelope, addressed to Miss Ellen Ternan, with a stage hand. It was an invitation for her to accompany him, with her mother and her sister, to the races the following afternoon. On the return journey to the Angel Hotel, he knew immediately what he must do in order to prepare for any hint of a scandal connected with Miss Ternan. When he returned to his room, he lit a gas lamp on the bureau, sat down and began to write.

The Angel Hotel
Doncaster
August 16th 1857

My Dear Miss Burdett-Coutts
   Our friendship is such, that I can no longer stay silent upon the truth about my domestic situation.
   Poor Catherine and I are not suited to each other and it cannot be helped. It is apparent to me that there are no two people who could be less compatible, have less in common or a greater lack of confidence in each other than we two. We have been living separate lives for some time now, maintaining appearances for the sake of the children.
   Sadly, there is an insurmountable barrier between us and despite my best efforts, it cannot be overcome. Don't think the worse of Catherine, as I don't think that she has it in her to be anything beyond what she is.
   At present, her mind is in a state of jealousy and confusion, and she is prone to make the wildest of accusations, so if she should seek you out with any of her stories, you must pay her no heed.
   I could never commit her to professional care like poor Mrs Thackeray, and that is why I am arranging for a separate residence where she can reside with Alice, our dear old servant, and I will ensure her comfort

without sparing any expense.

As yet, I have not broached the subject to her, for I am not sure that her mind is such that she can bear it, but when I return from Doncaster, I will seek Dr Bell's advice.

For now I remain, ever your friend
Charles Dickens

Dickens blotted the letter, put it in an envelope which he carefully sealed, and then he began all over again. On and on, late into the night he worked, until he had written much the same to almost everyone that he knew, creating a world that only he controlled.

Chapter 12

August 1857
Doncaster Races

'It was so kind of you to send a carriage for us, Mr Dickens,' Mrs Frances Ternan began. 'And it is a most unexpected surprise to see you and Mr Collins in Doncaster. What a coincidence it is that you should find yourselves here, at precisely the same time as ourselves.'

Mrs Ternan was not a fool, and knew with certainty that there was no coincidence.

'Yes, Mr Collins and I are here to report upon the races for *Household Words,*' Dickens answered enthusiastically. 'You cannot imagine how surprised I was to see Miss Ellen's name advertising her appearance at the Princess Theatre, and I decided there and then to invite you to be my guests today, as a way of thanking you for your wonderful performances in *The Frozen Deep*.'

Ellen Ternan was wearing a tartan day dress of vivid blues and greens, and a small hat made up of ribbon and delicate feathers. She had been thrilled when she had realized that Dickens had been secretly observing her at the theatre. Now she knew with some assurance that he admired her and it gave her a strange sense of power which she had never known before, and the knowledge that she could use that power to great effect.

Her hands had trembled when she had opened the letter addressed to her in his recognizable hand, and she had to admit some disappointment when she saw that the invitation was extended to her mother and sister also; but she was excited by the idea of being in his company once more.

During the rehearsals for *The Frozen Deep* she had often noticed him looking at her and had begun to wonder what he thought of her. Did he think she was a polished actress? She hoped so: she had so wanted to earn his admiration and good opinion. She had noticed that whenever he had addressed her family, it appeared as if he was talking only to her, but after the last performance there had been a party, and she was dismayed when Dickens had left early, excusing himself on the grounds of tiredness. It seemed that perhaps she had meant nothing to him at all.

The following day, however, a letter had arrived at the Ternans' hotel. He had given his earnest apologies for leaving so abruptly, but explained that he found endings very difficult, and that saying goodbye had always made him sad.

'Please excuse my little peculiarities. You can be sure that meeting you all with always stay in my memory.'

Ellen could not know how much he had wanted to address her directly, but there was far too much at risk if such a letter should ever fall into the wrong hands. So he had hoped with all his heart that she could read between the lines, for now.

*   *   *

Wilkie Collins had not slept well the night before. He had gone to bed early while Dickens was at the theatre, but awoken in a sweat in the middle of the night, not sure of where he was, and had called out for his mother. At the foot of his bed he could see a vision of a shimmering green woman with huge tusks, and he pulled the covers over his head and tried to think of Caroline.

Dickens had heard him shout out, put on his dressing-gown and knocked upon his door, enquiring whether all was well, but when no response came, he returned to his bed acknowledging that it was likely a result of his friend's addiction. Consequently, Collins was very withdrawn the following morning, and the Ternan ladies, who had noticed, were grateful of the animated conversation with which their host entertained them.

'Would you care for some champagne, ladies? I hear that it is all the rage on these occasions.'

Anxious that he would be left in the company of the Ternan ladies, and still looking over his shoulder in fear of the green tusked woman, Wilkie Collins insisted that he should fetch the refreshments and he quickly disappeared into the bustling crowds of gentleman wearing bold-check trousers and ladies in their exotic hats.

'Is your friend all right, Mr Dickens? He seems a little agitated,' Maria Ternan asked.

'He suffers with the most terrible rheumatism, Miss Maria, and in consequence sleeps very badly at times, but I can assure you that he is of the most impeccable character, and, of course, as you probably know, he is a very fine writer.'

Collins had employed a young man to accompany him and return the drinks to his associates, sure that his own hands were too uncertain for the job.

'Ah, my dear Wilkie, you are just in time. The race is about to begin!' Dickens said with excitement.

The bookmakers standing on their scaffolds, shouted that their books were closed, the crowds surged to the edge of the race track and, when the race began, a loud roar went up. Dickens was quite taken aback at the manner in which some of the women shouted and waved their parasols about, cheering on their chosen winner. He was glad to see that Ellen watched with a great deal more decorum than those about her: she knew his eyes were upon her.

Looking at her again, the noise of the crowds evaporated and in that moment it seemed as if the only person who existed for him was her. He edged a little closer, closed his eyes and breathed in the perfume of her hair, whispering to himself, *It was so wonderful to see you last night. I could not take my eyes off you.*

She did not turn, but smiled softly, reached out her hand and momentarily clasped his gloved fingers, releasing them just as the winning horse crossed the line, the crowds roaring with delight.

Her response was completely unexpected. Dickens had not meant for her to hear, but sensing his hand in hers, he was elated that she *had* heard. Now there was no mistaking the feelings that existed between them and if another word was not exchanged, it mattered not: they understood one another completely now.

Chapter 13

September 1857
Hanover Terrace, London

The woman in white stood in front of the flickering flames of the fire, her hair falling over her shoulders. Wilkie Collins had been glad to return from his excursion with Dickens, realizing how much he had missed her.

From Doncaster, he and Dickens had travelled to The Queen's Head in Cumberland. Dickens had persuaded a reluctant Collins to accompany him hill-walking. To his mind, Wilkie could not have imagined an occupation less appealing, but Dickens had been bursting with energy and enthusiasm after his afternoon at the races.

'It was a success beyond my wildest dreams, my dear Wilkie.'

Collins had not observed the affectionate exchange that had taken place between the two lovers, and assumed that Dickens was referring to his delight at a triple win on the horses. He had randomly picked the name of three runners, only to find that each had won.

They had been greeted at The Queen's Head by the genial landlord, Joseph Porter, whom Dickens quickly pressed into service as a guide for his planned walking expedition. After a breakfast of eggs and oatcakes, Dickens, who was not in the least deterred by the misty weather, paced back and forth outside the front door of the inn, keen to make a start. He threw his head back, letting the rain dampen his face.

'Come along, Collins, don't let the weather put you off. After all, this is the sort of atmosphere of which your famed melodramas are made. You never know, you just might find inspiration out on those murky hills.'

Wilkie was not at all enthused and trailed behind Dickens and Porter, who strode on ahead, onward and upward, talking incessantly. The rain had become heavier, the skies had darkened and the mist had thickened.

'Dickens?' Wilkie called, trying to hide the fear in his voice. He could hear his companions but they were no longer in sight.

He called out more forcefully, 'Dickens!'

At that moment he had felt the stones under his feet giving way and he lost his footing and slipped. He did not fall far, but a terrible pain shot through his ankle.

'Collins, are you all right? Where are you?' Dickens called.

Wilkie had shouted repeatedly until he was at last found by his walking companions. He had sprained his ankle badly and, in great discomfort, he was carried downhill between the two of them.

'Damn and blast!' Dickens cursed. 'My compass is broken. What a time for it to happen.'

Collins had never been a brave man, and in that moment he had wanted to cry. Porter said that he could hear the sound of a stream and that if they followed its course downwards, it would surely lead them back into town. The two men struggled on until they came to an abandoned dog-cart on to which they lifted Collins and continued along the stream's path. When at last Collins found himself being carried into the snug lounge of The Queen's Head, no place had ever seemed so welcoming in his life before.

Now, back in the safe haven of his own home, he was so grateful to be at Hanover Terrace, and in the company of Caroline once more.

'Wilkie, I have something to tell you.'

'Really, my dear?' His voice was full of contentment, he puffed on his cigar and he was enchanted with the way that the reflection of the firelight was dancing on her hair. These last few weeks since Caroline had come into his home, his life, he had known exquisite moments of peace and tolerated his pain a good deal better.

The reply from Ireland had never arrived and, glad of it, Wilkie had not asked why. Charlie, however, had wanted answers and pressed his mother to ask Mrs Graves about her relatives. But Harriet Collins had been reluctant.

'I have not seen your brother so settled in his moods for a long while, and if it discourages him from relying so heavily upon his tincture, then all the better.'

'But what will people say?' Charlie persisted.

'There is no shame in us having a lodger, and a destitute one should appeal to your sense of Christian charity, Charlie.'

'But her appearance, Mama, people stare so.'

'People stare at you too, Charlie; if only you would eat a little more.'

Disgruntled at such a personal reproof, Charlie Collins said nothing more about the woman.

His own romantic pursuits had not met with much success. He was now almost thirty years old and his only meaningful relationship had been with Maria, the sister of Dante Gabriel Rossetti. She was a very attractive woman, but, like Charlie, was deeply religious and had brought their relationship to an end when she had decided to become a nun at the Anglican Sisterhood of All Saints Convent.

He was also extremely dissatisfied with his career as an artist, never attaining the perfection that he sought in his art and, as his own harshest critic, he often abandoned his work, half-finished. For Charles Collins everything in life needed to emulate the perfection and purity of nature, and the presence of this unconventional woman in his house was most unsettling.

Wilkie drew on his cigar and asked gently, 'What was it that you wanted to tell me, my dear?'

Caroline's voice was nervous and uncertain. 'Well, it is more something that I have to show you, than tell you.'

She crossed the room to the door and opened it, and there in the doorway stood a child the very image of herself, dressed in flowing white attire, with loose blonde locks and the same angelic countenance.

'This is my daughter, Elizabeth, Wilkie.'

'Very pleased to meet you, sir.' The child's manners were impeccable.

Wilkie stood up and took her hand in greeting.

'And I am pleased to meet you too, Miss Elizabeth.'

She was as lovely as her mother, and there was no doubt in Wilkie's mind that Caroline *was* her mother, for they were the exact image of one another.

'And where have you been hiding, my dear?'

'I have been staying with Mrs Green at Lodge Road, but as Mama no longer has the means to pay for my lodging, she brought me here today.'

Caroline came to her child, knelt at her side and before the man who had been her saviour these past few weeks, looked up at him.

'Never once have you asked for more of my history, nor about the letter from Ireland, which by now I suspect that you realize will never come. You have been kindness itself, Wilkie, and if the discovery of my daughter's existence means that you—'

Wilkie put a finger to his lips.

'I think, my dear, that I prefer no explanation at all. Your entrance into my life has been the most wonderful thing that has ever happened to me. All that I need to know is if you are going to stay and for how long.'

The woman in white had been christened Elizabeth Caroline Compton and had not been raised in Ireland at all, but in the small village of Toddington, near Cheltenham. Her father was not a gentleman, as she had indicated by her manner, but a carpenter whom she had not seen in many years. She never had been married to a captain in the army and the man at Regent's Park had been one of a long line of opportunistic predators. The woman in white was fortunate that she had managed to spirit her daughter away to safe lodgings until today, when she had thought that she had at last found a man who would give her his name.

For reasons best known to himself, Wilkie Collins chose to remain blissfully ignorant of all of these details, and preferred to believe that she was what she had said she was: the widow of a gentleman.

'I will stay for as long as you allow it, and if you ask it, then I will not leave at all.' She smiled. At these words, Wilkie grew cold, and the sentiments that he had expressed to Dickens sounded in his ears.

'I have a horror of marriage, Dickens . . . to find myself in a permanent state of matrimony would somehow change how I feel about her, how I think of her . . .'

He threw the stub of his cigar on to the fire, and took out his pocket-watch.

'It is late, my dear, and I am tired. It has been somewhat a surprise, although a most pleasant one, to learn of your daughter's existence. Perhaps in the morning, we can talk over better arrangements for you and young Elizabeth. After all, we cannot expect my mother to make such a provision here at Hanover Terrace.'

The woman in white nodded sadly. She had played out this scene before: it seemed that she could not expect anything different from Wilkie Collins after all, but she lived in hope, none the less.

Seated on the end of his bed, Wilkie took off his thick-lensed glasses, put his head in

98

his hands and sighed. Caroline would leave him now, it was a certainty All that he had to do was ask her, to say those four words: *'Will you marry me?'* But even thinking upon them caused a knot in his stomach. He lay down and looked up at the ceiling He did not want her to go; he truly loved her; what her past had been mattered not to him.

He slept restlessly. In his dreams it was raining incessantly and he stood at the door of a church, a flower in his button-hole, the rain streaming down his face and soaking his clothes. His brother was at his side, his complexion whiter than ever, his flame-red hair in contrast to his paleness. The doors to the church opened before them, the congregation were seated and, to his surprise, the bride was already waiting for him at the altar. He felt his collar tightening around his throat as he approached her. He stood at her side, lifted her veil, and to his horror, found himself looking directly into the face of the green, tusked woman.

He sat bolt upright in bed and shouted, 'Caroline!'

Chapter 14

October 1857
Tavistock House

The Narrative of Charles Dickens Junior

I found my sister strolling in the autumnal garden and wondered how I could prepare her for what I had to say. She looked so pretty and carefree, and I was crushed by the knowledge that what I was about to share with her would change her world forever. I approached her with a tentative smile and encouraged her to sit on the garden bench with me.

'Whatever is the matter, Charley? Why do you look so serious?' she laughed, nervously.

'Mamie, something very sad has happened to Mama.'

'Oh, Charley, whatever is it? Is she dead?' My sister began to cry.

'No, no, Mamie, it is not as bad as that.'

'Then what is it?' she urged.

'Yesterday afternoon, she and Papa visited the zoological gardens and they ended up having the most terrible row. Papa left her in the carriage and walked home, but the driver returned with an empty carriage, and said that Mama had insisted on walking by the lake in the park.'

'Oh, Charley, she has drowned, hasn't she?'

'Shh, Mamie, I have told you. She is not dead.' I took a handkerchief from my jacket pocket and handed it to her. 'Papa insisted that the driver return, and upon doing so the man found her walking at the water's edge. Heaven knows what she would have done if he had been a moment later.'

Mamie dabbed her eyes. 'But why on earth would Mama consider such a thing? Doesn't she love us anymore?'

'Of course Mama loves us, but I think that she is not at all well. Yesterday Papa spoke of things which he should not have, things which he has been suppressing for too long, and she could not bear to hear them said. You know how she has always idolized him.'

'So where is she now?' Mamie asked sadly, looking at the withered leaves scattered across the lawn.

'She is sleeping in her room. Doctor Bell has given her a draught.'

'Can I see her?'

I hadn't the heart to tell her that there was more to know, but it had to be said.

'Wait a moment, Mamie, I haven't finished.'

I breathed deeply, angrily wiping a tear from my eyes, annoyed that I had been overcome by emotion.

'Whatever is it, Charley?'

'Papa has told our mother that he wishes to separate from her.' I squeezed my sister's hand

101

tightly. 'He is going to move us all to Gad's Hill and find somewhere else for Mama to go with Alice.'

Mamie stood up. 'It can't be true! I will go and ask Papa myself.'

I caught her arm. 'Mamie, it is true. There . . . there is someone else.'

She stopped dead in her tracks, 'Someone else? I don't believe you, Charley, Papa would never do such a thing. He is a man of principle.'

'I heard everything, Mamie. Our parents were shouting at each other, and in her rage, Mama threw a glass at Papa. He told her that he is in love with . . . ' I faltered, wondering how I could tell my sister that our father was in love with a girl no older than she was.

'Who is it?' Mamie's eyes flashed with resentment.

'It doesn't matter who it is, Mamie. You'll find out soon enough.'

Her anger turned to despair and she sank onto the bench, putting her hands over her face. The events of the preceding weeks played out in her mind, and suddenly she saw everything.

'Oh, God, Charley, I know who it is. It's Ellen Ternan, isn't it? Oh, poor Mama. Poor, poor Mama.'

I sat down next to her and we remained in silence for a little while wondering how this could have happened and how our lives were going to change. Neither of us could imagine our family being broken up in this way.

Mamie broke the silence. 'Well, I for one shall go with Mama, of that I am certain and Katie will surely come too.'

'It's not that easy, Mamie. You and Katie are not yet of age, and I know that Papa will not let you go as long as he has a say in the matter. I, however, am of age, and I have told him that *I* will go with Mama.'

Mamie's face was full of amazement. I had never stood up to my father in my life before, nor countered anything that he had asked of me.

'What did he say?' Her voice was hushed with awe.

'At first he was terribly angry, and said that he would never allow it, threatening me with all manner of punishments, but when I encouraged him to believe that people would think better of him if they thought that my going was his suggestion, he relented.'

Mamie shook her head in disbelief. 'Oh, Charley, what will everyone think? It is terrible.'

'Papa will be discreet, you can be sure of that. He will make people believe that the separation is for the good of Mama's health, nothing more. There will be no hint of Miss Ternan's existence.'

Mamie's face coloured with anger, 'He had better not bring her here, for I shall not say one word to her.'

'You don't understand, Mamie. If you behave in a way which gives any hint of Miss Ternan's place in our father's life, your own position in society will be at risk. Our name will be tarnished in such a way that all invitations will cease. Don't you see? You must behave as if nothing at all has changed. You must treat her as if she is your own sister.'

A figure appeared in the garden, carrying an easel and a box of paints. I had already told Katie everything and after her tears had ceased she had been very quiet.

'Does she know? Mamie whispered nodding towards our sister. 'Yes, I have told her everything.'

'Then what on earth is she doing?'

'Katie,' I called. 'Are you all right?'

'Of course I'm all right,' she snapped. 'Why shouldn't I be all right?'

She was struggling to set the easel upon the grass.

'Katie, shall I assist you?'

'I have already told you, I am all right.'

She continued to struggle with her task and, in her agitation, the easel toppled over and her box of paints scattered all over the floor. Her anguish finally overcame her and she dropped to her knees.

'Oh, Papa, Papa, how could you?'

And I felt so helpless to do anything.

104

Chapter 15

March 1858
Tavistock House

The Narrative of Charles Dickens Junior

There had been no Christmas celebrations in the house that December and all the colour seemed to have faded from our lives. Papa endeavoured to continue with his work but could not settle sufficiently to begin a new novel, being in a fury over his separation from my mother and her determined reluctance to leave him. In order to speed a resolution to matters, my father's friend, John Forster, who had a sound knowledge of legal matters, recommended a solicitor to draw up a deed of separation.

In the uncertain atmosphere that pervaded our home, I had found some unexpected relief in sharing a confidence with a childhood friend, Bessie Evans, who was the daughter of my father's publisher, Frederick Evans. Mr Evans had been proposed as one of the trustees to oversee my mother's interests, find her a new home and administer her financial affairs. While our fathers discussed these sensitive matters in the study at Tavistock House, I had been left to keep Bessie company in the absence of my sisters, who were visiting the Thackeray girls.

Bessie and I sat in the sitting-room endeavouring to make polite conversation about the weather and other such pointless topics. Occasional and uncomfortable silences punctuated our efforts, during which I found my eyes straying to Bessie's charming face and shapely figure; both of which I noticed had changed of late from girlish to womanly.

I could hear my father's voice gaining volume in his study and, in an effort to provide a distraction, I attempted an enquiry about Bessie's recent visit to Europe.

'And how did you find Paris, Bessie—er, Miss Evans?'

Sensing my difficulties, Bessie, who was of the most practical disposition, cut to the heart of matters.

'Charley, I have never been Miss Evans to you and I never will be. I have always been Bessie and I am Bessie still. Now, we can sit here and make foolish conversation about my trip to France or acknowledge what is taking place in your father's study. After all, we are no longer children and we both know the subject upon which our fathers are speaking.'

In that moment, she looked and sounded so very much like a woman and I realized that she was right. We were no longer children and I was suddenly angered that those days of innocence had been snatched from under me with no warning at all.

'You look so sad, Charley. Surely it would help to speak of what is in your heart?'

I nodded, glad to be relieved of the pressure to pretend.

'It all feels so uncertain, Bessie. My father is like a man possessed, as if his life is spiralling out of control. The house feels strange and empty without Mama, who has chosen to stay with my grandparents until matters are resolved. Only my aunt and little Edward seem able carry on as if nothing has changed. Francis is quiet—his stammer worse than ever—and Katie, Mamie and myself must say nothing of what we feel for fear of displeasing our father.'

'That must be a great burden to you,' Bessie said with understanding in her voice.

Walter, who had overcome a brief but frightening period of sudden deafness, had now left for India as a cadet in the East India Company. Sydney, Alfred and Henry were boarding in Boulogne, and Henry was receiving his schooling in Germany. As yet Papa had written to them only of Mama being unwell and needing to spend some time with my grandparents. My brothers were not fully aware of the circumstances that would greet them when they returned to England.

'Have your sisters not been able to draw any comfort from your aunt?' Bessie asked.

I laughed at such irony.

'My aunt is not the sort of woman from whom comfort is easily drawn, although I think Mamie finds her a little easier company than Katie. In fact I am quite concerned about Katie's wellbeing. She has not been herself at all since all this trouble began.'

I did not feel able to describe how my sister's behaviour was fluctuating between being either quietly withdrawn at home, or laughing loudly and gaily whenever she was in company. I noticed how she had also taken to carefully moving certain ornaments into a set position and would become quite agitated if she returned to find them moved, even an inch, after the servants had dusted. I was sure Bessie would think that my sister was losing her mind if I outlined such behaviour.

It had also been rather embarrassing to notice how Katie appeared to have taken to flirting with a friend of my father's, a Mr Edmund Yates, who was a married man. Mr Yates, who was a part-time writer and journalist, had come to know my father on the basis of Papa's friendship with his father. If Mr Yates had noticed my sister's behaviour, he did not comment upon it or respond to it, but I worried that she was becoming unstable. It was as if she were trying to elicit a reaction from my father whose own behaviour was making her feel so insecure.

'I'm sure your kind interest in your sister is a great comfort to her, and in time she will be her former self again,' Bessie offered kindly.

At the sound of the study door opening we both jumped a little, and the voices of my father and Mr Evans could now be heard in the hallway.

'*So that is settled then, Frederick, Catherine will receive four hundred a year, and a brougham, and if she takes up residence at Gloucester Crescent then she will not be too far from your own home for you to see to her requests if she needs anything.*'

Bessie looked at me with sympathy.

'It seems,' I said, sadly, 'that it is all settled.'

*   *   *

May 1858

Gloucester Crescent, London

'It's a lovely location, isn't it, Charley?' my mother had said on arrival, looking up at the small villa and trying unsuccessfully to sound cheerful. 'I shall enjoy walking in the park in the good weather, and inviting my oldest and dearest friends to visit.'

Gloucester Crescent had a pleasant aspect looking out across Regent's Park and, when at last she had her own things about her, Mama endeavoured to make the house her own. She had tried so hard not to let me see her unhappiness and to be cordial company whenever I returned from working at the bank. She would ask me about my day, and now I had moved into brokerage with the assistance of Miss Burdett-Coutts, I felt much happier and could speak of my work with some enthusiasm, although I still held longings to be a writer.

Matters at Gad's Hill, however, were not so harmonious. My grandparents had been outraged at Papa's treatment of their daughter, and argued with him furiously, but what was most perplexing was the response of my aunt Georgina. Did she take her sister's part and leave my father's house? No. Did she share her own parents' disapproval of my father's actions? She did not.

In the wake of the argument with Papa, Mama had accused my aunt of all manner of treachery, but my aunt remained coolly aloof, neither admitting guilt nor defending herself. It appeared as if Papa could do no wrong in her eyes and she vowed to stay firmly at his side. In doing so she placed herself in the most perilous position, for upon the public learning that my mother was no longer in the marital home, and that her sister had remained, Georgina Hogarth became subject to the most scandalous of gossip: that she was my father's mistress.

No one can imagine the extent of the outrage and indignation that my father displayed at such accusations. Upon my next

110

visit to Gad's Hill, he summoned myself, Mamie and Katie into his study and began an angry tirade while we stood before him like recalcitrant schoolchildren.

His face was blood red.

'Have any one of you been approached by a journalist? Come on, out with it, for, upon my word, I will have the truth.'

Mamie and Katie both became tearful and so it was my role to speak on their behalf.

'No, Papa, none of us has spoken a word to anyone.'

He paced about his study like a madman, gripping his hair and gesticulating wildly.

'I will not tolerate one hint of innuendo against your aunt or, for that matter, anyone one else that I might choose to call my friend.'

We presumed by this that he was referring to Miss Ternan, but dared not utter a word.

'Such friendship is marked by a simple innocence and nothing more. If such lies continue to abound about your aunt, or indeed any other such nameless person, I will go to the papers myself, and issue a statement categorically denying such accusations as grossly false.' His voice was full of rage.

I cringed at such a thought. It was bad enough that the whole of London seemed to be gossiping about my family's business, and yet here was my father threatening to publicize his personal affairs in the newspapers for all to read. How humiliated we children would feel to bear the surname Dickens if he followed such a course.

'And I will make this plain to you now,' my father continued, 'if you girls set one foot in your mother's home, or enter into the presence of your grandparents—and that applies to you also, Charley—I will disinherit you all!'

And he left the room with a slam of the door.

Mamie began to cry, but Katie, who had remained strangely detached from all emotion since the episode in the garden, became angry.

'Well, he will not forbid me. If I wish to see Mama, or our grandparents then I will. How dare he lecture us in such a self-righteous manner?'

As we left the study, Aunt Georgina crossed the hall, and while Katie flounced up the stairs to her room, and I put on my hat to leave, Mamie threw herself into Georgina's arms and began to sob.

'Oh, Aunty, it is all too much.'

*   *   *

Upon returning to Gloucester Crescent, I sat in the carriage, and looked beyond the passing scenery, reflecting on my father's anger and my aunt's place in our lives. I could hardly remember a time when she had not been a part of our family home, and had taken it for granted that she had lived with us with my mother's blessing. I acknowledged then how much children accept such situations unquestioningly.

I had been about ten when Aunt Georgina had accompanied us on a holiday to Switzerland and, after that, she never returned to her own home with my grandparents, but had remained with us, first at Devonshire Terrace and now at Tavistock House and Gad's Hill. Little by little she had adopted what had appeared to be a supporting role to Mama, and I recollected how often she would tell us that our mother was not well.

Now I wondered which had come first: was Mama in need of her sister's assistance because she was unwell, or did Mama become unwell at the growing interference of Georgina within her own household?

I called to mind the terrible day that baby Dora had died. Mama had been taking a rest cure for her nerves in Malvern and she returned to find that, in her absence, Dora had died tragically from a sudden convulsion. I think she partly blamed herself for not being there when it happened, but did she also blame her sister in some way?

From that moment on, I realized how Aunt Georgina had asserted her position more powerfully than ever, making herself my father's confidante in matters great and small, and it became apparent to me now, that poor

Mama had been too grief-stricken to object.

When I arrived at Gloucester Crescent, Alice opened the door with a look of relief.

'Oh, thank goodness, ye've returned, Master Charley. Y' mother is in the most terrible state.'

I ran up the stairs and found her sitting in her armchair, staring into space and upon her side-table was an open box holding an emerald bracelet and a card from my father, bearing the name of Miss Ellen Ternan.

Chapter 16

June 1858
Household Words

PERSONAL

For some years now, my wife has represented to me that it would be better for her to go away, for due to a mental disorder, she felt herself unfit for the life she has to lead at my side, and that she would be better separated from me.

Mr Charles Dickens would like to make plain that innocent persons, dear to his heart, have been made the subject of the most monstrous, grossly false, and cruel accusations arising from this separation.

Miss Georgina Hogarth, from the age of fifteen, has devoted herself to the care of her sister's children due to some peculiarity of character possessed by Mrs Dickens that made her inadequate to do so. What would have happened to my children were it not for this aunt, who has given up the greatest part of her youth for them, I cannot imagine, and I declare it now that she is faultless in her integrity.

In addition, the reputation of a young lady, for whom I have the greatest respect —I will not repeat her name—I honour it too much, has been tarnished, when there is not a more virtuous and honourable young woman, who is as good as my own dear daughters.

I declare in the name of both myself and my wife that any such rumours about Miss Hogarth, or any other such innocent persons whose names are being falsely linked with mine, are abominably false and that such rumours cast doubt upon the moral character of not only myself, but individuals who are equally innocent.

Whoever should dare to repeat any one of these falsehoods after this denial will find himself a liar before Heaven and Earth, and with the greatest certainty will become subject to legal action.

Charles Dickens

115

The Garrick Club — London

The smell of cigar smoke permeated the air of the richly decorated lounge and the rumble of deep voices, interspersed with vigorous laughter, denoted that this was entirely a gentleman's domain. The chandelier illuminated the heads of many notable figures from the art and literary world of the day. Upon the walls an art collection was on display and the establishment boasted a dining-room, as well as offering rooms where out-of-town members could stay the night.

The Garrick Club, named in honour of the eminent actor David Garrick, was formed at a meeting held at the Theatre Royal, Drury Lane, on Wednesday, 17 August, 1831, in recognition of the need to draw together like-minded individuals who would promote the sustenance and regeneration of theatrical interests. Among those present at that first meeting were Mr Samuel Beazley, an architect, novelist and playwright, whose keen eye for detail had been significant in the design of several prominent London theatres; Mr James Winston, an actor and theatre manager, and Sir Andrew Francis Barnard, a hero of Waterloo.

Along with Mr Beazley's understanding of the use of space and design within the theatre, Mr Winston brought his knowledge of theatre management to the table, and Sir Andrew moved among circles from whom many suitable prospective members could be drawn. At that first meeting, the participants suggested a number of eminent individuals who might be invited to become the first members of the Garrick Club.

Within six months, suitable members had been recruited, a property found on King Street in Covent Garden and a club house subsequently decorated and equipped to meet the discerning tastes of its members. On 1 February, 1832, the novelist and journalist Thomas Gaspey was the first member to enter at 11.00 a.m., and at 12.30 Mr Samuel Beazley ordered a mutton chop for his lunch.

As the years passed, the club opened its doors to the Shakespearean actor William Charles Macready, the author, William Makepeace Thackeray and the tenor, John Braham: all of whom were friends and associates of Mr Charles Dickens, who had been a member since 1837 and frequently renounced his own membership, falling in and out of friendships, only to rejoin. On this day in question, Mr Dickens was about to fall out of friendship once more.

William Thackeray sat with his legs crossed in a deep, back-buttoned leather club seat, reading *The Times*. He had been to pay his usual visit to the asylum that morning and, although he was unsure if his wife still knew him, she had looked serene and contented enough within her own world. He tried to believe that he had done his best for her. He shook his newspaper, as if trying the shake the image of his wife's uncomprehending face from his mind, and he focused his attention on the affairs of the empire.

Born in Calcutta, Mr Thackeray had been most disturbed by news of the ongoing affairs of the Mutiny in India. The 1850s had seen deterioration in relations between the British officers and the Indian ranks in the East India Company's Bengal Army. Many Indians believed that the British were seeking to destroy traditional Indian social, religious and cultural customs and, as a result, the Mutiny had begun when eighty-five members of the 3rd Bengal Light Cavalry, who had been imprisoned for refusing to use cartridges greased with the fat of animals which were sacred to them, were rescued by Indian comrades.

A whiskery old gentleman sitting opposite, looked over his newspaper and addressed his comments to Thackeray.

'I hear your old friend Dickens has published his affairs for all to read, eh?'

Thackeray raised his eyes.

'Gorn orf with his wife's sister, and now trying to cover his tracks by all accounts.'

Thackeray closed his newspaper and folded

it in half, laying it upon the table at his side, and picked up his sherry.

'I can assure you, Major, that Miss Hogarth's reputation is spotless. All this confusion has arisen over the fact that she decided to stay in the household for the sake of the children. After all, she has known most of them since infancy.'

'Hmm,' said the major with an air of disbelief. 'There's no smoke without *farr*, Thackeray. You can't tell me that a man leaves his wife in order to become a bachelor again. This sister-in-law of his is the other woman; mark my words.'

Thackeray lowered his voice and leaned forward. 'It's not his sister-in-law, Major, it's some young actress.'

'Whaddya say? Speak up, man,' the major barked.

'It's some young actress,' Thackeray hissed.

'Dickens and a young actress!' the major announced for all to hear. 'Well, there you have it, sir! Man's not a gentleman, then, is he?'

The chatter in the club dropped to a hush: Dickens was standing in the doorway, and Thackeray found all eyes turned upon him. Dickens turned abruptly on his heels to leave, his face coloured with rage, and Thackeray knew not whether to chase after him, or take up his newspaper again in shame.

His friendship with Dickens had stretched

back over the last two decades and their wives had been the closest of friends. When his dear Isabella had first become disturbed in her mind, it had been Catherine who had walked those horrific corridors with him to see his wife in Brompton Asylum. His daughters had practically grown up as sisters to Dickens's daughters, and the Dickens household had always been like a second home to him.

There were always petty disagreements among members at the club, and recently the young Mr Edmund Yates, who had been introduced to the club by Dickens, had written a rather biting profile of Thackeray in the periodical *Town Talk,* which hinted that Thackeray's literary success was on the wane. In Thackeray's opinion, Yates had ingratiated himself with Dickens by means of flattery and when the wounded Thackeray insisted that the club exclude Yates on the grounds of the article, he was most hurt that Dickens seemed to take the younger man's part.

The club insisted that Yates apologize or retire from membership, and when Yates refused to do either, Thackeray retaliated with some sneering remarks of his own in print. A committee meeting was set up to try to seek a compromise, but with Yates still withholding an apology, his membership was withdrawn; and when he boldly attempted to enter the club, he found himself refused entry by the secretary.

Thackeray had been hurt by what he perceived as disloyalty on the part of his old friend, but he acknowledged that the matter of Dickens's marriage was a much more personal topic; he could not allow a longstanding friendship to be marred by such a misunderstanding. In that moment he knew what he should do; he took to his feet and headed off briskly to look for Dickens.

Thackeray bounded down the steps and, scanning the street in either direction, saw his friend heading away.

'Dickens! Wait, why don't you? Let me explain.'

He began to chase after him, wishing that he had not grown quite so thick around his middle in recent years. With a rasping breath, he caught him up and took hold of his arm.

'You didn't hear the full story, my friend. You have misunderstood.'

Dickens pulled his arm away abruptly.

'I can assure you that I heard everything, and I think that I understood completely, Mr Thackeray, when you maligned my good name.'

'I was not maligning your good name at all,' Thackeray said, still catching his breath. 'I was in fact defending it.'

Dickens was not listening. His mind was already closed to the matter.

'Thackeray, I will ask that you never refer to me as your friend again and to mark from this moment forward that whatever there was that passed between us that constituted friendship, is now at an end.'

'But, Dickens—'

'Good day to you, sir.'

Dickens turned away and, with his hurried gait, disappeared into the city.

Chapter 17

June 1858
Park Cottage, Canonbury

Ellen Ternan was now residing in a house with her sister Maria, in Canonbury, Islington, after Dickens had encouraged her to settle in London. Her mother had travelled to Florence for the summer to visit her eldest daughter, Fanny, who was studying music, and Mrs Ternan had taken with her letters of introduction from Dickens, which he was confident would further her daughter's career. He had also offered some financial sponsorship, for which Mrs Ternan was immensely grateful.

Ellen was currently performing at the Haymarket after Dickens had spoken with one of his associates, Mr Buckstone, a playwright, and she could not help but be appreciative of all that Dickens was doing for her family. But what of their own relationship? He had visited her at Park Cottage whenever her sister was at home. However, his schedule was mercilessly tight and it often seemed that he had hardly a moment to spend with her before he was called away again. There was so much that they needed to say to one another.

She had been thinking of writing to him, and thanking him for his kindness, but asking that their friendship come to an end, for she felt a constant sense of uncertainty about his feelings for her; but he had warned her never to put pen to paper with regard to anything but the most formal of arrangements.

'Even the very tiles and rooftops know me, my dear; were they to hear even a whisper between us they would tell the world.'

But that morning a parcel had arrived for her. She opened it to find an exquisite emerald bracelet in a box. She took out the card upon which was written:

'To Ellen: Remembering Doncaster.'

Her heart leapt at the writing, she recognized it in an instant. Now she was sure that his feelings for her had not changed.

Taking it from the box, she thought about the magical moment when her fingers had entwined with Dickens's own and they had silently acknowledged their feelings for one another. She held the bracelet and, moving it back and forth in the light, suddenly noticed that it appeared marked. She frowned and inspected it a little closer, but then realized that such a beautiful antique would undoubtedly have had an interesting provenance.

* * *

A colourfully attired gentleman, with a fine top hat, was making his daily round of Holborn at his usual brisk pace when he came to a jeweller's shop. He stopped abruptly and peered into the window, his eyes, by degrees, taking in rings, brooches, pendants and bracelets. He was drawn back to a particular item and, bringing to mind a young lady whom he recalled appeared very fond of the colour green, decided to enter the shop.

A few moments later, the assistant had taken a bracelet from the window and allowed Mr Charles Dickens to make a closer examination. He admired the emerald stones, the antique faceting and the gold and silver setting: it was perfect. He retrieved a card from his inner pocket, wrote an inscription with a flourish, and sealed it in an envelope, requested from the shop assistant.

He was just about to leave his instructions for its delivery, when a commotion out in the street occured. A policeman was endeavouring to move along a blind beggar who was resisting.

Ever compassionate to the poor, Dickens left the shop in a hurry and went out to assist.

'What seems to be the trouble here, Constable?'

'This 'ere fellow has been 'ere all mornin', sir, and it's time 'e was a-movin' along; but 'e won't budge, sir, and I'm a-tellin' 'im that I'll be callin' for some assistance if 'e don't get up.'

'Now, now, Constable. I'm sure that won't be necessary. Perhaps a little charitable compassion is all that is needed.'

Dickens crouched down upon his haunches and, seeing the man's pitiful condition, he was immediately transported back to the most terrible place in his memory. The stench of a room, no bigger than ten feet square, sleeping four people head to foot on a filthy wooden floor. The sound of crying, not just women and children, but grown men, wondering how they were ever going to get out of this hell-hole of a debtors' prison.

He could hear his father's voice: *Well done, my boy! That's another shillin' you've earned today. You keep it up, son, and we'll be out of this place in no time.*

He returned to the present with a shudder and enquired of the man whether he had ever heard of the Association for Promoting the General Welfare of the Blind.

'I's a-heard of it, sir, but can't see my way to findin' it, if you know what I mean.'

'Then I shall call a cab and assist you there myself, my good fellow.' And true to his word, that is precisely what Dickens did.

While the man, whose aroma was rather arresting, reaffirmed his gratitude to his patron, Dickens reflected on the disgrace of his childhood years. He had been one of eight children: Fanny, born in 1810, followed by himself eighteen months later, a brother, Alfred, who had died at the age of six months; Letitia born in 1816, followed by another brother Frederick, in 1820. In 1822, Alfred Lamert was born and a sister Harriet had died the same year from smallpox; and finally in 1827, Augustus had completed the family.

Their father had found it difficult to provide for his growing family on his small income and, in time, his debts had become so severe that all the household goods were sold in an attempt to pay his bills. When he could not meet the demands of all of his creditors he was imprisoned with his family in the Marshalsea.

At the age of twelve, young Charles had been sent to work in a rat-infested, tumbledown blacking factory which looked out upon the coal barges on the river. He had been employed to paste the labels onto the jars of boot blacking, and when he thought now of the taunts that he had endured from the other children there, he felt sick to his stomach.

''Ere 'e is: the little gentleman. Keepin' 'isself to 'isself again.'

No one could imagine the shame that he had felt at his lowly position in life. All the hopes and dreams that he had cherished of receiving a good education and becoming a learned and distinguished man were crushed. He had been expected to be a man while still a boy and he had felt that he had no support or guidance from anyone.

He could see his hands now, the black polish ingrained into his skin and nails and remember how he had rubbed them raw, trying to clean them before climbing into bed. At night the hunger had gnawed in his belly, and in order to endure it he had imagined himself dressed in a brightly coloured waistcoat, with a fine top hat, dining in a restaurant and eating a hearty meal.

Sitting next to the beggar now, he could feel a spasm beginning on his left side. It was a spasm that he had felt for the first time when he had returned home from his first day at the factory, and he had lain in bed hearing the children laughing at him over and over again in his mind. He clutched at his stomach and drew in his breath sharply.

'Are you all right there, guv'nor?' asked the blind man, sensing his benefactor wincing with pain.

'Don't worry yourself about me, sir.' Dickens tried to smile through his discomfort. 'I am quite well and I think that just around this next corner we shall find the answer to your own troubles.'

The carriage arrived in the parish of St Pancras, and drew up outside a small, modest broom and basket shop. It could have easily been passed unnoticed as nothing out of the ordinary, but upon closer inspection a body would see that painted above its door was the title the Association for Promoting the General Welfare for the Blind. Both here and at a shop in Oxford Street, the blind recaned wicker chairs along with making brushes, brooms and baskets. Thus industriously employed, the need for begging was negated. With such an illustrious agent as Mr Dickens representing him, there was little chance of this poor unfortunate from the streets of Holborn being turned away.

*   *   *

But what of the bracelet? In his haste to assist the beggar, Dickens had forgotten to leave an address for its delivery.

'No matter,' said the owner to his young assistant, who was polishing the display cabinets. 'I am in Town later, and will call at Mr Dickens's office, where they will undoubtedly have the address for his wife.'

'Oh, sir, p'raps it's a token of his love, and that he wishes their separation to come to an end.' She had stopped her task, a far-away look in her eyes, and had clutched her duster to her breast.

The owner, Mr Edward Brown, who was too old to be caught up in such romantic nonsense, frowned and chastised the young woman, reminding her all such purchases by notable individuals were not a subject for idle gossip and were confidential within these four walls; and that he hoped she would remember that upon returning to her home later in the day.

She resumed her polishing and, after discreetly wrinkling up her nose at her employer, returned to the romantic notions that had made her toil more bearable.

*　　　*　　　*

By the time that Ellen Ternan opened the box that contained the bracelet, she had no idea that, in error, it had arrived at 70 Gloucester Cresent; that it had been opened by the sender's estranged wife, and that she had hurled it across the room in great distress. The sender's son had consoled his mother, and then had had the embarrassing task of returning the gift and explaining to his father that it had been sent to the wrong recipient. Instead of shame or remorse, his father explained that he often sent gifts of appreciation to fellow performers and that his son should not attach any romantic sentiment to it.

Charley Dickens had not the courage to

state that, while he had been attending to some business in Islington a few days before, he had by chance seen his father knocking upon the door of a house in Canonbury and when the door had opened, it was Miss Ellen Ternan who had stood on the threshold. The look that had been exchanged between the householder and her visitor had told Charley Dickens everything that his father was seeking to hide, from both his children and the world.

Chapter 18

July 1858
Gad's Hill Place

The large window looked out on the marshy landscape towards Gravesend and the red slate roof of the Falstaff Inn, where Dickens had enjoyed many a satisfying meal. A mahogany dressing-table, a gentleman's wardrobe and a set of heavily checked curtains gave the bedroom a distinctly masculine air, and with Catherine's departure had gone the perfumes, powders, pill boxes and general feminine clutter which seemed to Dickens to have spilled over every available surface. In its place was orderliness itself: a horse-hair clothes brush, a tortoiseshell comb, and a small tray which held a razor, shaving brush and mug.

At Dickens's bedside was his book of memoranda, lest he be struck by an idea in the middle of the night, as was often the case. At present he was working on a concept that had occurred to him during his performance in *The Frozen Deep,* and he had scribbled down the words: Resurrection, Fate, Injustice, Self-Sacrifice and Love, not yet knowing how they would be linked, but the seed of a story was there, nonetheless.

It was often the way when an idea was forming in his mind. He tried not to think upon it too hard in case it eluded him completely, and he would find that if he jotted down the vagaries which came upon him unbidden, when he was least expecting it, the story would appear in its entirety.

Since moving to the countryside, Dickens had become more conscious of his vulnerability and before he retired to bed, had begun to obsessively check all of the doors several times to ensure that they were locked. He had also taken to sleeping with a gun beneath his mattress lest there be an intruder. Last night, however, Dickens had slept quite soundly, feeling more his old self again, now that the furore around the separation was dying down.

*   *   *

A breeze lifted the curtain, gently inviting

131

the morning sunlight into the bedroom and Dickens opened his eyes gradually. At the side of his bed stood a small child, a halo of light about his head, and Dickens sat upright abruptly, his hand on his heart.

'Bless my soul! Plorn.' This was the pet name for his youngest son, Edward. 'You gave your papa quite a fright!'

Observing anxiety upon the boy's face, he ruffled his hair reassuringly.

'Come here, my lad, and tell me what is troubling you.'

Plorn, aged six, clambered onto the bed next to his father, drew up his knees and encircled them with his arms. He was small for his age, but loved nothing better than being out of doors at Gad's Hill, roaming the fields looking for rabbits.

'I heard it again last night, Papa.'

'What did you hear, my boy?' Dickens said with gentle encouragement.

'It was The Phantom again, Papa, moaning.'

Dickens suppressed a smile, 'Ah, The Phantom. Is he still haunting you?'

He acknowledged that his children had always been prone to the wildest imaginings in their young years, and put it down to their being his progeny. However, he was concerned that Plorn had held fast to his story for some days, and wondered if it were not a sign of anxiety that he was missing his mother.

A mournful, wheezing lament floated in on

the breeze at the window. Dickens and Plorn looked at one another, and Plorn clung to his father.

'There it is again, Papa. The Phantom.'

Dickens swung his legs over the edge of the bed, pulled on his dressing-gown and slippers and retrieved his gun from beneath the mattress.

'There is always an explanation for everything, Plorn. Now there is no need to be afraid, my boy, your papa is here.' Dickens was not ready to admit that his own heart was pounding within his chest. It was an unholy sound.

Father and son padded down the stairs, unlocked the back door and crossed the garden which led to the fields and marshlands. In the nearby village of Higham the bells of St Mary's church tolled, and the mournful lament rose up to greet them once more. On approaching an old stone wall, Dickens signalled to his son that he should remain quiet and still. Dickens took a step forward and shouted, 'If you value your head, by God, take heed now, for I will fire, I swear it!'

A wheezing cough emanated from beyond the wall and Dickens fired a warning shot into the air.

'I will not warn you again!'

Taking a cautious step forward, he bent over the wall, looked down and found an overweight, asthmatic sheep looking up at him sorrowfully. Dickens threw back his head and roared with laughter until he cried, calling his son to his side to come and see the object of his amusement.

'Here is your phantom, Plorn. The mystery is solved. Come and have a look.'

Plorn ran to his father, who embraced him and kissed his cheek, and upon looking at the woolly phantom, father and son laughed in unison.

Chapter 19

August 1858
Park Cottage, Canonbury

Charles Dickens and Ellen Ternan sat on a blue velvet love-seat, their knees almost touching, holding one another's hands.

'I think, my dear, that it is a probability that we will not see each other for a little while. You have your theatre commitments in Manchester, and I have my reading tour to commence. It will be difficult for us to write, as you know, but if Mr Collins is in Manchester, then I will entrust a note to him, although you must promise to burn it as soon as you have read it, my dear.'

Dickens was endeavouring to draw closer to his public by means of a reading tour, hoping that it would help to repair any damage to his popularity in the storm that had followed his separation from Catherine. He had begun in London and then planned to go up north for eleven days, followed by Edinburgh, Aberdeen and Glasgow. When he had stepped out onto the stage at St Martin's Hall, Piccadilly, even he could not have anticipated the thunderous applause and cheers that had greeted him, and Dickens realized that here was an avenue by which he could not only reach a wider audience, but also ensure financial security.

His financial commitments were now heavier than ever, having two homes to run, an estranged wife, two dependant daughters, a sister-in-law, and his younger sons' schooling to pay for. He had also found himself responsible for the abandoned wife of his youngest brother, Augustus.

Fifteen years before Dickens had written a letter of recommendation to Chapman and Company, a shipping merchant, trying to obtain a position for Augustus.

'I have a young brother who has recently finished his schooling in Exeter. He is bright and clever, has never given trouble to anybody, and has been well brought up.'

He had appeared to have had all the makings of a fine young man and four years later,

Augustus married Miss Harriett Lovell at Trinity Church, Marylebone; but when Harriett had suddenly gone blind, Augustus abandoned her and left for America with another woman. With a strong sense of duty for his family responsibilities, Dickens took over the financial care of Augustus's wife.

If Ellen Ternan had felt saddened at the thought of a summer separation, she tried not to show it. She knew that she must be grateful for all that Dickens had done for her already and that he could never entirely be hers alone. Dickens, however, found himself in unfamiliar territory. He had caught sight of himself in the mirror in Ellen's sitting-room as he had greeted her with a kiss, and had noticed how his curls were becoming more wispy and greyed at the temples. His face, although handsome, was lined, and he had not realized that the separation from Catherine had taken such a great toll upon his health. In contrast, Ellen was in the bloom of her youth and Dickens felt strangely insecure.

'You do care for me, don't you, Ellen? I don't think that I could bear it if you told me . . .'

Her voice was hushed. 'Dearest Charles, I care more than you could ever imagine. You have become everything to me.'

The warmth of his hand in hers was the only closeness that had ever been theirs, for they could never be alone for more than a few moments without interruption. His eyes were lost in hers, searching for an answer.

'I think about you every moment that we are apart, I keep looking for a way for us to be together. If only Catherine would—'

She put a finger to his lips.

'Shh, you mustn't.'

'Then tell me you have not wished for the same thing. You know that it is the only way. Oh, Ellen what are we to do?'

Ellen could not confess how often she had also reflected that the death of his wife was the only way that the man she loved would ever be free to marry her.

'My love for you makes me strong and determined, and helps me believe that one day we will be together. We must be patient, Charles, that is all we *can* do.'

She looked so beautiful, and he thought how sad it was that disappointment should ever leave its traces upon so lovely a countenance. He longed to kiss her, to take her in his arms, but he knew that if he did, his passion would overcome him. As if she had read his thoughts she lifted her face to his. He hesitated, but feeling himself uncontrollably drawn to her, he moved to kiss her. A sharp tap upon the door caused him to jump to his feet and Maria Ternan entered the room.

Dickens smoothed down his waistcoat, retrieved his hat from the sofa and made to put it on. The intensity that had passed between the two lovers was so recent that he was sure that it still lingered in the air, and that Miss Maria would certainly sense it.

'Ah, Miss Maria, how lovely to see you. I was just leaving in fact.'

Maria Ternan noticed the blush on her sister's cheeks, the uncertain manner of Mr Dickens and she knew exactly what had passed between them. She tried to hide her embarrassment at their obvious discomfort.

'Please don't leave on my account, sir,' Maria invited. 'I was just about to make some tea. Will you not stop to take it with us, Mr Dickens?

'Sadly, Miss Maria, I have business to attend to, but I wanted to pay a brief call to see that you are both well, just as I promised your mother I would.'

He shook Ellen's hand warmly, and said, 'Miss Ellen, I am so pleased to hear that your career is prospering, and you, too, Miss Maria. I look forward to reading the glowing reviews, ladies.'

Ellen smiled. 'Thank you, sir, you are very kind, as always.'

She accompanied him to the door and as Maria disappeared up the staircase in an act of discretion, Dickens hesitated for a moment filled with uncertainty.

'Will you always remember the day at the races?' he whispered. She drew up the sleeve of her dress to reveal the emerald bracelet.

'Always.'

Chapter 20

September 1858
Gad's Hill Place

'It's a pity that you have set your heart on renouncing a career as an artist, Charlie, for Ruskin has said that there is no one to match you when it comes to natural detail. Are you sure that you have thought this through?'

Dickens leaned forward his hands clasped together in a gesture of earnestness.

Charles Collins had just passed through a long period of dissatisfaction with his work. He had attempted a new portrait, with Millais' new wife—Effie Grey—as his model, but after two weeks, and scant progress on Collins's part, Effie refused to sit for him anymore and yet another unfinished canvas was added to his collection.

Seated in his study chair, Dickens wore a light grey woollen suit, with a matching waistcoat. Charles Collins was seated opposite him and, while Dickens had been talking, his eyes had been drawn to the rows of books that lined the study walls. It had struck him that several of the shelves contained dummy copies, which bore titles that undoubtedly reflected Dickens's sense of humour: *History of a Short Chancery Suit* in twenty-one volumes, *King Henry the Eighth's Evidences of Christianity,* and alongside these was placed a very narrow volume entitled *The Virtues of Marriage.*

'I said, have you thought this through, Charlie?' Dickens repeated.

Charles Collins brought his attention back to their discussion and replied, 'Oh, I have thought about nothing else for some time, sir. My mind is made up. I intend to concentrate on being a writer and, as I have said, I hoped for your thoughts on my contribution about Broadstairs for *Household Words.*'

'It was an excellent piece, Charlie, there's no doubt about it. In point of fact I am in the process of winding down *Household Words* in favour of a new periodical which I intend to name *All the Year Round. I* would be happy for you to be a regular contributor, if that is what you want.'

Dickens had had a difference of opinion with Frederick Evans, his publisher, who had not been happy with the publication of the letter concerning Dickens private life. Although Mr Evans had been invited to be one of Catherine's trustees by Dickens himself, Dickens was now seeking to distance himself from anyone whom he felt had allied themselves with his wife.

By withdrawing his own support from the periodical he would render it unviable without the strength of his name behind it, and was now seeking for contributors to his new project.

This was what Charles Collins had been hoping to hear, and his customary seriousness was replaced with a smile of relief. He leaned forward and grasped Dickens by the hand. 'Oh, thank you, sir. You can't imagine what it means to me. I shall consider it a real privilege to be in your employment.'

'Well, I have to admit that it seems a mortal shame that you have set your heart on abandoning your art, but the art world's loss will be the gain of *All the Year Round, I* suppose.'

'I very much hope so, sir.'

Dickens noticed that Collins had not touched the biscuits which had been placed on the tray with his tea, and wondered how anyone could resist Cook's melt-in-the-mouth baking.

The two men stood up and, as Dickens opened the door to his study, his daughter, Katie, was crossing the hall with her drawing book and pencils in hand. She was wearing a high-necked day dress of fine cream wool, edged with a golden brown trim, which echoed the autumnal colours in her hair.

'You have met my daughter, Katie, before, haven't you, Charlie?' Dickens gestured.

'Ah, yes, sir, but it has been a little while. Good to see you again, Miss Dickens.'

'She's becoming quite a fine artist herself, if my opinion counts for anything.' said Dickens, with obvious pride in his daughter. 'Why don't you ask Charlie for his opinion on your sketches, Katie?'

Katie was not at all embarrassed at being placed in an awkward position by her father, but smiled at Charlie, 'I would be honoured to have the opinion of an artist of the Royal Academy.'

Charlie was a little unsure whether she was flirting with him, or if she was in earnest, but, as Dickens turned to go back in his study, Charlie followed her out into the garden where they sat upon a bench and began looking through her drawings.

'Tell me something about your painting, *Convent Thoughts,* Mr Collins. It is so beautiful, I could have looked at it for hours when it was exhibited.' Katie's voice was filled with awe.

'Well I made a start with some preliminary sketches at first; studies of lilies and the reflections in the water, until I was satisfied with the effect that I wanted to achieve.'

'And the lovely model—can you let me into the secret of who that lady was?'

Charlie sensed that she was flirting again, but the topic of art gave him something to talk of which he found both easy and natural.

'Her name is Miss Ludlow and she is a friend of Millais. I was very fortunate to use her as a model for she was only in London for a few days, so I had to make sure that I captured the expression I was looking for very quickly.'

As he was talking, Katie was examining his features very carefully. She appraised his blue eyes and, although she found his physique a little too slight for her own tastes, his manner was gentle and kind. It was a relief to have something to focus her mind on other that the events of the last year, and to converse upon a subject that was so dear to her heart, with such an esteemed artist.

Charlie had not intended to stay but the afternoon passed so quickly with talk of his work that he found his confidence brimming when it was time to leave.

'I have enjoyed our discussion, Miss Dickens, it has been a most pleasant afternoon.'

'Please, call me Katie, and should you be passing again in the next few days, I would be most grateful of your assistance with sketching the detail of the geraniums at the front of the house—if you have the time.'

*   *   *

Dickens had been working in his study for the duration of Charlie's visit, and upon finishing his afternoon's work he pushed back his chair from his desk and, satisfied, stood up and stretched his back. Leaving his study, he strolled into the sitting-room, noted the time on his pocket-watch, and raised his eyebrows at the observation that the young man, Charles Collins, was still deep in conversation with his daughter out in the garden.

He noticed how she was listening attentively to every word that Charlie uttered, how she leaned forward to closely observe when he pointed to features of her drawings, and how her eyes returned again and again to his face.

Unexpectedly the painful thought came upon him that one day soon his little *Lucifer-Box* would leave him, and he was gripped by a sudden spasm in his left side which took his breath. Hearing the sound of youthful laughter, he dropped down onto the *chaise* and knew with both certainty and sadness, that there were some things in life that could not be controlled.

Chapter 21

January 1859

24 Albany Street, London

'Are you happy, my dear?' Wilkie asked, sipping at a glass of claret and talking a bite from a portion of cheese on a plate in front of him.

He was seated at a table with Caroline and Elizabeth at either side of him, playing a game of cards. Caroline placed a hand upon his and smiled.

'Never happier, my love.'

'And you, my little maid?' he asked Elizabeth.

'Yes, Uncle Wilkie, I am very happy too.'

'Ah, very good!' Wilkie threw back his head and laughed.

A large fire burned in the kitchen, its flames reflected in the highly polished copper saucepans which lined the shelves on the opposite wall. An inviting parlour, divided by a folding door, led to a breakfast-room; and a sitting-room decorated in the latest crimson-coloured wallpaper was furnished comfortably in anticipation of receiving visitors. Upstairs were two bedrooms, and an attic room in the garret for occasional guests.

The woman in white and her daughter, Elizabeth, had moved from Hanover Terrace to 124 Albany Street on the east side of Regent's Park. The name Mrs Caroline Graves was written upon the rent book and Elizabeth was recorded as 'a ladies' maid'. On the night that she had revealed the existence of her daughter, Caroline had gone to bed at Hanover Terrace convinced that the following morning Wilkie would ask her to leave. She had considered waking Elizabeth and taking their leave under the cover of the night as she had not wanted to bear the sadness of parting from Harriet Collins, who had become like a mother to her, nor from the man of whom she had grown so fond.

Wilkie Collins was not a handsome man by any means, and when he was in pain with his rheumatism his moods fluctuated wildly between self-centred moroseness and the fringes of insanity. The pain would begin in his feet, travel to his legs and back, and had even been known to affect his eyesight. Caroline, however, had come to adore him, finding him fascinating company; and, most importantly, she was grateful that he had never raised his voice or his hand to her. After what she had once endured, she was more thankful for that than anything else.

The night that Wilkie had been having nightmares about marriage, Caroline had lain in bed and relived the nightmare that had been hers at the hand of her captor. She remembered how she and Elizabeth had been sitting in Regent's Park near to the lake, when a dark-haired man with a drooping moustache had approached them to ask if they had seen a small dog run past.

Mother and daughter concurred that they had not, and he began to tell them that it had belonged to his recently deceased wife and consequently he was most attached to it. He had appeared to become quite distressed at its apparent loss, and Caroline asked whether he would like some assistance in looking for it. He assented, and they had scoured the bushes to the very fringes of the park without success. When the man said sadly that he could not expect them to expend their energy any further, he asked if they would take tea with him and his elderly mother as a means of thanking them.

Caroline, who was very wise when it came to matters involving gentlemen, agreed, but said that her daughter had to attend her singing lesson; however, if he would give her his address then she would call alone later.

The man's feigned sorrow disappeared with the production of his card from his pocket. He handed it to Caroline with a knowing look and with the greatest certainty that they understood one another perfectly. With Elizabeth settled with a Mrs Green of Lodge Road, who asked no questions about the comings and goings of her lodger as long as she was paid in advance, Caroline returned to the address upon the card. The dark-haired man with the drooping moustache opened the door and, just as she had expected, there was no sign of an elderly mother, nor evidence of a much-loved deceased wife.

The woman in white had endured much since Elizabeth's birth in order to keep them both from the workhouse, but what she had endured at the villa near to Regent's Park she knew that she could never endure again. If Wilkie could not offer her marriage and respectability, then she would be eternally grateful to him for rescuing her that night, and for his hospitality, which came at a price: the wives of their visitors could never dine in her company, and Harriet Collins would have to believe what she had been told, that Caroline Graves had returned to her family in Ireland.

From then on, Wilkie divided his time between Hanover Terrace and 124 Albany Street, telling his mother that he was staying with Dickens at Gad's Hill. While battling episodes of severe pain and laudanum-induced psychosis, he invested his remaining energies on writing a new serial for Dickens's *All The Year Round* for which he was destined to become most famed: the story of a beautiful young woman who ran out into the moonlight dressed from head to foot in white.

Chapter 22

Miss Angela Burdett Coutts
The Highgate Estate
Highgate
London
21st March, 1859

Dear Angela
It is true to say that you have been one of my husband's truest and kindest friends, and in the matter of the separation you have tried to remain impartial, for I know that you do not want to damage your own relationship with him, nor put your charitable works together at risk; but my position is a sad one and I would consider it a great act of charity on your part if you would kindly attempt to mediate on my behalf one more time.

You will understand and feel for me, I'm sure, when I tell you that I still love and think of Charles far too much for my peace of mind. Again and again, I go over the old days, wondering what more I could have done to please him and to be the wife that he wished, and no matter how long and hard I think upon it, no answer comes to me.

The life that I shared with him was one

of wonder and vitality, and now all of the light seems to have gone and my days are filled with solitude. Whatever you might do in the way of assisting me will bring my eternal gratitude.

I remain yours truly
Catherine Dickens

*Miss Angela Burdett-Coutts
The Highgate Estate
Highgate
London
6th April, 1859*

*My Dear Angela
Your letter, I'm sure, was motivated by the belief that you might be able to reignite any remaining embers of my marriage that still burned; but to suppose or suggest that my wife and I might meet in some neutral place to re-evaluate our position, is impossible for me to contemplate. That figure is out of my life forever and my desire is never to see her again.*

When I was very young I made an unwise choice that let to a miserable error. The sad consequences that could only be expected from such a choice are what I see before me now. I do not suppose myself to be entirely blameless, but I must now move on to be cheerful and active in all other

aspects of my life.
Your sincere and affectionate friend,
Charles Dickens

*　　*　　*

June 1859

Wellington Street. London

Dickens stood back and admired the new portrait which Forster had commissioned in celebration of his birthday in February.

He was now forty-seven years of age and the portrait depicted him as a man at ease, seated, one elbow casually resting on the arm of his chair and the other hand in his trouser pocket. The expression that the artist had captured was one of assuredness.

'What do you think, Mr Fields?' Dickens asked his American visitor.

Mr Fields, who was both a publisher and an entrepreneur, admired the portrait which hung in the offices of *All The Year Round,* at 11 Wellington Street, Covent Garden, London. Dickens had just agreed to write a short story for *The New York Ledger* entitled *Hunted Down,* for which he would be paid £1,000, an amount he would have once considered only a dream.

'I think that you look like a man who had reached the very pinnacle of his career, sir,' remarked the American, 'and I hope you know how much your work is admired in my country. If *All The Year Round* were to be simultaneously published in America then I believe it would do very well, sir.'

Dickens was confident that such a suggestion would not only yield additional financial benefits, but would undoubtedly work to repair his reputation overseas, for news of his domestic affairs had now reached the shores of America.

'Very well then, Mr Fields, let us agree to it.'

'And have you given any more thought to the idea of taking your readings to America? I know that I have asked you before and you declined, but it really would be a most profitable venture for you, Mr Dickens, sir.'

Dickens shook his head, 'My mind had not changed on that point, Mr Fields. At the moment I have a very private and personal reason for not wanting to leave the country'

'Ah, too bad, sir. I hope to persuade you one day, though,' the American laughed.

'Well, I think that that concludes our business for today, Mr Fields, and if you would care to dine with me at The Falstaff Inn, this evening at seven, you would be most welcome. I can certainly recommend a visit to the old ruins of Rochester Castle and the cathedral. I know how you Americans like your history.'

'I would be honoured, sir, thank you.'

'Dinner at seven, it is then, Mr Fields.'

Dickens stood up from behind his desk, shook hands with his visitor and then crossed the floor to the coat-stand in the corner of the room, from which he took a beaver-skin top hat and his greatcoat. Having finished his work for the day, his intention was to visit 'the very personal and private reason that was preventing him from leaving the country'.

Walking from the corner of Tavistock Street, Dickens took a route through Covent Garden, Bloomsbury and Soho. As he walked he was deep in thought about the development of his new story, which he had decided to name *A Tale of Two Cities* and was to be set in London and Paris during the French Revolution. As Dickens and kept a steady tap, tap, with his cane upon the paving stones, the phrase *'recalled to life'* came to his mind and repeated itself in time to his step, *'recalled to life, recalled to life'*. He smiled at the idea, and the shape of the opening chapters began to form in his mind.

In a short while he arrived at 31 Berners Street where Ellen Ternan was now installed and living within walking distance from his office. The door was opened by a maid who had been engaged for Miss Ternan personally by Dickens himself and he was shown into the sitting-room where Ellen was waiting to receive him. He noticed immediately that her eyes were red as if she had been crying and he took his place at her side on the sofa and with the greatest concern took her hands in his.

'Whatever is the matter, my love? Are you ill? Just say the word and I will send for the doctor.'

'No, I am quite well, Charles, it is something else, something that I have to tell you, but I want you to promise me that you will not be cross.'

'Very well, I will try, my dear. What is it?'

'I believe that a journalist has approached a policeman in order to ask him to question myself and Maria about our comings and goings, and about who our visitors are.'

A look of indignation crossed Dickens's face and he sprang to his feet immediately. 'This is outrageous! Give me the policeman's name at once and I will contact his superior.'

Ellen sighed, 'You see, I knew that you would be angry.' Dickens wrung his hands and paced about the room.

'What sort of questions did he ask you? Was he casting doubt upon your reputation? Did he mention my name, at all?'

'Charles, calm down. You are making the situation far worse that it is already.'

'If this appears in *The Times* then the whole sorry saga of my marriage will be trawled up all over again.'

'You are jumping to conclusions without any real evidence, my love. It may be nothing more than a policeman doing his job, or, at worse, an opportunist preying on two women living alone.'

'Well, if someone thinks that they can go poking about in my business, then they can think again. I will be contacting my lawyer and asking him to make some discreet enquiries and try to find out who it might have been.'

'No, I don't want you to do that, my love.' Ellen's tone was quite assertive. 'Perhaps it would just be easier if we just didn't see each other for a while.' She sighed.

Dickens sat down again, and shook his head, turning over ideas in his mind.

'I think that I have another suggestion which may help, although I do not think it will be to your liking, but it may be the only solution if we are to retain any sort of privacy.'

'Very well, Charles, I will listen.'

'I think that it would be best if I remove you from this address to another location, and . . . '

Ellen noticed his hesitation and prompted him. 'What is it, Charles? What else do you want me to do?'

'I'm not at all sure you will agree, but I think that perhaps you should give up your career on the stage, Ellen. I know that it is a lot to ask, but it would be impossible for *me* to achieve anonymity, but with one of us out of the public eye, then maybe we will be able to carry on with our lives without being a public spectacle.'

'I see.'

Ellen was very quiet and she knew that here

was the true test of her feelings for him. Could she really give up her own ambitions for a man who might never give her his name?

'It is all I have ever known, Charles, you do know that, don't you? All that I have ever dreamed of is being an actress.'

'I will not press you, my dear. It is your decision entirely, but think on it if it is not too awful for you to contemplate.'

Side by side they sat in silence, both wondering why the joy and happiness that they had hoped to find with one another seemed so elusive.

Chapter 23

October 1859

Gad's Hill Place

The slender figure of Charles Collins paced back and forth in the hallway at Gad's Hill Place. He felt light-headed and a little sick as he had not eaten breakfast that morning but had, instead, absorbed himself entirely in prayerful contemplation of the matter about which he was now waiting to speak to Katie's father.

The door of the study, Dickens's inner sanctum, opened abruptly and Dickens hastened Charlie into the room with an apologetic smile.

'So sorry to keep you waiting, Charlie, but I was determined to finish the chapter I have been working on all morning. If I allow anything to interrupt my flow of thought, I am done for, so thank you for your patience, my friend.'

At Dickens's invitation, Charlie took a seat, crossing his slim legs first one way and then another. He loosened his collar a little and then asked if he might have a glass of water and Dickens wondered what was making the earnest young man more serious than usual. He endeavoured to help him out by opening the conversation.

'So, have you a proposal for a new contribution to *All The Year Round,* Charlie?' Dickens asked, pouring a glass of water from a jug on his desk and pushing it toward his nervous visitor.

'Ah, it is not exactly a proposal about work, sir.'

He took a gulp from the glass. This was every bit as difficult as he had imagined.

Dickens shifted uncomfortably in his chair.

'I see. Then would you like to tell me what sort of a proposal you do have in mind, Charlie?' A recollection of his daughter Katie and the young man conversing together easily in the garden came to his mind. He was beginning to anticipate what was about to transpire, and he did not like the idea at all.

Charles Collins smoothed down his red hair and cleared his throat.

'You know, sir, that I have been calling upon your daughter, Katie, for a little while now, and I have come to admire her more than any other woman that I know.'

Charlie took another gulp of water and this time Dickens did not seek to assist him in the conversation.

'I am aware that I do not have much in the way of a career at present, but I am confident that with your help I will prove to make a most reliable contributor to your periodical. In short, sir, I wish to make a proposal of marriage to your daughter, and I ask for your permission to do so.'

Dickens stood up, placed his hands behind his back, and began to circle the room.

'I see. And have you any idea regarding my daughter's feelings for you, Charlie? She is a very spirited young woman, you know.'

'Yes, sir, I am aware of her zest for life, and I know that I lack a little in the way of physical energy myself, but I believe that we share a passion for art, and I think that I can confidently say that she admires me, sir.'

Dickens's face took on a look of uncertainty. 'I think, Charlie, that neither of us should assume what Katie thinks, at present. I have to confess that I am a little concerned about your financial prospects, so I would like to speak to Katie myself, and when I have done so, then you may approach her and make your proposal.'

'Very well, sir, I am happy to wait until then, but please remember that I do have some independent means which were left to me by my father.'

The redheaded man stood up and shook hands with the gentleman whom he hoped would soon be his father-in-law, relieved that he had overcome the enormous hurdle which had loomed so large before him earlier in the day.

*   *   *

Dickens found his daughter in the sitting-room carefully rearranging the ornaments to her satisfaction and she jumped with embarrassment when he entered. He smiled gently, and said with a tone of reassurance in his voice, 'I used to do exactly the same when I was a child, Katie. It would irritate me intensely if things were not as they should have been.'

She approached her father and put her arms around him, 'Thank you, Papa, you above all others have always understood me.'

His throat immediately tightened, and he called to mind the little girl with the auburn hair and the fiery eyes, who had cried and cried for him when she was stung by an insect as a child.

He held her at arm's length and addressed her.

'Katie, I have had quite a serious conversation with Charles Collins this morning. I expect you know that he wishes to propose to you, and he has asked my permission, but I am really not sure that he is the man for you, my dear.'

Dickens saw the look in his daughter's eyes change from delight to defiance.

'Papa, I have already made up my mind. I would consider it an honour if he asked me. He is a very accomplished man, you know.'

Her father knew that Katie would only resist him harder if he were to forbid the union, so instead he hoped to persuade her to wait a little longer before accepting the proposal.

'Yes, he is a fine artist, Katie, I grant you that, but he has not been able to sustain his career and as yet, has no stable employment upon which he could support you as his wife. If you would consider waiting a little while in order to let him prove to you that he can stick at something, then I will happily give my blessing.'

Katie broke away from her father and went to the window where she could see Charlie circling the garden.

'I do not wish to wait, Papa. I am ready to be his wife now, and whatever financial constraints are placed upon us in the early days will be an adventure.'

Dickens could see it now. It would end with him bailing out his daughter and ineffectual son-in-law in exactly the same way as he did for other members of his family. This was not what he wanted for her at all.

'Katie, please reconsider. I want you to wait.'

'And I have said that I do not want to wait, Papa. Charlie is waiting for me in the garden, and I am going out to him now and will *accept* his proposal. Please try to be happy for me.'

'Katie, I do not want to forbid you . . . '

But Katie was no longer listening; she walked to the door and closed it behind her. In despair, Dickens knew that he was caught in a trap of his own making: if he threatened his daughter — as he had threatened countless others before her — that he would no longer have dealings with her if she defied him, then he would undoubtedly lose her. She was every bit as determined as he was.

Turning away from the window, angry that he was so powerless, Dickens had no desire to look upon the scene that was about to take place.

Chapter 24

November 1859
Gad's Hill Place

Dickens opened his eyes and blinked several times. Well after midnight, he found himself wide awake in bed and he sighed with frustration. He had been struggling to sleep soundly for some days now since Charles Collins had proposed to Katie. He had also received word that his brother, Alfred, who was successfully employed as an engineer in Yorkshire, was suffering with suspected consumption.

Now these cares were weighing heavy upon his mind, creeping into his subconscious at night. He decided to get up for a while, threw back the covers and swung his legs over the edge of the bed. He put on his slippers and dressing-gown and crossed the room to the window, pulling back the curtains. Thin wisps of cloud floated past the haloed moon which dominated the night sky and, peering out into the darkness Dickens wondered about all of the other restless souls who, like himself, were looking up at that same moon, plagued by insomnia.

He called to mind a night similar to this one, when he had been sleeping at his office in the city and, troubled by Catherine's appeal to Miss Burdett-Coutts for a reconciliation, he had been unable to sleep and had wandered the streets in the rain . . .

*   *   *

Dickens thrust his chilled hands deeply into the pockets of his greatcoat as he walked though St George's Fields. The silhouette of Bedlam Hospital could be made out in the moonlight and, as he passed it, he reflected upon the notion that at night the sane and insane became as one, for when the sane lie dreaming in their beds, did they not also imagine that they consorted with royalty; and if the insane were to say 'I can fly', did not the sane believe that they too could achieve such a feat, when they were asleep?

Although he was glad that the days were gone when the public could view the antics of the inhabitants of Bedlam for the price of a coin, he wished that he could now peer through those prison-like walls and look upon their strange habits and rituals, for such individuals were a source of great fascination to him.

His thoughts turned briefly to Thackeray's wife, Isabella, who had been in Brompton Asylum for some years since she had tried to take another woman's child; but madness in the guise of someone that he knew was not a subject to dwell upon for more than a moment, for it then became a frightening reality.

From Bedlam Dickens made his way back across the dimly lit Westminster Bridge and on through the dark lanes of the City, where shawl-clad figures clasped infants to their breasts and men with lanterns picked through dust heaps in the hope of retrieving something to sell. He knew that he put himself in danger every night that he chose to walk such streets, but the danger was a source of excitement to him, and lifted him above the mundane weariness that was his existence. On these night-time excursions he observed life in all its tragic forms, fuelling his imagination and his writing.

He passed by rookeries, black and grim, where guttering candles at the windows revealed the hopelessness of the poverty-stricken within. He looked upon the homeless huddled in doorways and those queuing to gain entrance into a night refuge. Scenes like these had inspired him to begin his most recent novel *A Tale of Two Cities*, for were not the conditions that led to the French Revolution akin to what he saw around him in London?

The sound of his footsteps had a hypnotic effect upon him and he walked in a dream-like state until he found himself passing the cemetery of St Martin-in-the-Fields. He stopped at the wrought-iron gates which

164

were fixed together with a padlock, hanging crookedly from their posts. Peering through the dilapidated railings, Dickens knew that the comparatively small number of weather-worn, lop-sided gravestones in the churchyard belied the actual number of bodies buried there. The cemetery could have been no more than 200 feet square and yet *The Times* had lately reported that it was estimated to contain the remains of between 60 and 70,000 persons.

Until recently most of London's cemeteries had been so overcrowded that bodies were being buried in shallow pits beneath the floorboards of chapels and schools. The fetid air which had come to inhabit such places was a constant reminder of the grisly undertaking. Dickens shuddered at the thought.

He squinted through the gap in the rusty railings. A shadowy figure began to appear in the darkness before his eyes: a raggedly bald individual, with spikes of black hair around his ears, moving furtively among the tumbledown headstones and stopping to stoop over a freshly dug grave. Dickens gaze fell to its boots which were splattered with mud, and without warning the figure lifted his eyes, fixed them on Dickens and spoke.

'Ah, I see that you have come at last. Well, now you have caught me in the midst of my despicable act, you will know only too well what my profession is, won't you, Dickens? And with a little more thought in that imaginative brain of yours, in time you will also certainly discover my name. Am I right?'

Dickens nodded slowly and then said thoughtfully, 'Yes, I know what you are. You, my friend, are a "resurrection man", removing bodies from their graves for sale to medical men as cadavers. And your name . . .'

Dickens pondered for a moment, 'Your name is . . . Jerry Cruncher. A man who by day is a respectable porter for a bank, but by night carries out this despicable occupation.'

The figure bowed. 'At your service, Mr Dickens.'

Dickens blinked and the resurrection man was gone.

The author smiled, it was not a new phenomenon; if he waited long enough he knew that his characters would always find him. Tomorrow he would bring him to life again with the stroke of his pen. Dickens nodded to himself, satisfied with his night's work. He took one last look at the cemetery, turned away and headed off into the chilly night.

*   *   *

The resurrection man had now taken his place in *A Tale of Two Cities*, alongside the girl with the golden curls and the forgotten prisoner hammering on the soles of the shoes which he made with an uncontrolled obsession. Now

Dickens had penned the final chapter of the novel he knew that he did not have the energy to begin anything new. Each of his works was like the delivery of a child, and it took time to recover from the labour.

Looking out of his window and reflecting upon his night-time excursions, he came upon an idea.

'What a capital notion!' he exclaimed.

Over the years he had had many strange experiences which would be of great interest to the readers of *All The Year Round*. He called to mind the occasion, when as a young man, he had been called to be a jury member at the trial of a young mother who had allegedly murdered her newborn child. It was a distressing responsibility, having to both witness the child's corpse and observe the mother's pleadings that the child had been dead when it was born. The muddle-headed doctor who had completed the autopsy kept contradicting himself and it seemed as if the poor woman was about to be charged with murder. How relieved Dickens had been when the mother had been found not guilty.

The image of that little corpse also reminded him of his numerous visits to the Paris morgue and how he had been both fascinated and repulsed by what he saw there, and the greediness with which the crowds had wanted to know the cause of each death. On one occasion a white-headed old man had been pulled from the river and spectators had gathered around the body laid out in its dripping clothes.

Yes, the strange experiences and curious observations that he had made throughout his lengthy career would make fine reading. He would start to record them in the morning, and he decided to encapsulate them under the title of *The Uncommercial Traveller*. At last he had a new task which would occupy his mind and distract from the troubles which had roused him from his sleep.

The rain began to patter upon the windowpane; an owl hooted. Dickens shivered and returned to his bed, disrobing and wrapping the bedclothes tightly around him. He had not once missed Catherine since the day that she had left Tavistock House, but he did miss the warmth of another human body next to him, and closing his eyes, he tried to return to his slumber and to blot out the deep sense of loneliness that gnawed in the pit of his stomach.

Chapter 25

June 1860
Gad's Hill Place

Garlands of white flowers decorated the parish church in readiness for tomorrow's ceremony. The village blacksmith had fired of a round of shots at 7.00 p.m. to herald the coming nuptials, the table was laid for dinner, and the dining-room at Gad's Hill glittered with candlelight. Cook had been given strict instructions about the evening's requirements and Georgina had written out the menu for dinner in her careful hand.

Palestine Soup
Sole with Herb and Oyster Sauce
Chicken with Spinach
Pheasant with Oysters
Ginger Pudding

Dickens seated himself at the head of the table with Georgina taking her seat at the foot. On one side the men were seated: Wilkie Collins, balding and myopic, Edmund Yates, rugged and hirsute, a greying John Forster, and the nervous-looking Charles Collins. Opposite, the ladies: Mamie in her favourite violet evening gown, Mrs Yates, fastidious and neatly turned out, the talkative Mrs Forster and Katie, soon to be a bride.

The sight of each course was greeted with enthusiasm by the guests as it was set upon the table. Charles Collins, however, accepted only a small serving of soup, declined anything resembling an oyster as shellfish brought him out in a rash, ate a few mouthfuls of chicken and then said that he was far too full to manage any dessert.

Katie glanced at Mr Yates, who was wiping traces of ginger pudding from his bushy moustache, and was repulsed by the idea that she had ever had a foolish crush on him. She did not like the way that he appeared to trade on his connections with her father, and in her opinion, he was certainly not as cultured as her husband-to-be.

Mrs Yates darted her eyes with frequency in Katie's direction, recalling how the pretty young woman had once flirted outrageously with Edmund, but she was relieved to see that the bride-to-be now appeared to be taken only with her fiancé.

Forster, who had more than taken his fill of both food and wine, stood up and, interrupting the chatter of the guests, raised his glass

'Well, Dickens, my old friend, it is the eve of your daughter's wedding and I for one propose a toast. To the bride and groom.'

The guests raised their own glasses in response and Forster cast a sideward glance at Wilkie Collins, glad that he had managed to be first with his congratulations. Forster had never really forgiven Collins for taking his place in Dickens's affections as chief confidant and friend, a place that had been his alone until Collins had come on the scene. With Charles Collins marrying into the family that friendship would be inevitably be bound stronger by familial ties, and Forster, now settled in his marriage, was determined to find his way back into brotherhood with his old friend.

Forster was the son of Newcastle butcher, who had risen from his unremarkable background to attend university as a law student. Finding that he was better suited to journalism, his path had crossed with Dickens's in the year before his fame, when they found that they shared a love of literature and the arts. Through the years that the two men had known one another, Forster had been an invaluable source of advice to his friend in matters of business.

Their friendship had begun to cool, however, when he advised Dickens against taking up public readings, believing that it would diminish the author's credibility. Dickens had taken great exception to this, but since giving of his time to lecture for the Douglas Jerrold fund, Forster had slowly begun to find friendship with Dickens once more and he planned to make the most of it.

The guests chatted with animation between courses. Mrs Forster complimented Georgina on the menu, Yates conferred with Collins over ideas for a comedy sketch which he planned to pen, and Forster suggested ideas for European travel with Charles Collins. Dickens's head turned this way and that, nodding and contributing something to each conversation, not wanting to miss a thing.

'Yes, Mrs Forster, Georgina has indeed done a capital job . . .'

'Sounds like a hilarious idea, Edmund, you should do it . . .'

'No, you cannot better France at this time of year, Forster . . .'

'Any more wine, gentlemen?'

After dinner they played charades: Yates made a dignified Disraeli, Forster an impressive Prince Albert, and Dickens had everyone roaring with laughter when he entered the room wielding a fire-shovel as an axe, and wearing a black handkerchief on his head as 'the beheading of Charles I'. The men played billiards, with Dickens playing competitively as always, and then the dancing commenced. Dickens kept up an enthusiastic jig behind the others, clapping his hands and urging everyone on to greater vigour until the room was filled with boisterous laughter.

When the celebrations came to a close and the guests had left, Katie bid her papa goodnight, but with a note of seriousness in his voice he asked her to wait a moment.

'Katie, I have to speak to you.' He took her hand. 'If I do not say what is lying heavy upon my heart, then I will never forgive myself.'

Katie felt herself stiffen.

'Please, Papa.' She pulled her hand away from his. 'I know what you are going to say and I do not want to hear it.'

Her father had known that it would not be easy, but he was determined to try

'Katie, please, reconsider your decision. It's not too late. The ceremony has not yet taken place and there is still time to change your mind. Charles Collins is not the man for you, I am sure of it. If you marry him tomorrow, it will be a terrible mistake.'

She did not want to listen: Katie had imagined herself and Charlie as the perfect match. Her father had seemed so distant and preoccupied since her mother had been sent away, and she longed to be the centre of someone's world, to be the complete focus of their attention. This is what she had found in Charlie and she did not intend to let it go.

'I have given my word to Charles and I intend to keep it. And as for mistakes, Papa . . . '

His eyes flashed with anger and, at the sight of his face, she did not dare to say one word more.

She put a hand to his cheek, and kissed him fondly. 'Please don't let us quarrel, Papa.'

'But Katie . . . '

'Good night, Papa, I shall see you in the morning.'

He turned away with no response to her words, as if speaking of the morning would bring it so much sooner than he could bear.

*　　　*　　　*

A train, hired especially by the bride's father to bring guests from London to Higham, arrived early the following morning. The parish church filled with invited guests and villagers, chattering with excited anticipation of the arrival of the bride. The atmosphere at Gad's Hill, however, was filled with tension.

As Katie stepped into her wedding gown, she could hear her father downstairs snapping at family members and servants alike.

'Which one of you has moved my top hat from the hall table? I put it here only a moment ago . . . For pity's sake, will someone answer the doorbell, and direct the well-wishers to the church? . . . '

Katie knew that her father was not convinced about the match but she had set her mind to it, nonetheless, and determined that she would be happy. Looking at herself in the mirror she was suddenly struck by thoughts of her mother, sitting alone in her room at Gloucester Crescent, and she was saddened at the vision. Last night, in the midst of eating,

174

drinking and dancing, none of the guests dared to mention that several people who had been important in the life of Katie Dickens were noticeably absent: her mother, Catherine, her grandparents, George and Helen Hogarth, along with William Thackeray and his daughters, Ann and Harriett.

Katie had defied her father's wishes in order to inform her mother of the engagement, but when the news had been greeted by Catherine with the same measure of caution that her father had shown, Katie had not visited again and no handwritten wedding invitation had arrived at 70 Gloucester Crescent. It was as if Catherine Dickens had never existed at all.

Katie now wished that she had had the courage to ask her father if her mama could be invited, but she knew that he would not have given it a moment's consideration and now she was troubled by guilt. However, she reasoned that once she was married she would no longer be under her father's direction and she could visit her mama as often as she pleased. Taking comfort from such a thought, Katie took one last look at herself in the mirror.

In the absence of the Thackeray girls, Mamie had the honour of sole bridesmaid, and when Katie descended the stairs her sister was moved to tears.

'Oh, Katie, you look a picture, doesn't she, Papa?'

Her father grunted, hardly able to bring

himself to look upon his daughter, nor tell her how lovely she looked. In silence he assisted her into the brougham, and as they passed under the arches of flowers and greenery which decorated the route to the church, it was to Mamie that he addressed most of his chatter. How could he bear to hand over his bright vivacious daughter to such a sober individual as Charles Collins?

The groom waited, white-faced, at the altar next to his best man, Holman Hunt. When the organ announced the arrival of the bride, Charlie stiffened with alarm, and silently repeated to himself over and over that getting married was the right thing for him to do. Looking at Katie he could not deny that she looked beautiful, but he was filled with overwhelming fear: women were such an enigma.

Harriet Collins had been delighted that at last one of her sons was going to be wed, but, like Dickens, she also had her doubts about the match. Harriet had found Katie to be the most sparkling company when she had visited Hanover Terrace, but she harboured reservations about her son's capacity to make a bride happy.

Seated in the congregation, she leaned to one side and whispered in Wilkie's ear, 'Do you think that your brother is ready to be a husband?

'Mama, when it comes to the topic of

marriage, I am not the man to ask.'

'He looks very nervous.'

'And so he should.' Wilkie sniffed. 'The noose is about to be cast about his neck.'

'Oh, Wilkie! You are no help at all.'

How Charlie managed to get through the service he did not know. He was most unnerved by the thunderous expression on the face of his prospective father-in-law and the doubtful look on the face of his mother, and glanced anxiously from one to the other, trying to keep his eyes on his bride and say his vows. With the ceremony complete, the bride and groom stepped into a waiting carriage and began the journey back to Gad's Hill for the wedding breakfast.

'So, are you happy, my love?' Katie asked, taking her husband's hand, delight shining in her face.

'Of course I am, although I must admit that your father did not look happy at all, Katie.'

'Oh, you must not mind him, Charlie. You must realize that I am the first of his children to leave him. He merely needs a little time to adjust, my love, that is all.'

'I hope you are right,' Charlie replied doubtfully.

'Anyway, Mr Collins,'—Katie lifted her glowing face to her husband's—'I am not interested in what my father thinks; I am only interested in what you think of your bride. Now tell me, am I beautiful or not?'

Charlie swallowed hard and smiled.

'Of course you are, Katie, you never looked lovelier.'

The villagers of Higham lined the country lanes, waving handkerchiefs, cheering and clapping the bride and groom.

At Gad's Hill the guests, in turn, shook hands with the bride and groom, as they stepped down from their carriage on their arrival.

Katie thanked each one, smiling absently, and looking for her father.

Her brother Charley stepped forward to convey his good wishes, and Katie asked him anxiously, 'But where is Papa? I haven't seen him since we left the church. I thought he would be the first to greet me.

'Don't worry Katie, I'm sure he will be here in just a moment. You know how Papa likes everything to be just so. I expect that he is ensuring that all is in order with the refreshments.'

Katie stood on her tiptoes, trying to see past plumed bonnets and top hats. She did not want her father to be sad on a day which meant so much to her. Surely he understood that she could not be his alone forever. At last she saw his brisk figure walking in the direction of the marquee upon the lawn. She waved at him and smiled, but he looked past her entirely and continued on into the marquee.

Katie pulled upon her husband's sleeve and

whispered, 'I think that we should go into the tent, my dear.'

Charlie disengaged himself from the guests, encouraging them to partake of the wedding breakfast and one by one the wedding party moved into the marquee. As the afternoon passed no one could have failed to have noticed that, in between noisy bursts of merry-making and feigned bonhomie, the father of the bride did not look happy at all.

He threw his head back repeatedly, drinking glass after glass of wine, and became quite argumentative with Holman Hunt over the relevance of his art.

'Don't you think yourself rather a hypocrite, Hunt? Your paintings have a religious theme, and yet all of your friends know that you yourself never set foot in a church.'

Charley took his father by his arm and steered him in the direction of his Aunt Georgina.

'I think Papa is a little unwell, Aunt,' he whispered discreetly.

'Nonsense!' Dickens snapped. 'I am perfectly well.'

'Of course you are, my dear,' Georgina soothed, 'but I will fetch you a strong coffee, all the same.'

Katie, who had changed into a black lace going-away gown, was alarmed that her father's voice was becoming increasingly loud and belligerent; and in turn her father thought inwardly with sadness how fitting was the colour of her gown. The time had come for the bride and groom to leave.

'Goodbye, Papa.'

Katie embraced her father before climbing into the carriage and he could hardly bear the pain. How could she take her leave of him with such ease? He kissed her sadly and in a moment she was gone. The wedding carriage pulled away, amid much waving and farewells from the guests who then returned to their merry-making.

As the evening was drawing to an end, Mamie noticed that since Katie's departure her father had been absent for some time. She began to scour the garden in search of him.

'Have you seen Papa, Charley?' Mamie asked her brother.

'I last saw him with Georgina.' Charley nodded in the direction of their aunt.

'Oh, I've already asked Aunty,' Mamie replied. 'She said that he had promised to return to you. Perhaps he has gone for lie-down. I think he has had rather a lot of wine.'

Mamie entered the house and, climbing the stairs, she was instinctively drawn to Katie's room. She opened the door, her hand remaining on the doorknob and was saddened to find her father kneeling at the side of the bed, his face buried in Katie's wedding gown, sobbing silently.

'Oh, Katie, Katie, my own dear little

Lucifer-Box.'

He lifted his dampened face at the sound of the door and looked at Mamie with distress in his eyes.

'If it had not been for me, she would not have gone at all.'

Chapter 26

August 1860
Calais, France

Charles and Katie Collins sat out on the balcony of their honeymoon apartment and while Katie sketched the scene below,

Charlie was scribbling down ideas for a novel based upon their travels. He stopped writing for a moment and looked at his wife thoughtfully, wondering whether to give voice to the words on his hesitant lips: it was a delicate matter.

'I hope that you did not mind me taking a separate bedroom, Katie, but I have always been such a light sleeper that any movement from another person in such close proximity to me would only disturb me further. I hope that you understand, my dear?'

His wife tried to smile but she was concerned. They had been in Calais for more than a month and Charlie had bid her goodnight with nothing more than a kiss on her hand at ten every night since their wedding.

'Charlie,' she faltered, 'you do not believe yourself to have made a mistake in marrying me, do you?'

'Whatever gave you that idea, my love?' He laughed uncertainly, anxious as to where the conversation would lead. 'We are the dearest of companions, are we not?'

'Yes, we are the dearest of companions, but I hoped that once we were wed, that you would find more in me than just companionship,' Katie said with difficulty.

'And I do, my dear. I greatly admire your mind and your talent. Whatever I can do to develop those as your mentor, I would consider it an honour.'

Katie thanked her husband for his kind interest, and decided to try a different approach.

'Charlie, would you ever consider painting a portrait of me? Millais said that I was a most compliant model and although he was the harshest taskmaster, the completed portrait has drawn the highest accolades.'

Earlier in the year Millais had approached Dickens and asked if he would give permission for his daughter to act as his model. He made it clear that it would be a painting with great sensitivity and taste: that of a young woman and her fiancé, a soldier, saying farewell on the eve of a battle. Katie had been delighted with the result, and she imagined that if her husband should look upon her repeatedly so as to paint her portrait, he might come to notice her as a woman.

Charlie sighed and shook his head. 'Katie, I have told you that I will never pick up a paintbrush again. My art made me too unhappy and I have left it behind me forever now.'

Her idea was not going to work and, admitting defeat, Katie changed the subject. She laid down her pencil and poured a glass of water for the two of them from a jug on the balcony table.

'Charlie, we have not been very sociable since we arrived, and I wondered if we might accept the kind invitation of our landlord, Monsieur Defoe, and his wife. They have asked us twice if we wished to dine with them, and I do not want them to think that the English abroad are unsociable.'

Charlie took a sip of water and shook his head, 'Ah, my dear, you know that my digestion is not favourable to the rich French delicacies of Madame Defoe's table, and I really am a man who prefers to observe other men than to be among them. But I will not stop you, my dear, if you wish to have some company. I know how gay and bright you are, and I would not want to suppress that in you.'

'Thank you, my love.'

The heat of the sun was becoming as difficult to manage as the conversation and Katie excused herself from her husband's company, returning to the shade of the sitting-room. Thoughts of home moved her to pick up a pen from the bureau and she sat down to write to her mother-in-law.

August 14th 1860

My Dear Mrs Collins
I hope that this letter finds you and Wilkie in good spirits.

Although Charlie and I are living in an economical manner, we are quite content and managing very successfully without servants. I endeavour each day to encourage your son to eat well, just as you asked me to, and you will be glad to know that this morning, he had a little fried bacon.

Charlie is at his most contented when he is writing, and when I watch his absorption in his task, I am reminded of my father and it is a reassuringly familiar vision.

I am drawing a little, but not painting as much as I would like, as painting materials are very expensive here. Please continue to write, for I do so enjoy receiving news from home. I have not heard from Papa yet, and wonder if all is well with him.

He works so hard.

For now, I remain your fond daughter-in-law,

Katie

*   *   *

At Gad's Hill, Dickens breakfasted as usual at eight. Mamie and Georgina sat at the table gossiping about the latest fashions that had arrived in town, and Dickens perused his newspaper after eating a breakfast of omelette and baked mushrooms. Later in the morning, seated at his desk, he took receipt of the mail and among the letters came welcome news from Sydney, now a naval cadet like Walter, who wrote that his ship would be returning to England briefly to undergo minor repairs. He would make a visit home.

Dickens had had cause recently to write quite sternly to Walter, who had repeatedly sent his bills home to be paid. Dickens had made it quite clear that he expected his sons to learn to live within their means, and that he did not intend to bail them out anymore. He had not heard from Walter since, and was unsure whether this was a good sign or not.

He retrieved another letter from the silver salver, hoping that it might be news from Katie. He was still finding the subject of her marriage difficult, and had not yet been able to face the task of writing to her. He turned over

185

the envelope but did not recognize the hand at all. Using his letter opener, he broke open the seal and pulled out the note from within. The opening lines revealed that this was very sad news indeed.

Chancery Lane
Malton,
Yorkshire
21st August 1860

Sir
I am grieved to tell you that your brother, Alfred, sadly passed from this life on Monday evening. As you know, his health had been failing for a little while, but his breathing became quite laboured on Saturday and Sunday and the doctor was unable to give him further aid.
Can I appeal to you with regard to the funeral arrangements, as I have no family here in Yorkshire and feel quite unsure as to how I should proceed with such matters? I await your much needed direction.
Your sister
Helen Dickens

Dickens blinked away a tear: where had the years gone? He returned the letter to its envelope and cast his mind back to days of the Marshalsea Prison. He could see Alfred's dirty little face looking out of the window, awaiting his brother's return from the blacking factory. He recalled how he used to bring back a small basket of provisions which he had purchased with his earnings and how Alfred's eyes would sparkle with delight at the sight of the food.

Alfred had been the only one of his brothers to make anything of his life. Dickens had appealed to Miss Burdett-Coutts to assist him in securing a position as an engineer at the Malton and Driffield Railway. Unlike young Augustus and the feckless Fred, Alfred had not squandered this golden opportunity, and had risen to a supervisory capacity. He had a fine wife and family, but now they were in need of shelter, comfort and practical aid and immediately Dickens knew what he must do.

He took up a pen from his desk and began.

Gad's Hill Place Higham
Kent
24th August 1860

Madam
I am indeed sorry to hear of your loss. My brother was a good husband and father, a man of whom you could be very proud. I will make arrangements for Alfred to be brought back to London by train, and for the funeral to take place at Highgate Cemetery, where my father is buried. There

*will be provision here for you and the
children at Gad's Hill, and I will set about
securing a home for you close at hand,
where I can watch over you all.*

*I give you my word that you have no
further cause to worry about your future.
Please cast all your cares upon me,
madam, from this moment forward.*

I remain, yours faithfully,
Charles Dickens

Chapter 27

August 1860
Regent Street, London

Georgina Hogarth and the widowed Helen
Dickens approached The General London
Mourning Warehouse in Regent Street.

Georgina had been talking the whole time,
oblivious to the lack of response from the
grieving woman at her side, and conversing
about things which seemed so trivial and
unimportant to someone who had lost a father
to her five children. Helen Dickens did not
hear most of what had been said for she was
lost in her own thoughts, but she winced at
Georgina's insensitive suggestion that she
should be firmer with her children for Mr
Dickens needed complete peace when he was

writing.

As they had left Gad's Hill they had been advised by the brother of the deceased that any purchases must be sensible, for he had no time for the extreme customs of mourning which presently held sway over fashionable society

'I absolutely will not tolerate any revolting display of excessive grief,' he had warned.

With these words ringing in their ears the two ladies had set off for town. Coming to their destination, the ladies peered into the window and read the advertisement which outlined the stock.

The Proprietors of the General London Mourning Warehouse respectfully reassure their patrons, whose bereavements compel them to adopt mourning attire, that every article requisite for a complete outfit of mourning is available within this establishment, or can be obtained at a moment's notice. Ladies requiring silks are particularly invited to try the new Corpeau Silks introduced at this house in black and grey. Half-mourning and Fancy Mourning Silks of every description are also available. The Show-Rooms are replete with the latest fashion in grief, including mourning millinery, mourning jewellery, flowers, collars,

head-dresses and trimmings.

The ladies pushed open the door which gave way to an atmosphere of deep solemnity. A gentleman, who wore a suitably grave expression, nodded as a form of address, and enquired, 'May I ask, ladies, whether it is the Half-Mourning Department you are seeking, or the Inconsolable Grief Department?'

'We are looking to purchase something for the widow of the deceased,' Georgina replied, gesturing to Helen Dickens.

'Ah, my condolences, madam.'

He adopted an air of affected melancholy which he hoped matched the exact mood of her affliction.

'Then may I direct you to the Weeds Department, where you will find the widows' caps, gloves and the highest quality in bereavement silks.'

Helen Dickens immediately took out a handkerchief from her purse and began to sob quietly.

'Ah, dear me, yes, it is a most difficult time, is it not, madam?' responded the suitably grave gentleman.

Georgina rolled her eyes for this was the third outburst of grief that she had witnessed that morning.

'Do try to control yourself, my dear Helen.'

The ladies followed the assistant, passing rows of black cloaks, sombre-coloured shawls, mantles, veiled bonnets on stands, and display cabinets bearing muslin collars, cuffs and unadorned handkerchiefs. Helen gave a muffled sob at the sight of each item, her grief reaching its peak at the sight of rails of black dresses. In some households it was expected that the servants adopt mourning attire also, but such rituals carried no weight with Dickens. He had insisted that his sister-in-law leave the curtains open in her room, believing that fresh air and daylight were by far the best tonic for her grief, and although he was secretly given to his own superstitions on occasions, he had made it quite plain that she should not cover any mirrors at all.

The suitably grave gentleman eventually led the ladies to a counter behind which stood a younger version of himself, whom one could easily suppose to be his son, and addressed him.

'If you could assist madam, *whose dear husband has recently departed?*' His words had dropped to a whisper, he bowed his head, and the poor widow put her handkerchief to her nose once more. The young man stepped from behind his counter.

'There, there, madam. Pray compose yourself, and I will familiarize you with our full range of garments and accessories, made especially to fulfil the obligation which respectable society places upon us all at such a time.'

He clasped his hands together.

'Now, may I ask delicately, is this your first full bereavement, madam?'

The widow nodded and sniffed into her handkerchief. 'Yes, yes, it is my first.'

'I ask, madam, because, of course, it is considered bad luck to wear mourning attire which has been adopted on the occasion of a previous bereavement.'

'Bad luck for business!' Georgina muttered under her breath. The young gentleman tried not to throw a look of contempt her way and continued.

'Now, of course, for the first year, madam's activities will naturally be restricted to church services and receiving visitors who have come to pay their respects.'

The widow nodded sadly.

'We have here the weeping veil which, after one year and a day, madam will be able to draw back from her face when she leaves the house. Or madam may prefer a veiled bonnet for outdoor wear and a widow's cap for receiving guests at home?'

As Helen had begun to sniff into her handkerchief again, Georgina sighed and gestured to the cap and bonnet.

'These will do fine, sir. I do not think that the veil will be necessary.'

'But for the church, madam . . . ' The young man adopted an air of horror.

'My brother-in-law was quite clear in stating

his preference for a plain funeral, and nothing more.'

'As you wish, madam.' He nodded his head respectfully and removed a black bonnet from its stand and widow's cap from a drawer in the display cabinet, putting them on one side for wrapping.

'Very good, shall we now turn our attention to mourning jewellery? May I ask whether madam has some hair from the head of the deceased, which she might wish to be made into a locket?'

At this the widow lost all sense of composure and Georgina's patience finally snapped.

'No, sir, she has no such thing! And if you could assist us promptly with a plain black dress without collars, cuffs or unadorned handkerchiefs, we would be most grateful and will take our leave.'

*   *   *

Highgate Cemetery, London

Dickens was moved at the sight of the five orphans huddled around their mother, Helen, who was desperately trying to be both brave and dignified during the funeral of her husband. Mrs Elizabeth Dickens, who was by now seventy-one years of age and rapidly declining into senility, had talked throughout most of the service, and seemed to have little idea who it was who had passed away, or why she was there.

The party of mourners moved from the church to the cemetery, and gathered around the grave. A large man of middle years removed his hat, and spoke in a soft Yorkshire accent to express his condolences to the brother of the deceased.

'I'm most sorry for your loss, Mr Dickens, sir. I worked with Mr Alfred since he were a young apprentice and he were a fine, hardworking man. He'll be sorely missed at the railway.'

Dickens took the man's black-gloved hand and shook it. 'You are most kind, sir, thank you.'

Charley Dickens walked out of the church, a dark-haired woman holding his arm. She had a fine figure, but was not in the least vain of it, and a thick head of hair, but little time for braids or curls. Her face was obscured by the veil of her small, black hat, but to those who knew her she was recognizable as Miss Bessie Evans, the fiancée of Charles Dickens Junior.

The news of the engagement had been unwelcome to Charley's father who had not spoken to Frederick Evans since the end of *Household Words*. Dickens had warned his son that he would not attend the wedding if it went ahead, but ever the diplomat, Charley refused to quarrel with his father and hoped that he

194

might warm to the idea the least said about it.

Standing at the graveside, the committal began and the mourners bowed their heads. The oak coffin bore no signs of unnecessary expense and the bearers were plainly attired as Dickens had directed. As the coffin lowered into the ground, the echoes and shadows of Dickens's life played out before him and, when the first spades of soil were thrown into the grave and the mourners began to disperse, Dickens lingered, finding himself strangely rooted to the spot until the task was almost complete.

In response to the desire to think and walk a little, he asked his driver to take him to the Regent's Park. He was not yet ready to return home and face his sister-in-law's grief again. The swaying carriage travelled through the village of Highgate, headed on towards Camden and in time approached the park via Gloucester Gate.

A hansom cab stood idle at the gatehouse, its driver pacing back and forth looking anxiously toward the lodge. In a moment, the gate-keeper appeared with a pole hook and handed it promptly to the driver, who took it from him and jumped back onto the seat of his cab with great haste. Shaking his reins, the vehicle set off, rattling away at great speed.

Dickens had watched the whole scene with intrigue and, moved by curiosity, he instructed his own driver to follow the same route, which took him back towards the Chalk Farm Road and the canal. He was most grateful for this mysterious diversion.

The cab stopped at the canal bridge. Dickens stepped down from his own vehicle and approached the hansom: its horse snorted, steam rising from its body. Finding no sign of the driver, Dickens made his way down to the tow-path where he observed a pole lying on the ground and next to it, the lifeless body of a young woman. Her feet were crossed at the ankles, mud clinging to her shabby velvet dress and her hair lay ragged across her face. Dickens noticed how tiny her feet were, as if those of a child.

The cab driver, who had pulled her out, and was now crouched over her, gently pushed back her hair from her features and as he did, Dickens knew her at once. He advanced toward the body and knelt at its side.

'Sarah?' he whispered.

'You know her, sir?' the driver asked with shock, realizing exactly what sort of a woman she was.

Dickens nodded sadly and thought about the diminutive young woman who had stood in the kitchen of Urania Cottage, full of spirit, challenging the matron. He had not visited the home for some time: his relationship with Miss Burdett-Coutts had become a little strained since she had advocated on the part of his wife. He had found it easier to address matters concerning the home by means of correspondence instead.

Miss Burdett-Coutts had written to inform him some little while ago that Sarah had finally determined to leave Urania Cottage. There had been plans for her to sail to Australia in order to start a new life there with references from the matron and Miss Burdett-Coutts. However, it had been discovered that she had been stealing from nearby drapery shops; her deception had come to light when the matron observed her wearing items of finery that could not possibly have been her own.

Miss Burdett-Coutts had written and asked whether Dickens felt that Sarah should be allowed to stay.

It seems that in some of our charges, there is a sudden passion which breaks out when recklessness has been long suppressed. It emerges and becomes like a madness uncontrolled. Perhaps we have done all that we can for her . . .

By what he saw before him now, it appeared that the wilful Sarah had left Urania Cottage after all, and had returned to her old ways. Dickens wondered whether if he had gone to her once more he could have secured a different outcome.

*   *   *

197

The sound of a barge moving through the waters caused him to raise his eyes. It was pulled by a horse, led by a young man in muddy jackboots, a ragged cloth about his neck. He had dropped the reins momentarily to light a cigarette and was paying little heed to where the horse was heading. Dickens shouted to him.

'Grab the bridle, man. Look! The rope is dragging along the floor and will take the body with it if you do not pay attention to your duty.'

The affronted barge man took up the reins again, quickly altered his path and, passing the body, spat upon the ground, casting a look of contempt upon the rags and tatters which had once been a living, vibrant woman.

Chapter 28

August 1861

Kensington Gardens, London

An attractive auburn-haired lady carrying a basket upon her arm stood before the large front window of Beaufort's Drapery shop in Kensington. She was admiring a crème silk dress, with full sleeves and a high waistline, modelled on the very latest fashion from Paris. She could see her reflection in the glass and imagined how she would look wearing such an elegant gown; it was a pure delight to her eyes and heart.

A cheerful voice from behind addressed her unexpectedly.

'I think I recognize that fair figure as belonging to a certain Miss Katie Dickens, or more lately known as Mrs Charles Collins. Am I right, madam?'

Katie turned and to her surprise found Mr William Thackeray standing behind her.

'Why, Mr Thackeray, what a delightful surprise. How lovely to see you.'

He took both of her hands in his, and kissed her cheek in a fatherly manner. As a child, Katie had always been rather in awe of William Thackeray, as she had been of most of her father's friends, but now she was a married woman, and here they were meeting as adults on an equal footing for the first time.

The distinguished-looking Thackeray was delighted to see her again and all the fond memories of years past came flooding back to him.

'I was just heading for Kensington Gardens, my dear. Would you care to accompany me?'

Katie nodded and smiled.

'I would be delighted, sir.' And she took his arm.

'So tell me about your travels, Mrs Collins,

I understand that you and your husband have been in France.'

'Yes we returned in February and are now living with Charlie's mother. Oh, France was wonderful, Mr Thackeray—'

'Call me William, please.'

'Thank you, sir. As I was saying, France was wonderful. It was so good to see Paris again, and then we travelled on to Brussels, and finally to Switzerland, although the winter was terribly cold.'

With the practised air of one who hides her true feelings, she did not reveal how much she had missed home, and how tears had dampened her pillow on the cold dark nights alone in bed. Oh, how she had longed for the warmth of a man's arms, to hear the whisper of his voice, telling her over and over how much he loved her.

'Your mother never liked the winter either.' Thackeray patted Katie's hand fondly. 'You remind me of her in that respect. I expect that you have had much to tell her since your return.'

'Yes, of course,' she lied.

For Katie had not been able to confide to anyone the truth about her honeymoon. Visits to her mother were always difficult, trying to find subjects which did not lead to talk of her father, but she certainly could not have revealed her marriage difficulties to her mama, who was still so sensitive about her own failed marriage. She could say nothing, either, to her aunt, nor to Mamie, who was still unmarried. As for her father, she could hardly meet eyes with him, for they knew each other so well that she was sure he would read her thoughts. So instead, she endeavoured to fool him and everyone else with laughter and light-hearted chatter about her travels. She could not have borne to hear her father say the words, 'I told you so.'

'Did you know that my brother, Charley, is soon to be wed, sir?' Katie asked.

'Yes, I heard talk of it at my club. Am I right in believing that the bride is to be Miss Bessie Evans?'

'You are right indeed, sir. Of course, it is no real surprise, for they have known each other since childhood. But the matter has become a little complicated since my father argued with Mr Evans. He has now completely refused to attend the wedding. I suppose the only good to come if it is that Mama will be able to attend in his absence.'

'I see,' nodded Thackeray with understanding, knowing only too well how easily Dickens quarrelled with his friends.

There had been no contact between the two men since the incident at the Garrick Club. Thackeray had heard news of Katie's marriage when it was reported in *The Times* and he was saddened to realize that had it not been for the estrangement with her father, he and his daughters most certainly would have been present at Katie's wedding.

'And what news of your sister and your other brothers? Is all well with them?'

'Let me see. Mamie has been on crutches for a short while after falling from her horse, but thankfully it was nothing more than a broken ankle. Walter is in India, in the army, and Sydney a midshipman. Poor Sydney had us quite worried for a while, when he was taken ill with a fever, but he has made a full recovery and has now returned to his ship.'

'What a relief for you all. And how are the younger Dickens boys? Living up to the family name?' Thackeray winked.

'Ah, well, Francis is now seventeen and working at my father's offices. He had ambitions to be a doctor, but the poor boy still stammers so. It was hopeless.'

At this, Thackeray regretted his playful jest, for he had meant no unkindness, and could only imagine the burden of his father's disappointment that the boy would bear.

'Alfred is destined for agricultural college,' Katie continued, 'and Henry and young "Plorn" are still at school.'

As the two figures strolled among the trees and fountains of the park, the conversation turned quite naturally to the subject of Katie's father.

'And how is your papa, Katie, is he well?'

'He works too hard, as you know, but he will

never be persuaded otherwise. At present he is managing his periodical, *All The Year Round,* preparing for another series of readings, and writing the concluding chapters of *Great Expectations.* It is a wonder that he does not collapse with fatigue.'

Thackeray was quiet and thoughtful for a moment.

'Do you think that a reconciliation with him could ever be possible, Katie?'

'I think, William, that you would have to approach him first for, as you know only too well, he is unable to apologize.'

Thackeray's face flushed with the heat of his anger.

'Me, apologize!' he spluttered. 'How can I apologize when the misunderstanding was completely *his* error?'

Katie smiled discreetly, amused at the pride of men.

'I think that I can safely assure you, sir, that if you could find the humility to approach him, that he would forget your quarrel in an instant and show kindness to you.'

Thackeray grumbled, full of doubt.

'Papa has a reading at the St James's Hall, Piccadilly. I would be honoured if you and your girls would accompany me as my guests. It would be lovely to see them again, and would give you the opportunity to talk to Papa. What do you say?'

'I will give it some thought, my dear. In the

meantime, I would like to invite you and your husband to my home in Palace Green. I have always admired Charlie's work and I would deem it an honour if you would both dine with me on Saturday evening. Lord Leighton will be present and I am sure that he and your husband would have much in common.'

Katie was delighted at the invitation. Her father had cooled in his relations with Charlie since he had become her husband, so to hear warm words of approval from William Thackeray, along with an invitation to dine with an associate of the Royal Academy, was welcome news.

'That would be wonderful, William, thank you. I know that Charlie will be delighted to see you.'

'And I him, my dear. Now, let me accompany you back to that little dress shop, where I found you looking at something that was undoubtedly far too expensive, hmm?'

Chapter 29

December 1861
Manchester

Dickens sat in the breakfast room of St George's Hotel in Manchester, sipping at a cup of tea. He was particularly fond of St

George's for it afforded its guests luxurious comfort and, when it was desired, privacy also. A large gallery overlooked a spacious entrance hall which was reached by the principal staircase, the hotel's finest feature. Dickens particularly enjoyed the mild and equable temperature which was regulated by an excellent piped hot-air system and the coffee-rooms with their large paned windows which made for a light and airy atmosphere.

He was now on his second series of readings, which were proving to be as popular in the North as they had in London and the Midlands. The tour would continue into January of the following year and would take him on up into Scotland. Although he had a reading to deliver that evening, he planned to return to his room soon and commence work on the current edition of *All The Year Round.*

As he sipped his tea, he tipped his head slightly to the right as he swallowed, in fear of aggravating the facial neuralgia that had been troubling him for some months. Whenever the pain came, it was a sudden, sharp shock which emanated along the left side of his jaw and up into the back of his head. Sometimes it came upon him while he was writing and other times as he lay down to sleep. Since working on the concluding chapters of *Great Expectations,* the pain had been excruciating, but he had worked his way through it.

A waiter approached the table with a plate

205

of kippers.

'Your breakfast, sir.'

Dickens nodded in approval. 'And did you order me *The Times?*'

'Yes, sir, I will just fetch it for you.'

A few moments later, the man returned with the newspaper as Dickens was very gingerly attempting a mouthful of his breakfast.

'Here you are, sir. Is everything in order with your meal?' The waiter sensed that Dickens was on edge.

Dickens nodded, putting a hand to his cheek, 'Mmm, yes fine, thank you. Just anticipating a touch of neuralgia, that's all.'

'All, you have my sympathy, sir. My grandmother always swore by an application of peppermint oil for that ailment, sir. Mr Mawdsley, the chemist in Dale Street, is very helpful in such matters. If you would care to pay him a visit, I'm sure he can oblige you.'

'Oil of peppermint, you say? I might just take a stroll to down to Dale Street after breakfast. Thank you.'

The waiter made a little bow and before retreating, nodded toward the newspaper on the table.

'Terrible news, sir, isn't it?'

Dickens picked up the broadsheet and immediately noticed the headlines announcing the death of Prince Albert.

'Well, I never!'

No one but his closest aides had known that

the Prince had been diagnosed by his doctor with typhoid fever. Some months before Albert had been to the military academy at Sandhurst to inspect the construction of new buildings. The rain had beaten down incessantly and he had caught a chill. Two days later he had visited his son, the Prince of Wales, at Cambridge. Albert had heard talk of the Prince's involvement with the Irish actress, Nellie Clifden, and the gossip had now reached London. He was weighed down with anxiety over his rebellious son, a reluctant and absent-minded student, who seemed to care for nothing but fine clothes and unsuitable women. This was not what the Queen wanted from the heir to the throne.

Alfred and Bertie had taken a long walk and, once again, it had rained unceasingly. When Albert left Cambridge, his body aching from the damp, he hoped that his son had taken heed of what had been said, but he was not convinced.

As Prince Consort, Albert was a fine example to his son, adopting many worthy causes, such as campaigning for the abolition of slavery and education reform. He had made great contribution to the world of art and culture with the organization of the Great Exhibition and he had done much to support the Queen with the running of the royal household.

Dickens had read of the carriage accident

which Albert had recently been involved in which had left him badly shaken, but the newspapers had reported that he was making a fine recovery. No one knew that the Prince had been given such a dire diagnosis.

Dickens examined the article closely.

The news of the severity of the Prince's illness was unknown until a few hours ago. To the readers of the Court Circular it was known only that his Royal Highness was slightly indisposed. As the illness progressed, the Prince sank with alarming rapidity and at his bedside during these last hours were Her Majesty, the Prince of Wales, and the Princesses Alice and Helena. At a few minutes before eleven p.m. he ceased to breathe.

We can report that the Queen bears her loss with calmness and has only asked that her subjects reflect upon how great the loss to our country. In consequence of the melancholy event of the death of His Royal Highness, the theatres will be closed this evening, and again on the evening of the funeral.

'Close the theatres!' Dickens exclaimed with outrage. 'But *I* have a reading!'

Chapter 30

July 1862

Farringdon Street, London

The Narrative of Charles Dickens Junior

I became aware that I had been staring at my business accounts for some time, my pen hovering above the books, when my wife's kindly voice broke into my thoughts.

'Charley? Did you hear what I said?'

My life with Bessie had been one of great contentment since the day of our wedding. My father had kept to his word and declined to attend in the presence of Bessie's father, but it had been a pleasure to see Mama, happy in her role as mother of the groom, taking her place alongside other members of the family in the wedding party.

As a married man I had invested a measure of my savings in a paper-mill, hoping to use the knowledge that I had acquired at the bank to make a success in the world of business. However, there had been problem upon problem for which I had not been prepared: poor quality machinery, a fire in the drying room caused by a discarded match, and now unpaid accounts. Looking over the books in front of me I did not seem to have made a promising start. However, thoughts of another subject were troubling me.

Bessie withdrew her little finger from the mouth of our baby daughter, and repeated herself.

'I said, I think that Mary-Angela has another tooth coming through, my dear.'

'I'm sorry, Bessie, I must have been distracted. I was just thinking about my father. I'm a little concerned about him. He has not seemed himself at all.'

Bessie sighed. 'Your father does not deserve a son as devoted and forgiving as you are.'

'This incessant and unexplained travelling back and forth to Europe seems to be rendering him increasingly vague about matters.'

My wife's face took on a look of scorn.

'I think that your father is as sharp as ever, Charley. I would never underestimate him for one minute. He certainly still sees where there is an opening for a money-making opportunity. His reading tours have made him thousands.'

'Perhaps, then, it is not that he is becoming forgetful, but that he is seeking to hide something. It seems, sometimes, as if he can hardly look me in the eye.'

'Well, of course, he has got something to hide, hasn't he?' said Bessie, dandling the baby upon her knee. 'There is that young woman whom he cites as being nothing more than a

210

friend. None of the family or our associates has seen anything of her for months now. Perhaps his uncertain behaviour is centred upon that little riddle.'

I did not wish to be drawn too much upon that subject, but I had begun to have my own thoughts about it.

'It is most perplexing. Last month, my father told Forster that he was going to Belgium to visit a sick friend, but when he returned he said that his visit had been to Paris. Then only yesterday, he gave mention to the idea of visiting Geneva over the summer, but a few minutes later, he repeated exactly the same thing as if he had not told me at all, only switching his intended destination to Genoa.'

The thought had occurred to me unexpectedly as I was inspecting the accounts, that Papa had secreted away that young woman in a place where she might live as his 'wife', but I did not feel comfortable voicing my thoughts to Bessie. After all I did not wish to be indelicate. It seemed, however, that my wife had guessed at my suspicions, and as Bessie was very much in favour of plain-speaking she gave voice to them immediately.

'You believe these visits to be connected to that woman, don't you?' she asked.

Momentarily, I was unsure as to what my response should be. Although I was well acquainted with my father's shortcomings, I did not like others to think ill of him. But

Bessie was a bright and intelligent woman and I knew that I would be insulting her to deny what appeared to be staring us both in the face.

'Yes, my dear,' I sighed. 'I believe that his vagueness is quite deliberate and that there is every chance that the recently invisible Miss Ternan is living somewhere in Europe. If it is true, then I honestly do not know whether to be grateful for his discretion or angry at his pretence.'

Bessie stood up, and crossed the room, holding out Mary-Angela for me to take her. I was eager to do so and eased back my chair from the desk.

'It's your mother whom I feel for, Charley. Your father treats her as if she no longer exists.'

My wife had begun to make an inspection of the room, running her finger across the mantelpiece, her face taking a look of annoyance to find it so dusty. I knew that it would not be long before she spoke to Mrs Reed, our housekeeper, to tell her to keep a closer eye on the duties of our young housemaid; nothing escaped Bessie's notice.

'But he doesn't spare Mama financially, Bessie,' I offered, in my father's defence.

'It's not his money that she wants, it is his acknowledgement. She grieves for him dreadfully. I think that she still holds out a belief that they might be reunited one day. It

212

seems so cruel. When I visited her for tea last, she removed a crumpled note from her bosom, upon which was written a prayer. It seems that your father gave it to her many years ago, when he first discovered that she was expecting your arrival. She told me that she reads it every night before going to sleep.'

I found myself distressed at the thought and I drew my daughter toward my cheek, embracing her.

I found my voice to be hardly more than a whisper. 'I may bear the name Charles Dickens, and I know that I will never achieve all that my father has accomplished under that name, but I promise you, Bessie, that I will never do to you what he has done to my mother.'

Bessie smiled, crossed the room to my side and kissed the top of my head.

'I know that, my love, and while it is true that you are not your father, I can sincerely assure you that there is no one more pleased of that great mercy, than I.'

She held out her arms.

'Here, let me take the baby, and you can return to your books. I need to address Mrs Reed on matters of housekeeping.'

Chapter 31

New Year's Eve 1863
Gad's Hill

The guests had left; the children were now in bed. An hour before, the clock had struck midnight, and there had been raucous shouts of 'Happy New Year' and much embracing. Now it was quiet, and Dickens sat alone in the flickering candlelight of the dining-room at Gad's Hill.

He reflected upon the year that had passed. All year long he had struggled to settle down to writing a new novel, and in fact had only been able to do so in the last few weeks. There had been many family concerns that had weighed heavily upon him: Catherine's mother, Mrs Hogarth, had died in August, then his own mother, who had become increasingly senile, died the month following. He had also been exceedingly worried about Georgina.

His sister-in-law had been ill over the summer with a sudden weakening of the heart and Dickens had tried to keep from his mind the memories of the distressing manner in which his beloved Mary had died; the night when he had called her name over and over in disbelief that she had gone. If Georgina were to go in the same manner he did not know how he would cope. He was relieved to find that a short holiday in Dover taking the sea-air seemed to have aided her recovery.

He reflected with wonder upon the existence of Mary-Angela Dickens, his first grandchild. Although he could not quite reconcile himself to the position of grandfather, Dickens was quite enchanted with the little girl and began to forget that he had ever frowned upon the marriage of her parents.

The union of his daughter, Katie with Charles Collins, however, continued to trouble him. There had been no sign of grandchildren from that quarter, and Dickens had his own view as to the reasons. His son-in-law had finished his first novel, and continued to contribute to *All The Year Round,* but he remained weak in health, and although Katie earned small sums from her paintings, Dickens had begun to supplement their income; he could not bear to think of his daughter in such difficult circumstances.

As for friendships, he had finally made his peace with Thackeray. They had met unexpectedly at the Athenaeum.

'Come, Dickens.' Thackeray had held out his hand. 'We have allowed our foolish quarrel to continue far too long. Let us be friends again, eh?

How glad he was now that after a moment's

hesitation he had taken up Thackeray's hand warmly, for on Christmas Eve, William Thackeray had died. His daughters had found him, his arm thrown across his face, as though asleep in bed, but he had died of a stroke. Katie had been beside herself with grief, for William had asked her to visit him only the day before, but feeling low in spirits, she had declined. She sobbed upon her father's shoulder with regret that she had not accepted him.

'Oh, Papa. He had become such a dear, dear friend to me.'

Dickens turned away from his sad reflection and found his attention focusing upon his surroundings. Propped against the wall was a stick from which hung a length of black cloth. It had been carried about the room by young Plorn in a charade as the God of Discord. In the flickering light it cast an eerie shadow upon the wall and its likeness to a funeral staff came to Dickens's mind.

By degrees an awful premonition crept over him with an icy chill. He thought of his son Walter in India. It had been months since he had written and Dickens sensed strongly that his son was in trouble again. All that he had wanted for his boys was for them to be self-reliant, and yet he feared that his own father's blood coursed too strongly through Walter's veins.

When Charley had visited his brother three

years before, he had freed him from a series of debts, but now the lack of any correspondence in recent months led Dickens to believe that Walter was in straitened circumstances once more.

As young Francis had been unable to settle to working in his father's office, plans had been made for him to go out to Calcutta and join the mounted police. Although Dickens did not believe in New Year's resolutions, in that moment he was moved by sentimentalism, after all he had not seen his son for six years, and he resolved to send Francis with a cheque. Perhaps as a father he had been too hard on the boy.

His eyes returned to where the forgotten prop leaned against the wall. Still unnerved, Dickens stood up with annoyance, crossed the room and snatched it up, tearing the black material from it. He cast the material to the floor, set the denuded stick back against the wall and opened the door to leave. In the light remaining, the shadow took on a new form, the form of a soldier's rifle, and as Dickens closed the door, the stick fell quite suddenly with a clatter to the floor.

*   *   *

New Year's Day 1864
Calcutta, India

The body of a young man lay in an army hospital, a trickle of blood snaking from the corner of his mouth. He had been weakened by a fever for some weeks, but at a sign of recovery the attending doctor had suggested that the young soldier go home for a month. Time with his family would be good for him. It had been too long since he had seen them all. His mother wrote faithfully every week, and the soldier felt guilty that he had not replied more often. There had always been the call of another card game preying upon his time. He admitted to himself that he had also disappointed his father and he resolved then to become a better son.

Delighted at the news that he would be going home, the young man had propped himself up, keen to share his good fortune with his fellow patients.

'Do you hear that, my friends? I'm off home!'

'Good for you, lad,' nodded the wounded sergeant in the bed opposite.

'Ah, for a glass of that fine English ale!' called another.

'And what's more . . . ' He coughed, 'And what's more . . . ' He coughed more violently.

A gush of blood spurted from his mouth.

At the sight of the horror the sergeant

218

shouted for help. 'Quick! Doctor, he's choking.'

The infirmary doctor hurried back to his patient's side, and endeavoured to prop him up, but it was too late. The young man had fallen back dead upon his pillow. The doctor shook his head: the room fell silent with horror. The soft footsteps of a nurse crossed the ward to the bed where the body lay, and she pulled the bed sheet over the vacant eyes of Lieutenant Walter Dickens.

Chapter 32

June 1865
Staplehurst, Kent

Mrs Ternan laughed gaily as Dickens imitated the exaggerated manner of Monsieur Beaucourt-Mutel, the French landlord from whom he had been renting an apartment for the last three years.

Ah, it is very sad, Monsieur Tringham, that you leave us. It has been un grand plaisir *over these last few years to have you and your wife as our guests.'*

Dickens took out a large handkerchief from his jacket pocket and blew his nose with comic affectation.

'Oh, you have him to perfection, sir!' Mrs

Ternan, dabbed at her eyes.

The apartment just outside Boulogne had been the only way in which Dickens and Ellen Ternan had been able to live out their lives as they wished, away from the view of those who knew them and from those in Press who would wish to ruin the reputation of Charles Dickens. If it had not been for the frequent need to leave behind his life as 'Mr Tringham' and return to his life as a famous author in London then he would have found his life in France to be idyllic. In a small village, he was able to go about his life unnoticed.

In recent months, however, there had been some concerns about Ellen's health, and every time that Dickens came to leave her, he worried that on his return, she would be worse. His own health had been troubling him too, not only had he continued to be plagued by the recurring spasms of facial neuralgia, but he had also experienced severe swelling in his left foot. His doctor, Frank Beard, had warned him that he needed to rest, to cease his relentless travelling and start to take life a little easier. Ellen had urged him to listen and reluctantly they had both acknowledged that perhaps it was time to return to England for good.

Now, accompanied by Ellen and her mother, Dickens was travelling across Kent by means of steam train, and Georgina and Mamie would meet them on their arrival. Later, Dickens planned to install Ellen and her mother at St Leonard's-on-Sea for a while, thinking that a change of air would be good for Ellen's health.

Dickens threw back his head and laughed. 'Yes, I can still see Monsieur Beaucourt-Mutel with his funny little moustache, waving us goodbye and—'

Without any warning at all, the sound of a piercing whistle broke into his laughter and the carriage jolted, throwing Mrs Ternan and Ellen from their seats onto the floor and far into the corner of the carriage which was now tilting downwards. Mrs Ternan blinked rapidly as if trying to make sense of what had happened and then put her fingers to her head. At the sight of blood, she became hysterical.

'Mama? Oh, my God. Mama, you are bleeding!' Ellen cried.

The carriage rocked, creaking and groaning.

'Charles, what has happened?'

Strangely calm, Dickens said quietly, 'Pray, ladies, do not cry out. We cannot help ourselves if we do not remain composed.'

Ellen took her mother's hand, swallowed hard, and nodded. A single tear trickled down her cheek.

'Very well, my love,' Ellen whispered fearfully.

'Now, do not stir but remain perfectly still, while I see what can be done.'

Dickens stood up cautiously and looked

out of the carriage window. He could see that the carriages ahead of them had broken away and fallen from the bridge down into the river below. A guard ran through the swirling smoke, toward the carriage with a plank, and at the sight of him Dickens opened the door carefully.

'Here, man, give that to me. There are ladies here who need to escape.'

'Very good, sir.'

The guard laid the plank from the door onto the ground and gestured to Mrs Ternan.

'Madam?'

Mrs Ternan shook her head, 'No, no. Please, let my daughter go first.'

'Oh, no, Mama, I couldn't—'

'Please, ladies,' Dickens urged, 'I do not want to alarm you, but you must make haste.'

Mrs Ternan, reluctantly accepted Dickens's assistance to her feet and, walking very carefully, took the guard's hand to safety 'And now you, my love.' Dickens extended his hand to Ellen.

As she stood up, the carriage creaked and gave another jolt, causing Ellen to cry out.

'Charles! I'm frightened.'

'Calm yourself, my love, just take my hand and stand up.'

'Charles, it's going to fall, I know it.'

Dickens sought her eyes. 'Ellen, do you trust me?'

Her voice was hushed. 'Yes, my love.'

'Then focus your eyes upon my face and listen to my voice.' She nodded, her eyes full of tears.

'Now, take my hand and stand up carefully.'

Ellen reached out for his hand and grasped it, easing gently to her feet.

'Now take a few steps toward the door and place your foot upon the plank. I have your one hand, and the guard will take the other.'

'I'm frightened, Charles, I'm frightened,' she choked.

'You are almost there, my love, just another step.'

The guard held out his hand. 'Mr Dickens is right, miss, just another step.'

In a few moments Ellen was out of the carriage and, once on firm ground, threw herself into the arms of her beloved and embraced him.

'Oh, Charles, I thought it was the end.'

Even in this moment of distress, Dickens was conscious that the guard had recognized him and that there could be eyes upon this scene which would remember every word and gesture that was made.

'There, there, my dear, pray compose yourself. There are others who need my help.' He patted her hand.

Ellen smoothed down her skirts, 'Yes, yes, of course. I am being selfish.'

'I will come and find you and your mother shortly, my dear.'

223

As Ellen disappeared, Dickens climbed down the muddy embankment and took in the awful scene of the injured and dying. It was dreadful: he had never seen such horror before. A man who had found his wife dead was kneeling in the mud, holding her body and crying inconsolably. For a second, Dickens agonized over what he would have done if it had been Ellen, but he was distracted from the nightmare by the sound of moaning coming from the wreckage of a carriage. He urged the guards to investigate.

'Over here, I think that there is someone trapped!'

Wedged beneath the seating was a young man, his body twisted, his face covered in blood. The guards endeavoured to ease him free, taking great trouble to not cause further injury or pain, and Dickens kept up his spirits with words of encouragement.

'A few more minutes, young sir, and all will be well. Do not fear, these gentlemen will see you aright.'

When he was finally freed and laid upon the ground, Dickens took a flask of brandy from his pocket and held it to the man's lips.

'Thank you, sir,' the young man whispered. 'I believe that you have saved my life.'

Dickens was not listening: he had suddenly remembered that his latest manuscript was in the carriage in which he had been travelling. He hastily replaced the lid on the flask and made his excuses, gently taking the man's hand.

'I wish you well, young man, but I have something urgent which I must attend to.'

With his eyes fixed upon the swaying carriage, he made his way determinedly toward it.

'Mr Dickens, sir! Do not be foolish,' the guard shouted after him.

But Dickens took no heed. If he lost the manuscript, weeks of work would be gone, and he knew that he had not the time to make it up. The weight of the broken carriage strained upon the couplings of the adjoining carriage. Dickens edged his way toward the open door, his coat tails flapping in the wind. As he was about to step onto the plank, it fell from its position and tumbled down into the water below.

He watched it for a moment and, undeterred, placed a foot inside the carriage and reached toward the manuscript which lay crumpled and soiled upon the floor. With the nimblest of movements he snatched it up, then he turned and momentarily caught a glance of the swirling waters of the River Beult below him and began to edge back along the broken track to safety.

He found Ellen nursing her mother, who was still greatly shaken.

He crouched down next to her saying, 'The guard has just told me that an emergency train is on its way to take the surviving passengers to Charing Cross in London, my dear.'

'Oh, thank heavens!'

'When we arrive, I can arrange for you and your mother to stay in an hotel and I will send word to Mamie and Georgina to come and assist you with caring for her for a few days.'

'And what about you, my love? What will you do?' she whispered, now also conscious of those who might recognize Dickens.

'I will stay at my offices in Wellington Street for the night, and then return to Gad's Hill tomorrow. I can send a carriage to bring you all back from Town.'

'Very well, my love.' Ellen's voice was filled with sadness. 'It will not be easy for us in England, will it?'

Dickens shook his head. 'No, it will not be easy, but unchanging love will see us through.'

At these words, she put her hand instinctively to her wrist, where she always wore the emerald bracelet, but to her horror found that it had gone.

'Charles, my bracelet! The clasp must have broken when I fell.'

The emergency train was just pulling in and the guards were beginning to ready the able passengers to board. Dickens glanced up toward the carriage from which they had escaped, and Ellen placed her hand on his arm fearful that he would attempt to retrieve it.

'There is nothing you can do now, my love. We must leave it there.'

He looked at the sadness in her eyes and, as the terrifying thought that he could have lost her swept over him again, Dickens was overwhelmed with love for her. He longed to take her up in his arms and hold her, but he knew that he could not, and his heart was filled with bitter resentment.

*　　　*　　　*

After a fitful night's sleep, Dickens awoke with a start. He reached out his hand to the space next to him, but Ellen was not there, and he remembered that she was installed with her mother at the Griffin Hotel. He lifted his head from the pillow, feeling faint and nauseous. The thought of the journey back to Gad's Hill gave him a rush of terror, and he wondered how he would manage it. A tap on the door made him jump.

'Dickens? It's me, Wills, are you all right?'

William Henry Wills, worked at the offices in Wellington Road as a valued assistant on *All The Year Round.*

'Yes, thank you, Wills. A cup of strong tea will soon set me right, if you would oblige.'

'Very good, sir. I will return shortly.'

Dickens dropped his head back on his pillow. He knew that Wills was a reliable and discreet friend and associate upon whom he could rely, and he wondered if he should confide in him that Ellen was still very much a part of his life, and that she was now back in England. He had no idea what he was going to do; what *they* were going to do. He had recognized that he could not return to the incessant travelling back and forth to France.

His whole body ached, and his foot throbbed angrily, reminding him mercilessly what he knew in his heart to be true: that his health was failing and he was becoming an old man.

Chapter 33

August 1866
Palace Green, Kensington

'May I introduce you to Mr Valentine Prinsep?' Ann Thackeray gestured toward the dark-haired man of fine physique who was seated in the sumptuous living room at Palace Green. Valentine stood up to take the hand of Katie Collins and, as he did so, she inwardly estimated that he must have been over six feet tall.

'How do you do, Mrs Collins. I have heard so much about you.'

'Really?' This was the only reply that Katie

could manage, as she took in Mr Prinsep's impressive stature.

'Yes, I know of your husband's work, but Ann has told me that you also have quite a talent for painting.'

He sat down again, folding one long leg over the other.

'Then she honours me with a compliment that I cannot own, sir. Although I wish that I could be credited with such.'

'Perhaps you are too modest, madam.' His voice was deep and resonant.

At Ann's invitation, Katie took the seat opposite Mr Prinsep and, after a moment's hesitation, politely enquired, 'May I ask, are you a member of the Prinsep family of Little Holland House, sir?'

She found herself unusually self-conscious and placed her hands one way and then another in her lap.

The Prinsep family were well known in Kensington, for their beautiful home in extensive grounds attracted many associates of the Royal Academy. They were also connected to both the Kipling and Tennyson families, and Mr Prinsep's distinguished Anglo-Indian heritage was evidenced by his dark features and dusky skin.

'Yes indeed, Mrs Collins. Perhaps you might also know of Mr Watts who instructs me in art? He came and lodged temporarily with my family as a guest, and I managed to persuade him to stay on and tutor me.'

'Yes, I have heard of him, although I myself have not yet had the pleasure of meeting him. He is well known to my husband.'

Ann momentarily excused herself to arrange for more tea to be brought it, and left her two guests alone.

'Ah, yes, of course. May I say what a pity it is that your husband ever stopped painting. I so admired his eye for detail. It is such a loss to the world of art.'

'It is kind of you to say so, sir.'

'How is Charles these days? I heard that he had travelled to Wiesbaden earlier in the year for his health.'

'Alas, sir, it did not help his constitution as much as we had hoped. He has not been able to get out of bed today at all, which is why I find myself making this visit alone. I don't know what I would do without Ann's friendship.'

Just as Katie had taken in the impressive stature of Mr Prinsep, he in turn had noticed her petite figure, and the charming way in which she looked at him from under her eyelashes. He sensed a sadness that lay deep within her and, as a man of the world, he knew precisely what that sadness was.

'You must find yourself quite lonely at times, Mrs Collins.'

'Oh, I cannot complain, sir.' Katie was blushing. She could not remember a time since her youthful infatuation with Edmund Yates when she had felt such a lack of composure in a man's presence.

'Well I can tell you that at Holland House there is always something amusing happening; the house is never empty. You must come as my guest, madam, with Miss Thackeray at your side, of course.'

'Thank you, Mr Prinsep, I would be honoured.'

The door opened and Ann Thackeray entered the room, followed closely by a maid carrying a tray of tea. Ann immediately noticed the flush of colour in Katie's cheeks and was pleased. For too long her pretty friend had looked pale and worn out from nursing a sickly husband. She had often wondered what the vivacious Katie Dickens had seen in the ineffectual Charles Collins. Since the day that Ann's father had met Katie outside the dress shop, the Collinses had been regular visitors to Palace Green and old ties were resumed once more between the girls; but, prior to his death, Thackeray had noticed that Katie had lost the spark which he had so admired in her youth and sensed that her marriage wasn't what it seemed.

The maid set the tray upon the table, and Ann began to pour out the tea for her guests.

'I have invited Mrs Collins to Holland House, Ann. What do you think?'

'I think that she will be the belle of the ball,

231

and impress all your illustrious friends with her beauty and talent,' said Ann, handing a cup of tea to Mr Prinsep, who nodded in acknowledgement.

'Her beauty I can testify to,' remarked Valentine, 'but as for her talent I have yet to witness it. You must certainly allow me to view some of your work, Mrs Collins.' He took a sip of his tea.

For Katie this was certainly a wonderful opportunity to raise her profile as an artist for she knew that there would be many influential members from the world of art at Holland House. But at that moment, Katie was unsettled to find that what was completely irresistible to her was the opportunity to be in Valentine's company once more, for in his presence she remembered exactly what it felt like to be a woman; and it felt wonderful.

Ann handed a cup of tea to Katie, who was trying to disguise the fact that she was trembling a little, and upon taking it she upset the cup of tea into the saucer.

'Oh, Ann! I am sorry; how clumsy of me.'

'Not at all, dear, please let me call for the maid to bring a cloth.' She rose quickly from her seat and left the room.

Katie looked up to find Valentine regarding her with a hint of amusement in his eyes.

'Mrs Collins, I do believe that if I don't see you again, I will lose the will to paint.'

'Please,' she appealed, taking a handkerchief from her purse and trying to mop up some of the tea from her dress, 'don't say such things, sir. You are merely playing with me.'

'Not at all. I had heard of your beauty and fire, and know I have seen it for myself. It is a terrible crime that you have married a man who does not value you as a woman.'

Katie did not know whether to feel shame or anger. It seemed to her as if marriage had become a laughing matter among the artistic circle. She shook her head, her eyes flashing.

'I will not listen to such talk. What could you possibly know about my life or my marriage?'

'I simply say what I sense, madam.'

As she stood up, Valentine immediately got up from his own seat and crossed the room to her.

Katie raised her hand in protest.

'Please, Mr Prinsep. Do not come one step closer. I have a husband who is very ill, and I must return home to him immediately.'

Valentine Prinsep took no heed of Katie's words at all, but took her hands in his.

'Please promise that you will come to Holland House.' His voice was a whisper. 'I have to see you again.'

She pulled her hands away and turned her face from his. 'I can promise nothing.'

'If I swear that I will not speak upon the

233

subject of your marriage again, unless you give me leave to do so, will you promise to come then? I want to watch you paint, to see you hold a brush in your hand. I will ask Mr Watts to assist you, Katie. Please, will you say yes?'

'I will think about it. I can promise no more.'

The door opened and Ann entered with a cloth, but seeing her guests up on their feet she remarked, 'Oh, Katie you are not leaving already are you?'

'I'm so sorry, Ann, thank you for your hospitality, but I need to return to Charlie.'

'But what about your dress?' Ann held out the cloth.

'Don't fret, dear, it's fine. Now, I really must go.'

She raised her eyes to find Valentine's gaze fixed upon her. 'Goodbye, Mr Prinsep.'

'Goodbye, madam. I will make arrangements with Ann to bring you to Holland House in a few days. Until then, Mrs Collins.'

*　　　*　　　*

Katie wrapped her coat around her and began to walk back to the tiny house in Thurloe Place. She hoped that her husband had found the energy to get up, that he would be seated at the table writing when she returned, that he would greet her with the news that he was feeling much better. She needed to believe that when she walked into the house that nothing had changed, but something had changed: she had experienced a strength of feeling which had taken possession of her.

Valentine's voice echoed in her head.

'You must find yourself quite lonely at times, Mrs Collins . . . !

She wrestled with feelings of guilt. In Valentine's eyes she had seen passion reflected and she could feel it drawing her to him.

At Thurloe Place, Charlie was seated by the fire in an armchair when she returned, and he smiled at the sight of her.

'Hello, my dear. Did you have a good afternoon?'

'Yes, I did, thank you.' She removed her gloves, coat and bonnet and tidied her hair. 'Did you manage to take some of the soup which I left for you?'

'Yes, I did, my love. It was most thoughtful of you.'

He inspected his wife's face closely.

'You look a little flushed, dear, is everything all right?'

'Yes, I took a brisk walk home and it was a little breezy. I think that the wind had probably caught my face.'

'Well, it certainly suits you, if I may say so. I think that the visit to Palace Green has done you good, you must go out more often. Did anyone else join you and Ann for tea?'

Katie hesitated for a moment.

'No, my love. Ann and I were quite alone.'

Chapter 34

March 1867
Elizabeth Cottage, Slough

The small cottage, nestled among roses and neat shrubbery, was overlooked by the village church of St Laurence. A more picturesque setting could not have been wished for. The attractive young woman who resided there, however, was restless. She looked at the clock and found that it had been only minutes since she had last inspected it. Crossing the room to the window she looked out upon the mundane village life which was taking place outside and sighed.

The rent book in the bureau drawer bore the name of Mr John Tringham, so there was no need for her to concern herself with pecuniary matters. A maid was on hand to assist with cooking and housework, so there was no need for her to put her hand to any household task. In fact, every need that she had was taken care of, except the need which pressed upon her more heavily than all others: she had no purpose.

At the age of twenty-seven, Ellen Ternan's life had become nothing more than a waiting game. Since the accident at Staplehurst, she had been moved from place to place by an ever anxious Dickens, who felt that this was the most efficient means of keeping their association a secret. He was especially pleased with her current location, for it was within easy reach of the railway line, and he could travel from London to Slough in less than half an hour. Yes, for him it was most convenient.

Mrs Frances Ternan had been re-engaged as an actress at the Lyceum Theatre, London. An associate of Dickens, Monsieur Charles Fechter, was seeking a mature actress to feature in a performance of *The Master of Ravenswood* and Dickens had remembered that Ellen's mother had played the part once before in her own career. He suggested her name to Fechter, who was pleased at the recommendation, but Ellen was disappointed. Until now she had said nothing. Perhaps given time, Dickens would do the same for her. After all, she could hardly have played the part of an old, blind woman.

Whenever Dickens visited her, he would read from his latest work, ask for her opinion, share news of his associates, but during each of his last visits there had been no hint that he planned to recommend her name to anyone, and how could he? Ellen Ternan did not exist.

From the window she saw the handsome

figure of a middle-aged man, dressed in a green frock-coat, his hat at a jaunty angle, approaching the cottage. She had not anticipated him today. Sometimes his visits were announced and at other times unexpected, but Ellen would inevitably be at home, for where else had she to go? Perhaps today he would have news for her and, if not, then she would take courage and ask him about returning to the stage.

Opening the door to welcome him, she was greeted with the words, 'Good morning to you, my dear girl. And how are you today?'

He did not wait for her answer, but continued, 'Do you know, I have seen the most interesting looking dame, dressed in black, with the bonnet and shawl and costume of thirty years ago. She was followed by a little troop of dogs, which she kept in strict order and she so amused me I wanted to say "Halloa" and ask her name, but she disappeared into a narrow alleyway between the shops. I must seek her out again one day. What a character!'

Dickens became aware that Ellen had not greeted him with her customary cheerfulness, and seemed unusually quiet. In fact, if he had given it some little thought he had reflected upon a similar observation the last time that he had visited her.

'Are you well, my dear? You seem a little out of sorts.'

He removed his hat and gloves, putting them on the table beneath the window, and taking her hand he led her to the sofa, where they sat down.

'Ellen, are you unhappy?'

She hesitated for a moment. Her heart had been filled with so much resentment only minutes before his arrival.

'I am sorry to say, Charles, that I am not happy at all.'

Her hands were folded in her lap, and she looked at the wrist where she had once worn the emerald bracelet.

'Did you say that you are *not* happy?' A look of complete shock fell upon Dickens's face. He thought that he had misheard her, for never once had she indicated the slightest displeasure with any arrangements that he had made.

'Yes, Charles, I did.'

'But what on earth have you to be unhappy about? Don't I provide well for you? Do you not have everything that you could wish for?'

'No, Charles, I don't have everything that I could wish for. I want to live a normal life. I find myself shut up for hours here alone. Even my mother goes out more than I do.'

'That is quite unjustified. You know that you are free to come and go as you please.'

'And who would I visit? I have no friends to speak of in the locality and now I have no career.'

'But I have never made you do anything that you did not want. Your independent spirit is what I have always admired most about you, so it is unkind of you to infer that you have been influenced by me.'

'And how could I not be influenced by you? I was nothing more than an impressionable girl of eighteen when I met you, and you were a great man.'

A look of pain crossed Dickens's face.

'It seems,' he said bitterly, 'that now I am not so great in your eyes, after all.'

'My sister, Fanny, says . . . ' Ellen held back the words she had been about to speak, for she knew that they would provoke him.

'Go on,' Dickens insisted, feeling his temper rising. 'What did your sister say?'

'She said . . . that I should free myself from you now, while I am still young enough to be married.'

At this Dickens was furious. He stood up and began to pace the room.

'Then your sister is an ungrateful wretch. I paid for her to go to Italy, I wrote letters of introduction for her, and she repays me with such unkindness as that.'

'She never asked for one penny from you,' Ellen protested. 'When you did such things for her, you did them of your own volition.'

'I did them for you!' Dickens became aware that he was pointing his finger and shouting. He shook his head sadly and lowered his voice.

'I did them for you.'

'Then I can only assume that you think me an ungrateful wretch also,' Ellen whispered.

He returned to her side and they sat in quietness for a moment, both shocked at what had passed between them. Dickens put his hand to Ellen's chin and lifted her face.

'Ellen, you have been my life for the last nine years. We have never quarrelled. Please don't let us quarrel now.'

'I am sorry, Charles, truly I am. I should be grateful for all that you have done for me, and for my family.'

He was struggling to think of what he could say that would alter the mood between them, for it was unbearable, and then an idea came to him.

'I have been thinking about taking a trip to America, a reading tour. You know that it has been on my mind for some time. I think that I would like to go before I become too old to make the journey. What do you say if I take you with me?'

Ellen's face brightened at the news.

'Oh, Charles, I can think of nothing that I would like more.'

'I have engaged a new manager to look into it for me, and I am going to send him on ahead to make all the necessary arrangements. If I ask Mamie to come as a companion to you, then everything should be in order. The trip would do her good too. She has still not accepted a suitor, and I worry for her. It would give me great pleasure to have my two ladies with me.'

Dickens was relieved to see the look of contentment return to the features of the face which he loved so well. He was aware that he had roused her hopes, and he prayed that he would not have to see disappointment in her eyes once more, for he inwardly recognized that taking her to America would not be as easy as she believed. For now, however, he would allow her to enjoy the prospect. He could not bear to believe that the feelings that Ellen Ternan had for him were beginning to alter.

Chapter 35

May 1867 Marylebone Church, London

Wilkie Collins stood at the altar in Marylebone Parish church, reluctant to look upon the face of the priest, for holy men always made him feel uncomfortable. Instead he looked up at the oil painting by Benjamin West, which hung behind on the anterior wall: an image of the Holy Family. Wisps of cloud moved across the sky above their heads and changed before his eyes like tufts and curls, and Wilkie became aware that he was sweating profusely. A few years before, that same painting had been viciously scored with a knife at the hand of a madman and, although it had been restored, Wilkie wondered whether the work of art had played similar tricks with the mind of that tortured individual.

There had been a church on this site for more than 600 years. This holy place had witnessed the marriage of the artist, Francis Bacon, the baptism of the poet, Lord Byron and in more recent years the baptism of Dickens's son, Alfred. Today the vaulted gallery was empty of worshippers and the congregation was made up of no more than a handful of associates.

Unusually for Wilkie Collins, it had not been long since he had last been in a church. His mother had passed on, and in the final days of her life he had felt as if his own life had been draining away, so close had been their bond. Not only had he been in emotional pain but he had been plagued once more by his night visions of the green tusked woman, and racked with the physical torture of his rheumatism. It had only been the call of his writing which had moved him to lift his head from his pillow, drag himself to his desk and to live through another day.

When he had returned home from the funeral, Caroline had been waiting for him in the sitting-room, drinking a cup of tea. She was strangely cheerful and he had not understood it at all for she had been very fond of his mother. Although Caroline had remained hidden away over the years, she had never forgotten the kindness with which she had been received on that first night at Hanover Terrace and she had always enquired after Mrs Collins whenever Wilkie returned from visiting her. So Wilkie had been completely perplexed by Caroline's manner and wondered if it was a touch of nervous hysteria, which women were prone to at times of grief.

'Do you feel all right, my dear?' he had asked on his return home, taking off his scarf and gloves and dropping them onto the sofa.

'Of course, my love,'—she put down her cup, stood up and took his hands in hers—'for now at last you can ask me what you could never ask me during your mother's lifetime.'

Wilkie began to feel distinctly uncomfortable.

'Caroline, I have told you before—'

'My love, I have always understood that you feared that your mother would discover my history, but now she is gone, Wilkie, you are free to follow your own heart.'

Lost in her own excitement, she sat down on the sofa again and, looking into his face, her eyes shining, said, 'You may kneel to ask me if you want, or sit here next to me. I don't mind.'

He was very quiet, and lowered his eyes.

'Wilkie?'

In the hush of the church, the priest whispered something which brought his attention back to the occasion.

'I asked if everything was well, sir?'

However, it was not to Wilkie to whom the priest was speaking, but the man at Wilkie's side, Mr Joseph Clow: the man who was about to become the husband of the woman in white.

*　　　　*　　　　*

The bell above the shop door tinkled to announce the arrival of a new customer. Caroline Graves entered the pharmacy of Clow and Son, as she had done on many occasions before, to replenish Wilkie Collins's supply of laundanum. Joseph Clow looked up and was pleased to see the beautiful widow, Mrs Graves, at the counter. He greatly admired the dedicated care that she demonstrated toward her uncle, Mr Collins.

Joseph had never any desire to be a chemist's assistant, but his father was ageing and required assistance in the shop, particularly since he had slipped on a wet step and had broken his leg. Usually, at the sound of a customer entering, he would shout from the back room, asking who it was, and then giving strict instructions to his son as to doses, measurements and mixing. However, on this occasion, his father had fallen asleep, and Joseph was relieved that he would be able to give Mrs Graves his full attention without being made to look like an imbecile.

'Ah, good morning, Mrs Graves, what a pleasure to see you.'

Joseph Clow had dark, curly hair and light blue eyes which, on any other man, would have been an attractive combination; but whereas his left eye was good, he was unable to fix his right eye upon any one thing, leaving his customers unsure as to which eye they should look into when addressing him.

'And how is your uncle, Mr Collins, this day?' His eye rolled.

'I am sorry to say that he is not well at all. His mother—my aunt, of course—recently passed away, and in his grief his pain is harder to bear.'

'My sympathies, madam. Perhaps you would like me to increase his dose slightly today?'

'Yes, perhaps that would help.' Caroline Graves nodded. 'And how is your father, Joseph?'

'He is getting a little stronger each day, madam. He is able to walk a little if he leans upon me.'

'What a blessing you must be to him,' said Caroline thoughtfully, the beginnings of a splendid idea starting to form in her mind.

'I aim to be useful where I can, madam.' He began to make up a tincture of laudanum.

'Joseph, I wonder if you could also do something useful for me.' Joseph almost upset the bottle upon the counter. He would do anything to be of use to Mrs Graves.

'Why yes, madam, if I can.'

'You see, I always take a walk in the park each evening for a little exercise, but my uncle is unable to accompany me at present due to his indisposition. I don't suppose that you would consider taking his place until he is better? I know that he would be greatly indebted to you if you would oblige. There are so many unscrupulous people about: it's just not safe for a woman to be out alone.'

Mr Clow's eye rolled and he stammered, 'M-Mrs Graves, it would be an honour.'

Not only did Joseph Clow accompany Mrs Graves on her walk that evening, but every evening for the two weeks that followed; and when she suggested that she might be receptive to an offer of marriage, Joseph Clow found himself stuttering over an awkward proposal, completely unaware that he was the key player in a well-thought-out plan. The woman in white now had what she needed: an incentive for Wilkie Collins to marry her.

Seated at his desk, she found him writing.

'Wilkie, there has been a development in my life, of which I think you should be aware.'

He looked up from his work.

'Really, my dear?'

'Yes, really. I have been made an offer of

marriage by Joseph Clow.'

'The chemist's son?' He began to laugh. 'You are jesting with me! I have never heard anything so ridiculous. Married to a squint-eyed buffoon.'

'I am completely in earnest, Wilkie. I wish to be married and if you will not marry me then I will accept Mr Clow's offer. His family also own a distillery, you know, so he has prospects of an inheritance.'

Wilkie shook his head.

'Caroline, I will not be bluffed into making an offer. I have never misled you regarding my intentions, and I hope you will admit that I have looked after you well in all other respects.'

'Then you give me no choice, Wilkie, for I have given Mr Clow my word.'

*　　*　　*

The priest indicated to Wilkie Collins, by means of a whisper, that the bride had arrived. He was about to give her away and Dickens, who was seated among the congregation, muttered to Georgina at his side. 'If I had penned this myself, no one would have believed it. Wilkie's affairs defy all reason.'

For what Dickens also knew was that not far away, in a house in Bolsover Street, sat a well-proportioned, dark-haired young woman by the name of Miss Martha Rudd. Wilkie had first met her when he travelled to Norfolk to carry out research for his novel, *Armadale.*

When he had arrived at The Chandler Inn, not far from Winterton, the dark-haired barmaid had commented upon the state of his muddy boots. Wilkie had playfully asked her if that was an invitation to clean them, and she had laughingly rebuked him for his cheek. Over the months to come, he had travelled back and forth to Norfolk, guilty at his secret delight over Caroline's reluctance to accompany him as she was suffering from a little nervous indisposition.

Martha and Wilkie walked along the beach together, hid from one another amongst the rocks and when Wilkie complained of pains in his feet she had taken off his sandy boots, damp with salt water, removed his socks and massaged his feet: Martha Rudd and Wilkie Collins were falling in love. He brought her back to London and installed her in the house in Bolsover Street. When he had confessed all to Dickens, his friend had not known whether to laugh or reprove him. But Martha Rudd was under no illusions: she knew that her life was to be precisely that of Caroline Graves, a hidden one.

Wilkie accompanied the verger to the church door, where the woman in white now waited. He could not help but be reminded of the night when he had first set eyes upon her. Now just as then, she looked completely angelic. His eyes met hers and she willed him to speak; to put a stop to the ceremony; to offer to take the place of Joseph Clow at her side.

Although he loved her, as he had also grown to love Martha Rudd, he knew with as much certainty as he had ever known that he could never be a married man. He walked her down the aisle, and when the priest welcomed the congregation, he lifted his face and set his jaw with determination: Caroline Graves was about to become Mrs Joseph Clow and Wilkie Collins would do nothing to change it.

Chapter 36

August 1867

Gad's Hill

'Have you really thought about this, Dickens?' Forster asked, drawing deeply on his cigar. 'After all, you are not a good traveller these days, and if the crossing is anything like your last visit to America then the whole idea is bound to be a disaster.'

Forster took in the well-arranged surroundings of Gad's Hill and wondered why his friend was so determined to go ahead with an idea which was sure to be a strain on his health, even if it would yield huge financial rewards. There was little point if it ended in his death.

Dickens tried to hide his irritation. A reading tour of America had long been an idea he had entertained, and now he had employed a new manager, Mr George Dolby, to journey to America and make the necessary arrangements ahead of his arrival. He needed words of encouragement and support, and Forster was being anything but encouraging.

'My friend,' said Dickens, trying not to sound irritated, 'you should know after all these years that when I set my mind to something, nothing will dissuade me.'

That morning, he had received a letter from Catherine, who had also heard of his plans: she wished him success and a safe journey. After reading it, his first instinct had been to discard it without response, but he hesitated for a moment, mindful that Catherine had endured the loss of both her mother and their son, Walter. His conscience moved him to acknowledge her note, albeit with some reluctance.

Dear Catherine
Thank you for your letter.
I accept your good wishes for a safe journey.
Kind regards,
Charles Dickens

His thoughts about Ellen, however, demonstrated greater depth and concern. He had given much thought as to whether the woman he loved should be his companion on this trip. If Mamie were to accompany them, it would lend an air of respectability to the arrangement, but Mamie stated that she could not bear the thought of the journey and had flatly refused to consider it. Dickens had worried greatly as to how he would tell Ellen that the prospect of her travelling with him was becoming a distant one. He called to mind the disturbing argument that they had had, the promises that he had made to her regarding his visit to America, but in his heart he had realized that to take her with him would be too great a risk to his reputation.

Seated in this study, looking through his correspondence, Dickens made a tentative explanation to Ellen who was perched on the edge of his desk.

'Ellen, my love, there has been difficulty in our travelling arrangements which I had not anticipated.'

Ellen's eyes fell to the envelope on the desk containing the brief note addressed to Catherine, and wondered if Mrs Dickens was ill.

'Is it your wife?' she asked, well aware how Catherine's death would alter her own prospects, and a little unnerved that the thought was not as appealing to her now as it had once been.

Dickens frowned, and then remembering the letter replied, 'Oh, no, my dear. That note is nothing but a minor inconsequence. I'm afraid that it's Mamie. She has refused to consider the journey at all and, of course, that puts your accompanying me in an entirely different light.'

Dickens had begun to trip nervously over his words as he noticed the dark look which entered Ellen's eyes, and immediately pushed back his chair and circled the desk to placate her.

'Oh, my dear, I know that this is a disappointment to you, as it is to me. God only knows how much I wanted you to be with me.'

He lifted her chin with his hand in an attempt to seek her eyes, but she turned her face from him abruptly.

'Ellen? Oh, Ellen, my love, don't be upset with me.' He placed his hand on her arm.

She pulled away from him, her cheeks burning and, walking to the window, she folded her arms.

'Charles, Mamie is your daughter, and you should *make* her come. She is still under your roof after all.'

'But Ellen, Mamie is a grown woman. It wouldn't be fair to—' She turned on him, her eyes full of angry tears.

'Fair? You talk about what is fair! Is it

253

fair that I have built up my hopes about this trip, only to have them torn down at the last minute? Perhaps you had no intention of taking me at all, and you were merely indulging me 'til such time that you could find the courage to tell me the truth. I am not your uncomplaining little wife, my dear, and my emotions are not to be played with!'

Dickens was filled with horror: never before had a woman spoken to him this way. Should he assert himself, or would he lose her forever if he did? His voice was very quiet.

'My plans are to arrange for you to travel to Florence with your mother to visit your sister, Fanny. When I arrive in America, if I feel that your presence there can be kept discreet, then I will send a telegram. All Well means, you come, and Safe And Well means, you don't come. At least in my absence, however long that may be, you will be in good company with your family.'

Ellen, who was shocked by her own outburst, nodded without speaking, and with a silent nod in return, Dickens left his study.

*   *   *

In Boston, the city's bookshops were already beginning to display Dickens's novels in their large windows overlooking the busy sidewalks, and the tobacconists had bought in stocks of the *Pickwick* snuff boxes and the *Little Nell* cigar. Outside the Tremont Hall, queues had already begun to form at the box office where tickets for the readings were about to go on sale.

At The Parker House Hotel the manager, Mr Herbert Savory had instructed his staff that everything must be perfect in readiness for the visit of Mr Dickens, and that he must be given absolutely no cause to criticize American hospitality. Mr Dolby had also made it explicitly clear to Herbert Savory that on this visit Dickens would not tolerate the invasion of privacy that he'd endured as a younger man.

Mr Savory, seated in a chair which could not be drawn up too closely to his desk, due to the impediment of his ample stomach, addressed the hotel's chef with regard to the planned menus.

'If Mr Dickens chooses to dine alone, he will have a personal waiter who will be on hand to serve meals in his room, so it is important, Chef, that the food is prepared to the same standard as if he was eating in the dining-room.'

The chef nodded. 'Yes, of course Mr Savory. I will be ordering in a selection of meats which I understand are among Mr Dickens's favourites, along with the English Breakfast Tea which his manager, Mr Dolby, has advised is his preference in the mornings.'

'Excellent.' Mr Savory smiled, and turned his attention to the chief lobby attendant,

Scott, who stood next to the chef, awaiting his own set of instructions.

'And it will be your job, Mr Scott, to nominate an attendant who will be posted at Mr Dickens's door to discourage any uninvited attention. This has come at the special request of Mr Dolby who wishes to deflect any intrusive and unwelcome attention from other guests or newspaper men.'

'Very good, sir,' nodded Mr Scott.

'Well then, it seems, gentlemen, that we are ready for Mr Dickens's arrival.'

Herbert Savory reached across the desk and helped himself to a generous portion of meat loaf from a plate which Chef had placed there.

He took a large bite, and nodded with satisfaction. 'Yes, I think that we are ready.'

*   *   *

9 November 1867

The Cuba
Liverpool

Dickens had been accompanied to the docks in Liverpool by Katie and Charlie. It had been a complete wonder to him that his son-in-law was still alive to make such a journey, for the likelihood of his death had been predicted by the doctors on many occasions over the last year. In recent weeks, however, Charlie had regained a little of his former strength and the doctors had been able to give no firm diagnosis beyond a weakened constitution.

Dickens had been worried to leave Katie, for she had seemed depressed and anxious of late. He hoped with all his heart that his daughter would not have to face the death of her husband in his absence. He had no idea that it was not her husband's health which was worrying her, but her troubled conscience over her year-long relationship with Valentine Prinsep. With Valentine she had begun something which she had been convinced would comfort her through the death of her husband, and yet Charlie was still very much alive, and any prospect of marriage to Mr Prinsep seemed further away than ever. Her father had no idea how closely aligned his daughter's life had become to his own.

Dickens had never liked goodbyes, and this one was particularly difficult. In this familiar setting, the shadows of past years stirred up recollections of his journey with Catherine twenty-five years before. Katie had been little more than an infant at the time, and now here she was wishing him bon voyage with a husband of her own at her side. In his state of disturbed anxiety, his daughter's face kept changing into that of Catherine's and, unnerved by it, Dickens had been very short-tempered with a porter who had been trying to assist with the luggage.

'Are you all right, Papa?' Katie asked with concern, well aware that her father's health had been deteriorating of late.

'Yes, yes, of course, my dear. But let us make our farewells brief, for I believe that it is time for me to board the ship.'

'Goodbye then, Papa.'

Katie embraced her father, and found herself choked at the parting.

'Goodbye, my little Lucifer Box.' He swallowed hard.

He held out his hand to his son-in-law. 'Charlie? Take care, my boy.'

'No fear, I have a loyal nurse, sir.' He nodded to Katie. Katie watched with sadness as her father boarded the ship.

*   *   *

Dickens was pleased to find that he had been assigned the second lieutenant's quarters. It was much roomier than the tiny cabin he and Catherine had shared all those years before, and had a window which opened onto the deck.

Prior to his journey, he had thought a great deal about the ills which he had endured on that trip and had determined to be better prepared for them by means of a well-stocked medicine chest, containing salts, laudanum and ether.

He admired the polished, dark-wood fittings

and orderly layout of his cabin, and reflected upon the arrangements that had already been made ahead of his arrival in Boston, the first being a dinner with his American publisher, Mr Fields. At least he would have a fortnight to recover from his journey before the readings began.

The ship set sail and after unpacking his bags and a short nap on the bed, Dickens left his cabin to make circuit of *The Cuba*. Night had begun to fall and he nodded to the young man who stood, at the captain's request, outside the cabin door, protecting the privacy of the ship's most famous passenger. Looking across the deck, bathed in the moonlight, Dickens imagined the slender figure of Consuela Swift in her blue velvet gown, looking out to sea.

Twenty-five years before, on board *The Brittania*, the beautiful young Spaniard had been accompanying her husband, Dr Thomas Swift, to Philadelphia where he had been about to start work at the Institute for the Deaf. At the request of Catherine Dickens, he had visited her husband who had lain in his cabin suffering from seasickness. A lively friendship between the two couples sprang up from there on, and Dickens had found himself a little in love with the charming Consuela Swift.

He smiled at the memory and forgetting about the pain in his foot, he took her imaginary figure in his arms and danced around the deck, whispering, 'Madam, you have not lost your style at all.'

'*And you, sir, are as handsome as ever.*'

'Ah, Consuela, where have the years gone, my love?'

'*They have made no impression upon you at all, dearest Charles.*'

'You flatter my vanity, as always, madam '

He ceased his dance, inspected his watch and made a little bow. 'I must leave you now, my dear, but what a delight it has been to waltz with you once more.'

Noticing that he had been observed by the young attendant throughout the whole performance, Dickens was completely amused and raised his hat.

'Good evening, my friend and how are you? Tonight I think that
I shall seek out some company, for I find myself a little alone.'

'Ah, very good, sir,' the young man replied in wonder. 'Then I shall see you later.'

The attendant nodded and then watched as Dickens continued to bob his head and gesture to himself as he disappeared in the direction of the dining-room.

*   *   *

The journey across the ocean spanned almost two weeks and, as he had anticipated, it was

260

not an easy crossing. A gale sprang up, the ship rolling and tossing for days, but with his preparations close at hand, Dickens avoided the seasickness which had plagued him years before. When the ship arrived safely at Boston, he was relieved, but his heart sank at the sight of the crowd of pressmen and well-wishers gathered to greet him.

Amidst a welcome display of rockets and flares they shouted: *'Welcome back to America, Mr Dickens!'*

'Yes, welcome back, sir!'

'Are you going to write a novel while you are here, Mr Dickens . . . ?'

'We are sorry not to see Mrs Dickens, sir . . .'

Dickens stiffened at the words and in that moment, filled with indignation, he knew for certain that it would be impossible for Ellen to join him. It appeared that the Press were as impertinent as ever, and were undoubtedly waiting for the slightest hint of scandal.

'Can we have a few words from you, sir?'

But Dickens had neither the patience nor the energy to talk. He spotted a tall, well-set man waving enthusiastically to him from the wharf and with relief, he recognized the energetic individual as George Dolby, his manager.

'Ah, there is my tour manager, Mr Dolby. He will answer any questions that you may have about my schedule, gentleman. I thank you, sirs, and good night to you all.'

As Dickens made his way through the crowds, George Dolby prompted the driver of a waiting cab to load Dickens's luggage and then began fielding questions from the journalists. Dickens, meanwhile, climbed inside the cab, his pounding head falling back against the seat, and he groaned.

When the newspaper men were finally satisfied, Dolby joined Dickens in the cab in buoyant mood.

'An excellent reception, wouldn't you say, Dickens?'

'Mmm, excellent.' His eyes were closed, his head still dropped back with fatigue.

'Do you know, the queues for ticket sales to your readings snaked back almost a half-mile along Washington Street?'

'Really?' Dickens could not even feign enthusiasm.

'Yes, and would you believe that there are even scoundrels attempting to purchase as many tickets as possible, with a view to resale with profit?'

Dolby rattled on incessantly about dollars and cents, literary dinners and invitations to speak. Driving through the gas-lit city, they headed for the Parker House Hotel, his voice a constant but distant accompaniment to the sound of the cab wheels on the road: Dickens was sleeping.

Arriving at the hotel, he was gently prodded by Dolby.

'Here we are, Dickens, and there is Mr Savory, waiting to greet you.'

Dickens opened his heavy eyelids and saw at the foot of the hotel steps, a man who reminded him of his very own plump creation, Mr Pickwick. The cheerfully rotund Herbert Savory stepped forward to the carriage door as Dolby opened it.

'Ah, Mr Dickens, sir, we have been anticipating your arrival with great excitement. May I say what an honour it is to have you in my hotel, and may I also say that you have long been a personal favourite of mine. Your novels line my very own bookshelves, sir.'

He shook Dickens's hand with great enthusiasm and then gestured to his staff.

'Now, Scott here will escort you to your room, and will wait for whatever instruction you may wish to give him regarding your comfort, sir, and I can assure you that no request of yours will be too much trouble.'

Dickens nodded and tried to smile as he stepped down from the cab. He had no desire to be personally escorted to his room, nor have anyone wait upon him for instruction. He wanted nothing more than to take a bath, eat, and be alone, but all the same he thanked the effervescent Mr Savory with as much courtesy as he could muster.

An hour later, wearing a dressing-gown and night-cap, Dickens sat in a fireside chair. His mood was a reflective one and, eyeing the desk in the corner of the room, he was moved by the compulsion to write. Dolby had ensured that an adequate supply of ink and paper were at hand, and taking a seat, Dickens picked up a pen and began to unburden his heart.

Ellen, my dearest love
I hope that this letter finds you well.
   I cannot tell you how desperately I wish that you were with me. It is a wonder to me, how a man who is surrounded by company at every turn can find himself filled with so much loneliness.
   Even now I long to begin checking off the readings, for they are what stand between me and the moment when I can take you in my arms again. Already I regret ever undertaking this tour, I am so dejected and depressed in spirit . . .

The ink had run dry on the nib of his pen, and looking at what he had written, Dickens realized that it was pointless to continue. He could not post such a letter, for there were troublemakers at every turn, waiting to intercept such a missive. He could not take the risk. He pushed back his chair, crossed the room to the fireplace, crouched down and put the letter to the flames. He watched as the fire quickly devoured the paper, and with sadness he knew that in its place he would send a telegram with three words: Safe And Well.

Chapter 37

Evening had fallen, and an earlier winter storm had laid a blanket of snow across the city. Dickens turned up the fur-lined collar of his greatcoat and stepped out onto Union Square: the pavements glistened in the street lamps, but Dickens took little heed of his surroundings: he was upset; something had happened which had concerned him greatly and he now had a destination in mind which he hoped would bring him a solution.

He had given four highly successful readings in Boston, and he was now installed at the Washington Hotel, New York, where he was about to read at the Steinway Hall. However, he could not settle his mind on anything except the problem which was causing him unease.

A solitary figure huddled in a doorway played an Irish jig upon a penny whistle and Dickens dropped a coin in the tin placed on the frozen ground as he passed. On the corner of the street, a trio of night-watchmen surrounded a fire-basket, warming their hands, their breath turning to vapour in the icy air. Dickens raised his hat and asked, 'Good evening, gentlemen, could one of you assist me with the directions to the police station?'

'If you take a left turn here, sir, you'll find the police station just along that street,' one of them obliged.

Dickens thanked him and continued in the direction indicated. He soon came to a large municipal building with the sign identifying its purpose above the door. The desk-sergeant, who was preoccupied with writing an entry in a heavy ledger, did not look up as Dickens entered, but acknowledged his presence with the words, 'I'll be right there with you in just a moment, sir.'

Dickens paced back and forth in the vestibule, while the assiduous policeman finished his task, closed the ledger with a thud, and looked up.

'There, now, so what can I do for you, sir?'

Before Dickens had the opportunity to make his request known, the policeman exclaimed, 'Why it's Mr Dickens, isn't it? I've seen the posters advertising your readings, sir.'

Dickens felt a little uncomfortable because the purpose of his visit to the station touched upon his greatest desire, the desire to retain his privacy in the area of his personal life. But he had no choice but to identify himself now.

'So how can I help you, Mr Dickens, sir? I hope that you haven't fallen prey to an act of crime already. I hear you've only been here a day or two.'

Dickens looked around him uneasily,

wanting to keep the matter as private as possible.

'Well, I don't believe that a crime has been committed, Sergeant. I think it is more of an error on my part. You see I have lost my personal diary. It's not particularly valuable, although it is rather handsomely bound in leather, but it contains details about my day-to-day life, which I would prefer not to fall into the hands of anyone unscrupulous.'

The sergeant could not imagine how this apparently respectable Englishman could have anything shameful which he might wish to hide from the world outside, but as a policeman he had learned that appearances could sometimes be deceptive.

'I see, sir. Can you recollect when you last had the diary in your possession?'

'Yes,' Dickens replied emphatically. 'I had it earlier in the day while I was walking about the town, but when I returned to my hotel, I later noticed that it had gone, and I believe that it may have fallen from my pocket. I have asked the hotel manager if it has been handed in at the desk, but as yet it has not. I just thought that there might be a remote possibility that someone might have brought it here.'

The policeman noticed that as Dickens was talking, he was wringing his hands together and a note of desperation had entered his voice.

'I'm very sorry, sir, but nothing of that

description has been handed in today. If you want to leave details of where you can be contacted, I'd be happy to let you know if it turns up.'

Dickens nodded, disappointment registering on his face.

'I can be reached at the Washington Hotel, just off Union Square. Whoever returns it would be handsomely rewarded, I can assure you.'

The sergeant made a note of the address, volubly adding as he wrote, 'And a handsome reward . . .'

He dotted the end of the sentence with a sharp tap and then, satisfied that his business of policing had been completed, he asked with a hint of embarrassment in his voice, 'Can I ask if you'd mind putting your autograph on this piece of paper here, Mr Dickens, sir? Only my wife is awful fond of your books, and she'd be real pleased if you would oblige.'

'Yes, of course, no trouble at all. What's her name?'

'It's Doris, Mr Dickens.' he replied, the colour rising in his face.

Dickens wrote out a greeting and signed his name with a flourish, pushing the paper back across the desk to the policeman who looked at it with admiration and then thanked him.

'Don't worry, sir, if the diary makes an appearance, you will hear of it immediately.'

'Thank you, Sergeant.'

Dickens stepped out into the snowy streets once more. He was desperate to know the whereabouts of that diary if only he knew where he had dropped it. He had always been very careful to record the entries in shorthand, but nevertheless he did not like the idea of someone picking through the personal details of his life, trying to piece together what significance the assorted abbreviations might have. There were jottings about his visits to Elizabeth Cottage, repeated entries regarding money that he had given to Ellen and he cringed at the idea of what an inquisitive snooper might make of that.

He walked briskly along the street, his eyes and nose streaming with the biting wind but he resisted the idea of taking a cab; he always found it much better to walk when he had something on his mind. Eventually he came to his hotel, but when the doorman greeted him cheerfully, Dickens did not even raise a smile. He put his head down and headed straight for his room: he wanted that diary back. [The leather-bound journal written in shorthand was never to pass through his hands again: years later it would reappear at an American auction house where, just as he had feared, the personal details of his life became public property.]

April 1868

Florence, Italy

Ellen Ternan sat reading a novel on the patio of the Villa Ricorboli, her blonde head and fair skin shaded from the sun beneath a white lace parasol. A wrought-iron table and chairs were set out overlooking the fine gardens, which were beginning to bud with the onset of spring. The winter in Florence had been severe, leaving both Maria and Mrs Frances Ternan with heavy colds and, in consequence, Ellen had been disappointed to spend the early months of her time in Italy performing nursing duties, rather than attending dinners and balls as she had hoped. With both fully recovered, she was relieved to be enjoying the warmer weather at last and to be out of doors.

The month before, Ellen had celebrated her twenty-ninth birthday, and the neighbours had been very kind in arranging a party where she had been able to socialize and meet other families from the town. A small parcel had arrived for her from England, a silver jewellery box, chosen by Dickens before his departure, which had been left with Forster to forward to her at the time of her birthday, should she not have been invited to America.

Since her arrival in Italy, Ellen had received

several letters from Forster who updated her with Dickens's progress. Although she was pleased to hear that his tour was proving such a success she imagined what an intolerable mood he would be in with the pain of his foot and the inconvenience of a streaming cold. Perhaps it was as well that she was not with him, after all.

She closed her eyes and let her head fall back for a moment, inhaling the spring air. A cheerful voice broke into her momentary reverie.

'Buon pomeriggio, signorina.'

Ellen opened her eyes and saw before her a young man of about twenty. He was dressed in a light-coloured linen suit, held a straw hat in his hand, and was pushing his fingers through his mid-length dark hair. Giancarlo, the eldest child of the neighbouring household was the well-educated son of a Florentine banker.

Ellen sat up erect and smiled.

'Why, Giancarlo, how lovely to see you.'

'And also you, Signorina Ellen. Since your birthday party a few weeks ago, I have seen you only from my window.'

'You have been watching me, then?' Ellen smiled.

The young man gave a little cough of embarrassment. He could not admit that he had often hoped for a glimpse of the pretty young English lady who had favoured him with so many dances on the night of her party.

'Oh, not at all, *signorina, I* mean only that the weather has not been good for walking, so it is only by chance that I see you from my window.'

'Yes, it is a pity. I so enjoyed our walks together when I first arrived. We must take it up again now that the weather is a little kinder.'

The young man's face lit up.

'I should like that very much, Signorina Ellen. And may I ask, how are your mother and your sister?'

'Yes, they are fine, thank you, Giancarlo, much recovered now My sister, Maria, has travelled into town to post a letter to England. Her husband is engaged with business matters and unable to join us at present. Mama is in the house with Fanny and my niece.'

'I am pleased to hear that your family is well; I will let my mother know of it.'

An idea came into Ellen's head.

'How would you care to join my family and me for supper and cards, this evening, Giancarlo? And your parents, too, of course.'

'I would not miss it for the world. I will ask my parents when I return home.'

'At seven then, Giancarlo.'

'*Si,* at seven, *signorina.*'

Giancarlo nodded and made a little bow, before continuing in the direction of the town.

Mrs Ternan approached the table with a plate of bread rolls and a cup of coffee, and sat down next to her daughter.

'You should not encourage him, Ellen. It will only end in his disappointment.'

Her voice held a note of disapproval.

'Oh, Mama, I find it completely amusing that he believes me to be so close to him in age. How could a woman not be flattered to be considered almost ten years younger? Besides, I am not a married woman. Why should I not enjoy the attentions of a single man, if I so choose?'

'Precisely because he is almost ten years younger than you and because at any moment your status could be changed.'

Mrs Ternan took a sip of her coffee.

'Mama, we have been through this so many times before. For twelve years I have waited for Mrs Dickens to cease to be a feature in Charles's life and she continues to thrive as healthily as ever. How much longer can I be expected to put my life on hold waiting for a proposal? The best years of my youth are almost gone.'

'I believe that it would kill Charles if you were ever to break his heart by encouraging someone else. You owe him much, Ellen, we all do. Without him we would still be trying to make ends meet on the meagre earnings of a touring actress.'

'Mama, we have no idea what we would have been without him. But I for one would certainly have been married.'

A look of concern crossed Mrs Ternan's face. She put down her cup and saucer, and leaned forward with earnestness in her voice.

'You have no such idea at all, Ellen. Charles entered our lives at a time when they were filled with uncertainty. The very nature of our career made a prosperous match unlikely for you or your sisters. As it is, you have been well cared for all these years, and both of your sisters have elevated their own status through their connection with him. Would you wish all of that had not been so?'

'Of course not. I don't resent Maria being in possession of a house with servants and a carriage, and I am pleased that Fanny is happily married and settled here in Florence.'

Ellen watched the elegant figure of the handsome young man which was disappearing along the country road in the distance.

'But what I do begrudge is that I, who have made the biggest sacrifice, have benefited the least of all.'

Chapter 38

New York, America

May 1868

'My dear American friends, I am ashamed to say that as a young man I found little good to record about my visit to your country in 1842.'

Dickens tucked his thumbs in his waistcoat pocket and glanced at his speech notes on the table in front of him.

'On my return, however, I realized that I was far too full of youthful arrogance and I must acknowledge that there have been impressive changes in this fine country of yours since that time and, hopefully, changes for the better in me, too.'

At this the patriotic audience laughed and clapped their hands.

Dickens was about to return to England a very rich man. Neither he nor Dolby had anticipated how successful the tour would be: in just over four months he had earned almost £20,000.

The night before his departure, Dickens had spoken at a farewell dinner given in his honour at the Delmonico Restaurant. An hour before his arrival, he had felt so ill that he believed he could not leave his hotel, but still full of cold, his foot swollen and aching, he did not want to leave his hosts with any cause to write a bad report about him and he made a determined appearance leaning upon Dolby's arm.

With one hand on the table in front of him for support, he continued his speech. 'I could not have hoped to have been received with greater kindness or hospitality and for this I thank you all.'

The audience raised their glasses and toasted Dickens's good health. He inwardly prayed that their good wishes would have some sort of miraculous effect upon him as they had no idea just how terrible he felt.

For health reasons he had decided to cancel part of his tour to the west of the country, including Chicago: how angry he had been when a scurrilous story ran in the *New York Herald* that it had been with the intention of avoiding his brother's impoverished widow that he had shunned that part of the country. Dickens had been full of outrage at the article, for the public had no idea that Augustus' legitimate widow was still being cared for out of Dickens's own pocket back in England and the woman in Chicago who was parading herself as his sister-in-law was merely the woman with whom Augustus had been living until the time of his death. Thankfully that evening there was no talk of any such scandal, and Dickens was glad that the story seemed to have died down.

The following morning Dickens and Dolby were accompanied to the harbour by Mr Fields, who had also profited handsomely from the tour as his American publisher.

'Well you got me here in the end, Fields, and it has been an unmitigated success, wouldn't you say?'

Mr Fields shook Dickens by the hand with enthusiasm. 'I would indeed, Dickens, I would indeed.'

From among the crowds on the quay, bouquets were thrown. Dickens shouted his thanks, and put his hat upon a cane, waving in the air, before boarding *The Russia*. Halfway up the gangplank, he stopped for a moment, turned and looked out at the cheering crowds. He was greatly moved.

'Dolby, I could not have anticipated nor wished for greater success.' His voice quivered with unexpected emotion. 'I am indebted to you for your excellent management of all my affairs during the tour.'

Dolby shook his hand in acknowledgement.

'It has been my pleasure, Dickens.'

With a final wave goodbye, he continued along the gangplank. 'Now, Dolby, my friend, I have only one destination in mind.'

'Home, sir?'

'A little cottage in the picturesque village of Slough, Dolby.'

Chapter 39

Gad's Hill

May 1868

A basket-phaeton, a modest form of transport for a very important passenger, bobbed its way along the country lanes of Higham toward the station. The village's most famous resident had returned from America and the villagers had expressed a wish to make up a welcome party to line the route to Gad's Hill. Mamie, Katie and Georgina, however, knew that it was Mr Dickens's preference to make a low-key return and so had remained vague about the exact date of his arrival.

They were unaware that this was precisely the same ploy which Dickens himself had used since leaving the ship at Liverpool, in order to buy himself a few leisurely days in the company of Ellen Ternan before his official return to Gad's Hill.

The crossing to England had been calm and uneventful, having a restorative effect on Dickens, and he had stood at Ellen's door a bronzed and handsome man of fifty-six. Overwhelmed with the joy of seeing her again, if her own greeting had been somewhat reserved, he had not noticed. For Ellen there would be no more walks with Giancarlo, and she did not expect to receive anything from Italy written in his hand. Mrs Ternan with great alarm had watched the friendship growing, and casually let slip the truth about Ellen's birth date. As she did so, Ellen saw the light of admiration fade in the large, hazel-coloured eyes of Giancarlo, and in its place hurt and disappointment.

The basket-phaeton turned into the drive at Gad's Hill and Katie, who had darted back and forth to the porch since its departure from the house ran down the front steps at the sight of it.

'Oh, he is here! He is here!' she exclaimed, her excitement bringing the other two ladies out of doors.

Dickens was delighted to see the double-fronted house again with its bay windows and its porch lantern gently swaying in the breeze, but he was especially pleased to see his daughter Katie. He had been relieved that, during his time in America, there had been no bad news regarding the death of Charles Collins. Whatever reservations he had about his son-in-law, he was glad that Katie had been spared the pain of widowhood. However, she had also been denied the chance to make a marriage with Valentine Prinsep.

He stepped down from the phaeton and Katie flung herself into her father's arms.

'And how is my little Lucifer-box, eh?' he

laughed, kissing the top of her head.

Seeing Mamie and Georgina coming down the porch steps he held out his arms to greet them.

'My dear Mamie.' He kissed her fondly. 'And my own dear Georgie.'

Georgina offered her cheek to be kissed, saying in her efficient manner, 'Welcome back, Charles, have you eaten?'

'My dear, I have saved myself entirely for whatever you and Cook have rustled up in my honour. Please lead the way to the dining-room.'

'You look very well, Papa,' Mamie said admiringly.

'Yes, indeed,' Dickens retorted. 'I do believe that the doctor who attended me in America thought I would be dead before I reached England's shores. But as you now see, I am a man who looks six years younger, wouldn't you agree?'

The ladies nodded in agreement and, chattering with excited animation, they led him into the house. What he had not told them, however, was that he was having some difficulty seeing clearly out of his left eye, and that he could not control his left hand with precision. It had caused him great anxiety but for now, he was just content to be home.

*　　　*　　　*

280

After enjoying a noisy lunch with the ladies, he headed for his study in search of a little respite and was pleased to find that, although the room was spotless, nothing had been disturbed. A pile of letters awaited his attention in his correspondence tray, and it was the subject of correspondence which he now had on his mind. He had been giving some thought to the future of his youngest son, Edward. Henry was destined for Cambridge, but young Plorn was showing no such promise and Dickens had a proposal in mind which he planned to outline in a letter to his son, Alfred, in Australia.

He pulled out the chair from his desk and sat down again. Looking out on the verdant garden, everything felt familiar and welcoming. He eased himself back a little in his chair, closed his eyes and, feeling the warmth of the sun streaming onto his face through the window, he began to doze. A smile played about his lips and Marley's ghost addressed him.

'Ah, I see that you are sleeping, are you? At least one of us is able to sleep easy. You, my friend, condemned me to these confounded chains—'

Dodger interrupted him. 'Talking of chains, mister, if that ain't the finest bit of gold I've ever seen hanging off a waist-pocket—'

The kindly voice of Arthur Clennam interposed, 'Let him sleep, boy. Can't you see that he is tired?' And he put a finger to his lips.

*   *   *

New South Wales, Australia

August 1868

Alfred D'Orsay Tennyson Dickens stood in front of the bedroom mirror, and adjusted his new cravat. He reached for a bottle of macassar oil placed on his dressing-table, poured a little into his hands and applied it to his wavy, russet-toned hair. After drying his hands, he learned closed to the mirror, pursing his lips in order to inspect the condition of his moustache. His patted his impressive sideburns and nodded with satisfaction.

Alfred had been named after the flamboyant Count D'Orsay, a close acquaintance of his father's at the time of his birth. Perhaps the name bestowed upon him had also endowed him with the same extravagant tastes as his namesake, but Alfred was equally mindful that he was, after all, the son of England's most famous author and as such he should look the part. When he had left for Australia, he had no idea how angry his father had been to receive a bill from the gentleman's oufitter for a silver-topped cane, an onyx tie-pin, three silk cravats, and a beaver-skin top hat.

Alfred had been in Australia for three years and had had some moderate success as a station manager, overseeing the management of extensive farmland, and he was shortly anticipating the arrival of his brother, Edward. Young Plorn was now sixteen years of age and Alfred wondered whether his youngest brother had overcome any of his timidity. He certainly hoped so, for life so far away from England was not always an easy adjustment to make.

The latest letter that Alfred had received from his father spoke of his pride that Henry had just been offered a place at Cambridge. Alfred recognized that he had not been much of an academic success himself, failing his engineering entrance exams quite miserably. Twenty-one year old Sydney was enjoying life in the navy as a midshipman, and Francis was now in India in the Bengal Mounted Police, but it seemed that his father believed that it might make a man of Plorn if he were sent abroad and he had asked Alfred to find him a position.

Alfred reached for a set of gold cuff-links from the tray on the dressing table and smiled to himself as he clipped them into place. They had been an expensive indulgence to which he had treated himself on a recent visit to the city. He acknowledged that as a station manager he might not have the income of a successful gold prospector, but he could worry about paying his account at the store next month, for

now he had plans. Taking up his cane, Alfred
folded up his jacket over his arm. He planned
to spend the evening in a local bar, and fully
intended to make the most of the time left
before he was tied to overseeing the care of his
brother.

He took a final look at himself in the mirror.
He was grateful for his good looks; they had
undoubtedly won him a lot of female attention
since his arrival and he certainly could not
complain of loneliness. His eye fell upon the
letter on the dressing-table which bore his
father's handwriting. Opening the dressing-
table drawer he casually tossed the letter it
into it and firmly pushed it shut. Although the
name Dickens afforded Alfred a certain air of
celebrity, he was glad to be out of his father's
shadow and as far away from his controlling
hand as possible.

Chapter 40

90 Gloucester Place London
1st September 1868

My dear friend Dickens
I welcome you back to England, confident
that your visit to America could have been
nothing other than a tremendous success.
I have often reflected on the undertaking

of such a tour myself, but the perilous state of my health has hindered my ambitions in this respect so far. The pain in my joints is no easier, and when it is combined with neuralgia, I must confess that I medicate myself so heavily that I cannot remember a thing the following day. My physician has advised me to start taking a daily injection of morphine in order to lessen my dependence on laudanum, which I acknowledge has come to inflict the most frightening effects upon me. What I have written under its influence, God above knows! Thankfully, my most recent novel— The Moonstone—has been a tremendous success in serialized form, as you will know.

I cannot tell you how much I am missing Caroline, as much for her beauty and companionship as well as her efficient running of my household affairs. Her careful eye was often of value to me when I needed someone to look over my manuscripts, something with which Martha—for all I am fond of her simple ways—could never be entrusted. To think that Caroline is now the wife of that little chemist: I would take her back tomorrow if she would return to me.

How ironic it is that, determined as I was never to let a woman claim me in wedlock, I am shortly to be claimed by Martha in fatherhood. But I shall resist marriage to the end, and have decided instead to adopt the name and position of William Dawson, travelling barrister-at-law, for the purpose of registering the birth and giving Martha the name Mrs Dawson. Under the title of Wilkie Collins, however, my life will go on as before.

I think back with humour on our adventures of old, and miss our nights-about-town and our literary collaborations. I know that you have never favoured the match between your daughter and my brother, Charlie, but I hope that it will never be the cause of any cooling in our friendship. My regard for you is ever what it was.

I must let you know that I am greatly concerned about my brother's health, for you are sure to have heard that he is no better. Perhaps you could refer him to our own Doctor Beard? He makes no progress at all under the care of his own dithering physician. Thank heaven that Katie is such a devoted nurse. Let us hope for the best.

I send you my good wishes,
Your friend,
Wilkie Collins

*   *   *

November 1868

Little Holland House

Kensington, London

Katie Collins, dressed in a brown wool day-dress stood at the window, twisting at her wedding ring and looking out upon the large, elaborate gardens of Little Holland House: a house brought alive with its vibrant-coloured furnishings, and the echoes of intellectual and artistic debate. The doctor had come out in the morning mist to Charles Collins at Thurloe Place, but there was still no certain diagnosis of his condition. He had been vomiting in the night, and Katie had hardly slept: changing his night clothes and bedding, cooling him with a damp cloth and offering him a little brandy. At the conclusion of his morning visit, the physician had recommended that the patient's stomach required 'as much repose as possible, and a plain diet with little to irritate the digestive tract'.

Katie had wondered how much more repose her husband's stomach could take. She had taken to watching him eat, convinced that when she was not present, he disposed of whatever she put on a dish for him. She had asked the doctor for a prognosis and the faltering medic had been equally uncertain about that.

'Oh, who can say, madam? I knew a fellow who went on like this for three decades or more. A plain diet is the answer, madam—mark my words—a plain diet.'

She had closed the door after him and turned back into a house whose walls seemed only to be painted in shades of grey and echoed with the sounds of sickness. Katie was exhausted. She did not know if she could go on for many more days, let alone decades. She had not envisioned that her role as a wife would take the form of a life-long nursemaid. She did not want to see Charlie suffer, but his illness was suffocating her and wringing out of her every ounce of joy. She was struggling to find pleasure even in her painting.

She thought about her mother, Catherine. Loyalty had characterized her life, and it characterized it still. Katie knew that one word from her father would bring her mother immediately to his side once more, with all that had gone before forgotten in a moment. But she was not from her mother's mould: it was her father's spirit which beat strongly in her impetuous heart.

Valentine Prinsep had been watching her carefully, thinking how beautiful she looked, her gown complimenting the autumnal colours of her hair. He guessed at what was troubling her. She had been standing silently at the window for several minutes now, and he had noticed that she had been particularly distracted during the time that Mr Watts had been instructing her at her art earlier in the morning.

'Katie, my love, you are not yourself, today.'

She felt Val's hand upon her shoulder; when he moved to kiss her neck, she pulled away and he frowned.

'My dear, won't you tell me what's troubling you?'

She began to pace the room anxiously.

'Val, the guilt is too much for me to bear. All these lies are tearing me in two.'

'Come, my love, what lies have you told? Didn't you tell Charlie that you were coming here today?'

'Yes, I—'

'Did you tell him that you were coming for instruction with Mr Watts?'

'I did, but—'

'Well, then. Here you are; at Little Holland House, having had instruction from Mr Watts. That is the plain truth, my dear.'

'Val, you know my meaning. This . . . '— she struggled for an appropriate word— 'attachment between us. It's all wrong.' Val took her hands, and shook his head.

'Katie, please don't talk of our relationship in that way. What I feel for you is nothing more than honourable. If you were free tomorrow, I would marry you and make you my wife.'

Distress inhabited her every feature.

'But even then I am not sure if I would say yes. I could only become your wife if Charlie dies, and then my happiness would be dependent upon his death. Oh, then the guilt would be worse than ever!'

She dropped onto the sofa and began to sob.

'Oh, Val, why is it so hard to find contentment?'

He sat down at her side and began to stroke her face.

'You are a sensitive and passionate little flower, my dear. You feel things very deeply. It is both your worst fault and your greatest strength, and I love you for it. Come now, let me call for some tea, and we shall paint some more. You are overwrought and tired from your duties.'

'I don't want tea and I don't want you to indulge me,' she cried angrily, 'I want you to understand what I feel!'

'Katie, I know what you feel.' He took her hand. 'You feel guilty at betraying your husband, I understand that. But ask yourself, can you truly be unfaithful to a man who has never been your husband? Charles Collins took to his sickbed within weeks of your marriage, and you have been completely loyal and dutiful in nursing him. Has he ever asked you as a wife to do more for him than that?'

'No.' Katie's response was a thoughtful one, and she brushed away a tear.

'Then once and for all, relieve your mind on that point. If you wish to remain at his side and nurse him until the end, then I will wait for you, however long that may be, but you are not betraying him.'

Katie threw her arms about Val's neck, and sobbed upon his shoulder.

'Oh, Val. What would I do without you?'

He removed her arms from his neck and looking deep in to her eyes, addressed her with all seriousness.

'Katie, my love, I can only say that I cannot imagine anyone else as my wife.'

Chapter 41

September 1869
Gad's Hill
The Narrative of Charles Dickens Junior

The garden at Gad's Hill overflowed with colourful bloom: pink and white geraniums edged the path leading from the conservatory to the garden gate. My father had invited family members and close friends to stay with him at Gad's Hill, but when they had all arrived he had been distant and preoccupied, not at all his usual self. He had been so intent on working that morning that immediately after breakfast he had excused himself and bid his guests to enjoy his home at their leisure. The new novel on which he was presently working seemed to be driving his existence and draining every last drop of his energy.

My brother-in-law, Charles Collins lay on a *chaise* brought out from the conservatory into the garden. A check blanket covered his wasted legs and he was absorbed in writing a contribution for *All the Year Round*. In order to boost his meagre income, my father had offered him the opportunity to illustrate his new novel, which was to be named *The Mystery of Edwin Drood,* but despite completing the frontispiece, Charlie had been unable to find the strength to sit up for long enough to attempt anything more. My father found it very difficult to be sympathetic: if *he* could work through his pain and fatigue why couldn't Charlie, he had complained to me?

Mamie and Katie had just finished a game of croquet on the lawn with Mr Marcus Stone and Mr Percy Fitzgerald. Mr Stone, a young artist who had illustrated some of my father's earlier novels, was someone for whom Katie had occasionally sat as a model. Mr Fitzgerald, a writer and an old friend of Papa's was known to ardently admire Mamie; but despite making his admiration for my sister clear with an offer of marriage, she resisted him, just as she had resisted all of the other offers she had been made from various suitors. She and my aunt appeared to love only one man and, of course, no one could compare to Charles Dickens.

Mrs Ternan, seated on the garden bench, was engaged in animated conversation with Georgina about her latest theatrical appearance and was laughing loudly. Katie broke away from her partners in croquet, and joined me instead.

'That woman is insufferable.' She nodded discreetly toward Mrs Ternan. 'I don't know how Aunt endures her company.'

'You know Aunt. If it pleases Papa to invite Mrs Ternan, then Georgina will fall over herself to make her welcome.'

'And how is life working for Papa?' My sister teased, changing the subject.

'Just about bearable,' I replied with a grimace.

My business ventures had failed miserably and I had become bankrupt. It had been most humiliating to accept employment in my father's offices, but Bessie said that I should forget my pride and think of the practicalities: we now had a second daughter to feed. At least my involvement in the making up of *All The Year Round* brought me a little closer to my own secret ambition to be a writer, an ambition which had never left me.

'Where *is* Papa? It is not like him to be so unsociable when we have guests?' Katie asked.

'He is working on his novel and as usual will not spare himself.'

'Have you spoken to Miss Ternan?' Katie

glanced in the direction of Ellen who was walking the circuit of the garden apparently deep in thought.

'I have said a polite hello and enquired about her health. Like you, Sister, I have learned with the passing years to accept her presence in our father's life. I suppose she must feel a little uncomfortable being with his children, especially without Papa at her side to support her.'

Katie's voice dropped to a whisper.

'Do you really believe, Charley, that our father was living a double life at the time when he was travelling back and forth to France some years ago?'

I shrugged my shoulders. 'I suppose that we will never know the truth of that matter. I had my suspicions at the time, Katie, as I have told you before. And don't you remember how ill and seemingly preoccupied with worry Aunt Georgina became, over that summer? I have even wondered . . . ' My voice faltered.

'Yes?' Katie encouraged.

'Oh, I don't know, but I have even wondered whether at that time there could ever have been a child.'

'I see,' said Katie, casting a speculative glance at Miss Ternan who had now joined the company of her mother and my aunt.

My sister was not as shocked at the notion as I expected. She passed no opinion, nor judgement, which was not in her usual nature at all. And I began to wonder if Katie had secrets of her own to hide.

As for the sorry figure of Miss Ellen Ternan, she was soon to become a widow without ever having been a wife.

*   *   *

At the foot of the garden a Swiss-chalet—which had been a gift to Dickens from his friend Monsieur Charles Fechter—was positioned so that from the upper storey Dickens could write and glance out across the countryside of Gravesend. Seated at his desk, his head bent down low over his work, the sound of Katie's footsteps ascending the stairs caused him to turn a flushed face toward her and smile. She had been worried that he was neglecting his guests.

'Ah, if it isn't my little Lucifer-Box. How lovely to see you, my dear. Forgive me for being so unsociable, but I feel such an impulse to make use of every moment that breath is in me to work at my novel. God willing, I live to finish it.'

'Oh, Papa, please don't say such things. You are still quite a young man.'

He pushed back his chair and rose, taking his daughter into his arms with a kiss.

'I'm sorry, my dear, it was not my intention to alarm you.'

'You are working far too hard, Papa. I

want you to think again about recommencing your readings. The performances are a huge undertaking. I know that John Forster and your doctor have both advised against it. Why will you not listen?'

'Ah, my dear, it is only when I work, when I perform, that I feel truly alive. Do not fret, Katie, your papa is in an inestimable condition. Allow me to conclude this chapter that I am working on, and I promise to come and take lunch with you all presently.'

'Very well, Papa.'

Katie kissed her father, and took leave of him with a little heaviness in her heart. Dickens returned to his seat, took up his pen and peered at the page in front of him trying to find his place. Words and phrases danced on the sheet, the vision in his left eye alternately blurring and clearing again. He endeavoured to adjust his paper but his left hand would not obey him; he tried again, without success. He clenched his fist and banged it on his writing desk.

'Damn you, Edwin Drood, I will pursue you to the death.'

March 1870

St James's Halt, London.

A long queue had begun to form outside the St James's Hall, Piccadilly. The gas jets flickered at the foot of the stage, upon which was placed to the right a reading desk covered with a maroon cloth and bearing a glass of water. This evening was to be the occasion of Dickens's final reading. Seated at his dressing-table, he looked at his reflection in the mirror: his pallor was grey and his face deeply lined. He bore all the marks of a man who had not spared himself for one moment. His throat, sore from nights of animated readings, ached, and he called for Frank Beard, his doctor, to dress it with a hot mustard poultice.

'It is not too late to cancel the evening, Dickens,' Beard advised, setting the poultice about his patient's neck. 'I cannot be held responsible if your health fails you. After all, I have warned you of the risks.'

Dickens was also aware that his left foot, swollen and painful, throbbed angrily. Beard had informed him that it was a sign of the progressive vascular disease from which he had been suffering for some time.

'I would rather die than let my audience down, Beard, you know that.'

'And you may well do that, my friend, before their very eyes.'

Dickens laughed hoarsely. 'I will try my best not to inflict that drama upon them, sir, but no more talk of this matter, Beard. My mind is made up, you will not dissuade me.'

Charley Dickens looked at his father anxiously.

'Doctor Beard and I will stand in the wings, Papa. If at any moment you feel unwell, just indicate it and we will come to your aid.'

At this Dickens's patience finally wore out. 'I have no intention of being ill, so will both of you stop fussing?' he snapped.

The audience had begun to file into the hall and Dickens, inspecting his watch, asked Beard to remove the poultice. Immaculately attired in his evening suit, a flower in his button hole, he inspected his watch for a second time, and left his dressing-room to stand in the wings of the stage. It was a habit which he had adopted early on in his reading career, as a way of forming a connection with his audience before his performance began. Standing in the shadows of the stage he could see their illuminated faces watching for his entrance with hushed expectation, and his eyes scanned their faces as if each one were his personal friend.

Tonight he was overwhelmed with the sad thought that this was the last time that he would look out on such an audience and that he was about to part from them all forever. His readings had been such a large part of his life over the last decade and a half that he could hardly imagine life without them. With one last glance, he took a deep breath and walked onto the stage. At the sight of him, the audience rose to their feet in unison, greeting him with such cheering and applause that he could not begin until it ceased.

When all was quiet and still, their faces looking up at him full of anxious anticipation, the grudging voice of Ebenezer Scrooge cut into the silence.

'It has been seven years this very night since Jacob Marley died.' Dickens shivered, rubbed his hands together and, stooping, spread them out over an imaginary fire in a grate.

'If those two good Christian gentlemen who called here this evening believed that old Marley would have been any more charitable with his money than I am, then they would have been sorely mistaken. Jacob Marley believed, as I do, that the idle should look to their own labour to relieve their poverty, and not rely upon the charity of those who are industrious.'

Dickens scowled and blew upon his hands. He directed his narrowed eyes at the audience.

'Perhaps you believe, as my pocket-picking clerk does, that it is your right to ill-use your employer every twenty-fifth of December? Taking a day's pay for no work: it's nothing more than thievery.'

He reached for an invisible poker and stabbed at the dying embers of the fire.

'Christmas? Bah! Humbug!'

He became very still and squinted, looking into the imaginary flames.

The audience watched every movement of his features, waiting for his next words.

'That face! I know it. It can't be so.' He stared into the flames again, his voice becoming a whisper. *'It's Jacob Marley!'*

His face took on a look of sheer fright, and as his voice alternated flawlessly between that of the caustic Scrooge and the portentous Marley, the audience was transfixed. No longer were they sitting in a gas-lit theatre, but they were transported to the dark and chilly sitting-room of Scrooge's house.

'I have little comfort to offer you, Scrooge. These chains I wear in death were forged in life, and they will be yours also if you do not take heed,' Marley warned.

The entranced faces watched as the first of the three spirits which Marley had heralded, took Scrooge by the hand and showed him his life past. When Scrooge's tears began to fall at the sight of a forgotten boy sitting in a bare and melancholy room, the spellbound audience could not know that the tears which were stinging Dickens's eyes were his own, springing forth from the painful memories of his own wretched childhood. Standing in the wings, Charley and the doctor looked on, unable to believe that this vibrant individual on the stage was the same man who had struggled to his feet, his voice weak and hoarse only moments before the performance.

When Dickens began to limp pitifully as Tiny Tim, the audience saw before them not a full grown man, but an underfed boy wearing an iron calliper. With every breath that he took, Dickens's creations came alive, animating his features and inhabiting every gesture of his body. He rose above his sadness, his pain and his weariness and performed as well as he had ever done: a reading filled with passion, animation and power.

When, at last, the chastened Scrooge raised the meagre salary of his impoverished clerk, the audience cheered, waving their handkerchiefs in the air. The miser announced that he would be a better master, and their hearts melted. And when Dickens announced that Tiny Tim did not die but went on to live a long and happy life, the audience dabbed at their eyes and smiled.

With the promise of a reading from *Oliver Twist* to follow, Dickens announced a short interval. Withdrawing from the stage, he stumbled into the wings, his son and the anxious doctor taking his weight and leading him to a chair. His brow was beaded with perspiration and he pulled at his cravat loosening its grip on his neck.

'Fetch him a glass of water, Charley, quickly!'

Dickens waved his hand, his voice husky once more. 'I am quite all right, Beard. I have told you not to fuss.'

The doctor's face was grave, his voice serious. 'I must repeat my warning to you, sir. You are gravely ill, and your heart is under great strain. I believe that I must forbid you to continue.'

At these words, Dickens moved the doctor to one side with a flaying arm, and pushed himself to his feet.

'And I must repeat to you, Beard, that I will never let my audience down. Now let me pass, please.'

Charley had returned with a glass of water and pleaded with his father to listen. 'Please, Papa. Beard only has your interests at heart.'

But Dickens was not listening. He stumbled towards the wings of the stage, steadying himself with a hand upon a beam and then stepped back out onto the stage before his audience.

'What is he doing?' the doctor hissed to Charley at his side. 'He must be mad. If he continues with this performance he will surely collapse.'

It was with the voice of Bill Sykes that Dickens now began. If he had been unsteady upon his feet only moments before, his audience had no hint of it now for he stood before them erect, with the sturdy physique of a murderer. A voice full of treachery echoed across the auditorium.

'There's light enough 'ere for wot I've got to do.'

A voice answered in response, quivering with fear.

'Why do you look at me like that, Bill?'

Dickens's nostrils began to flare and dilate. 'You know, you *she-devil!*'

A snarl had become a shout.

'Oh, Lord, Bill. I've been faithful to you, God knows I have. I swear it.'

Nancy's voice was filled with terror.

Dickens's chest was heaving and, at the sight of it, the doctor in the wings took a step closer to the stage.

'Is he acting, or is it real?' he hissed at Charley.

Dickens reached out a trembling hand and grasped at Nancy's hair, pulling her head back violently. He placed his face close up to hers, and although there was no one there the audience could see it all and watched in awe.

'You were seen tonight, my girl. And every word you said was 'eard.'

'Oh, Bill, I beg you to spare my life. You can't mean to kill me, Bill. Think of everything I've given up for you. Oh, please, Bill, please!'

Dickens shook his arm violently as if flinging her off.

'Bill, it ain't too late to repent. For God's

sake, stop before you spill my blood.' She was clawing at him again, trying to lay her head upon his breast.

Dickens reached into his pocket and, drawing out an invisible pistol, he raised his arm and beat it twice with the greatest force upon the pathetic face that was upturned toward his. The audience raised their hands to their mouths in horror. As she fell to the ground Dickens staggered backwards, shielding the sight of her gashed and bloodied head with his hand.

*   *   *

The characters faded away again beyond the footlights, and disappeared. Dickens lowered his hand, his eyes piercing the darkness as if he were searching the blackness to see if they had really gone. A momentary silence was broken by a flood of applause, the audience rising to their feet, cheering again and again. He nodded in acknowledgement of their love, absorbing the applause which he knew would be his for the last time, and then quieted them with his hand: it was time to say farewell.

The applause faded gradually and he spoke.

'My dear friends, I cannot disguise the heavy heart with which I close this period of my life. For some fifteen years you have been my faithful and devoted audience and it is my heartfelt wish that you know of the love with which I have carried out my labours in connection with you. Although you will see me no more on the stage, I believe that I will never be far away from you in the words of my novels. The sadness that I feel at such a final goodbye is painful, but from these garish lights I must vanish now for evermore, with a grateful, respectful and affectionate farewell.'

He raised his fingers to his lips and imparted a kiss to them.

'My work here is now at end.'

He made a small bow, and his audience began to applaud him over and over.

The gas-lights flickered and Charles Dickens vanished into the shadows.

Epilogue

June 1883

Rochester, Kent

An attractive woman of middle years, dressed in a blue and green gingham gown, circled Rochester Cathedral, her closed parasol occasionally chafing against the flagstones. She was experiencing a little physical discomfort today and her slender fingers gripped the handle of her parasol more firmly than usual. A railway accident at Staplehurst some years before had caused her to be thrown to the carriage floor, and had since left her with recurring pain in her right arm. She never spoke of it though, nor complained of her pain. In fact, her husband and her two young children had no idea that she had ever been in such an accident. It was one of many things which they did not know about her hidden history.

Coming to the cathedral door, Ellen Ternan stopped and inspected the pendant watch which hung from her neck: she was waiting for someone. Also in Rochester that morning Georgina Hogarth, dressed in black, her hair now greying, was making her way toward the cathedral too. Her eyes were not what they

307

had been, and she did not know if she would recognize the woman whom she had come to meet. Their encounters had been infrequent in the years since Dickens's death, but neither had seemed able to break the connection which linked them to the same man.

Georgina found herself watching over Ellen's wellbeing from a distance, sure that Charles would have wanted her to do so. However, there was a principal motive which had never left her: the motive to ensure that old secrets remained hidden. With the years that had passed since his death, Georgina had guarded her brother in-law's reputation zealously. Assisted by Mamie, she had gathered together Dickens's correspondence and carefully chosen to publish, in volume form, only those letters which represented him as a man beyond reproach.

Now Miss Ellen Ternan was married to Mr George Wharton Robinson who had been led to believe that his wife was as much as fourteen years younger than her actual age. Georgina was confident that Ellen would not reveal an episode in her life which would contradict this convenient fabrication. Nevertheless, she watched over her still.

Standing at the cathedral door, Ellen remembered the last time that she had been in this ancient city: a morning similar to this one, the sun sending down its rays in sparkling shafts though the trees. Thirteen years had passed since that day, and she had not known it then, but three days later Dickens would be dead. They had wandered along Crow Lane together and, with an air of reflection in his face, Dickens had stopped outside the wrought-iron gate of Restoration House and smiled. He had taken the name of another house nearby, *Satis,* and—appending it to the property before him—he had created a home for one of his most famous characters.

'You know, my dear girl,' he had said, 'I can still picture Miss Haversham now, just as I did the first time I saw this house. If we entered inside, it would be no surprise to me to find her still sitting in the flickering candlelight and dressed in her cobwebbed gown.'

Ellen had looked up at the imposing brick facade of the house and nodded thoughtfully. She had just been about to make a response when Dickens's expression had changed abruptly, and he had raised his hand suddenly to his head as if he had been struck sharply in the eye. Ellen had been greatly concerned and, despite his repeated reassurance, she had known in her heart that he was not at all well. They had crossed the cobbled stones of the lane to the lawns opposite and, taking a rolled-up blanket from the basket on her arm, she had laid it on the ground, encouraging him to sit down.

His visit that day had been with the intention of making some notes for his latest novel, *The Mystery of Edwin Drood.* He had walked the circuit of the city, as he had done many times before, exploring narrow lanes and scribbling down his ideas; but the jottings he had made during that visit had remained in his notebook, as if the greatest mystery of all was to leave his final story unfinished.

Dickens had been prepared for his death, his affairs were in order and his will had been both generous and discreet: one thousand pounds was to be put in trust for Ellen. No one could publicly express disapproval, for the same amount had been left to his daughters. And wasn't that what he had always maintained Ellen had been to him? Nothing more than a daughter.

But Ellen had not been prepared for his death and for weeks she had found herself imagining that she could hear his footsteps approaching the house. At any moment she had expected him to appear at her door, his face flushed with excitement at some news he had to share. So great had been his presence in her life that she had begun to see and hear him everywhere; and believing that she was going insane, she had travelled to stay with her sister and brother-in-law in Italy.

Even here, she had been unable to escape her past. A visit to the town had unexpectedly brought her face to face with Giancarlo, strolling arm-in-arm with his new wife. After exchanging polite greetings and enquiries about each other's family, both had walked on, looking back fleetingly and wondering what might have been. Returning to England, unsure which direction her life would take, she was introduced to a young theology student George Wharton Robinson. With the practised art of an actress, Ellen had found an answer: she transformed herself into a much younger woman, and thus erased her past.

The sound of slow footsteps caused Ellen to break off from her reverie and she turned to see Georgina Hogarth approaching. Georgina raised a trembling hand to shield the sun from her eyes.

'Is that you, Ellen?'

Ellen approached her warmly with an outstretched hand. 'Yes, Georgina, it's me. How lovely to see you.'

Georgina took Ellen's hand briefly.

'You are looking well, dear. Motherhood suits you.'

The two women began to walk side by side along the leafy lanes of Rochester.

'Thank you, although I must confess it is very tiring. My little girl is walking now and I can't take my eyes off her for a moment.'

'And you have a boy too, am I correct?'

'Yes, Geoffrey is almost nine.'

'A boy and a girl. Then your happiness is complete.'

Ellen was unsure whether Georgina was asking a question or making a statement. She had never shaken off the feeling that Georgina was always making an estimation of her motives.

Georgina continued, 'When you wrote last, you said that you and your husband were running a boys' school in Margate.'

'Yes, that's right. And I am pleased to say that the establishment is running very successfully. Many of our young men are now at university.'

Georgina inwardly reflected how Dickens would have approved of such a venture. Casting her eye over Ellen's figure, she thought that he would also have also been glad to note that time had not been unkind to the woman he had loved. She looked much younger than her forty-four years.

'And how are your sisters, Maria and Fanny? I trust that they are both well?'

Ellen hesitated for a moment: her sister Maria had left her husband in Oxford without any warning, and was now living in Italy not far from Fanny.

'Yes they are both well, thank you.'

Ellen had learned only too well that it was not always providential to tell the whole truth.

The two women came to a tea-shop on the High Street. 'Shall we take tea here?' Ellen gestured.

Georgina nodded, and entering they took a seat by the window. The waitress approached, took the order and shortly returned with a tray, placing the cups in front of the ladies.

'I have been wondering, Georgina, if you might agree to present a prize for literature at the school. There are many manufacturing families whose boys are students and I think that your connection with Charles would be a great draw on prize-giving day.'

Georgina was hesitant for a moment: she picked up a teaspoon from the tray, removed the lid from the teapot and began to stir the tea.

'Perhaps it is a little indelicate of me to ask, but there is no temptation on your part to make public anything of your own friendship with Charles is there?'

Ellen shook her head firmly. 'My husband is vaguely aware that Charles was a kind patron to our family when I was a small child. Beyond that I am always silent on the subject.'

Georgina replaced the lid on the pot and began to pour out tea for them both.

'Then, yes, I will consider your request.' Georgina nodded. 'Do you take milk, dear?'

'Yes, thank you. And thank you for agreeing to attend the prize-giving. The school will be very grateful to you.'

Taking a sip from her tea, Georgina changed the subject.

'Did you know that my sister, Catherine, passed away? I don't think she ever really recovered from young Sydney's death at sea.'

'Yes, I read of it in the newspaper. The children must have been very sad at the loss of another brother and then Catherine also.'

'Katie took her mother's death very badly for she had become quite close to her in recent years.'

Ellen called to mind the vibrant, auburn-haired young woman who had been so like her father in looks and manner.

'I heard that sadly Mr Collins also passed away after his own long illness.'

'Yes, Katie is re-married now Another artist, wouldn't you know?'

Ellen was curious.

'Was it Mr Prinsep? I remember how much she admired his work?'

'No, it was not Mr Prinsep. Katie was introduced to an Italian artist, Mr Carlo Perugini by Lord Leighton and they fell in love very quickly. We were all rather surprised at the speed of the marriage. But I suppose poor Katie had been sad for so long at Mr Collins's illness, she was desperate to be happy again.'

'Well, then I am very pleased for her. And what news of the boys?' asked Ellen with interest.

Georgina's face brightened. 'Plorn and Alfred are in partnership together out in Australia, and Henry is making a great success of his career in law. I must confess that I was a little concerned when Francis became quite reckless with his inheritance, but thankfully I managed to use some influence to secure him a place in the Canadian Police Force.'

'And how is Charley? I hear that he has had a third book published.'

'Yes, I like to think that his father would have been proud of that. He often felt that Charley lacked determination.'

'Well, I'm sure that Charles wouldn't have minded being proved wrong in that respect,' Ellen replied.

For a few moments, an awkward silence fell over the two women and both sipped at their tea again, neither sure what more there was to say. It was Ellen who finally spoke.

'They were rather extraordinary years, weren't they, Georgina?'

Georgina nodded and answered gently, 'Yes, quite extraordinary.'

'I find myself thinking about Charles every day and smiling to myself over some thing which he would have found amusing or, in turn, enraging.'

Ellen laughed and both women came to life again, reminiscing about things which Dickens had said and done.

'Do you remember how he seemed able to hear everything that was said at the dinner table, turning his head this way and that without ever seeming tired?'

'Yes, his energy was boundless,' Georgina agreed. 'And if there were guests at Gad's Hill they always felt obliged to be doing something.

315

If ever Charles caught Wilkie Collins napping in the library, poor Wilkie used to jump to his feet at once!'

They laughed in unison and then when the laughter gradually subsided they were quiet again.

Ellen asked softly, 'Do you think when we are gone, Georgina, that he will be remembered long into the future?'

Georgina smiled wistfully.

'It is true to say that he had his flaws, my dear, but he asked only to be judged upon his works. And I believe that on that basis, yes, my dear, Charles Dickens will be remembered long into the future.'

Appendix

Chapter 1

Charles Dickens Jr, known as Charley, was born in 1837 and was the eldest of Dickens's ten children.

The play *The Frozen Deep* was a collaboration between Wilkie Collins and Charles Dickens, first performed on 6 January, 1857 at Tavistock House.

The drug laudanum was a combination of opium and alcohol, used by Collins to ease the symptoms of gout and rheumatism. He was to become increasingly addicted to the drug for which there were no legal restrictions until 1868.

Chapter 2

In a letter to Wilkie Collins, dated 22 April, 1856, Dickens describes the occasion when he first saw the woman with the Indian shawl in the city of Paris. He described her as 'handsome, regardless and brooding' and told Collins that he meant to walk about in the night to look for her, in order that he might know more about her. If he ever found her again, an account does not exist of it.

Chapters 3

Urania Cottage was situated in Lime Grove, Shepherd's Bush. The home for fallen women was opened from 1847 until 1862 and opened its doors to more than eighty women. Despite the offer of an education, and a new life overseas, it was not unusual for some to return to their former life.

Chapter 4

The former home of Charles Dickens at Gad's Hill bears a plaque which alludes to the words of John Dickens who said that his son might live in a house like that, if he worked hard enough. Charles Dickens lived there from 1857 until his death in 1870.

Chapters 5 and 6

Mary Hogarth, the sister of Catherine Dickens, occupied a special place in Dickens's heart. In a letter to John Forster he wrote that 'I don't think that there ever was love like that which I bear for her'. Maria Beadnell was the daughter of a wealthy banker who considered the unknown journalist, Charles Dickens, to be an unworthy son-in-law. Dickens subsequently married Catherine.

Augusta de la Rue, who was known to fall into fits and to experience night terrors, was treated by Dickens with a form of mesmerism during his initial visit to Genoa in 1844. Dickens revisited the de la Rues in the year 1853 when he travelled to Italy in the company of Wilkie Collins. The meeting between Catherine and Augusta in 1857 is fictional.

Chapter 7

According to biographical sources, the effects of laudanum caused Wilkie Collins to hallucinate and to experience the most terrible nightmares.

Chapter 8

In 1857 Dickens invited Hans Christian Anderson to stay for a fortnight at Gad's Hill. Anderson outstayed his welcome by another three weeks. In a record of his visit, Anderson spoke highly of Catherine Dickens. His reaction to the criticism of his work and Dickens's response to this is factual.

Dickens was known to treat his servants very well, and the incident of the young maid who injured her arm is based on fact.

Chapter 9

The meeting between Wilkie Collins and a woman known as Caroline Graves, who ran out into the night dressed in white robes is well documented.

Chapter 10

Dickens met the young actress Ellen Ternan when she took part in performances of *The Frozen Deep* to raise money for the Douglas Jerrold Benevolent Fund. Dickens's refusal to meet Queen Victoria while wearing his costume is well documented.

Chapters 11 and 12

Dickens and Collins travelled to Doncaster with the purpose of reporting
upon the races. During the same week, Ellen Ternan was appearing at a theatre in Doncaster in a play entitled *The Ladies Club*. A newspaper account of the time reports an

occasion when Dickens was seen sitting in a box at that same theatre.

Chapter 13

Wilkie Collins sprained his ankle while walking with Dickens on Carrick Fell in Cumbria. During this trip Collins took notes which formed the basis of articles about the North of England, intended for publication in the journal *Household Words*.

Caroline Graves described herself as the daughter of a gentleman named Courtenay, and claimed her late husband, George Graves, was of independent means. She was in fact the daughter of a carpenter, John Compton, and had been christened Elizabeth. The incident between Caroline Graves and the man in Regent's Park is fictionalized.

Chapters 14 and 15

Charles Dickens Junior joined his mother at Gloucester Crescent. The rest of Catherine Dickens's children remained with their father at Tavistock House, and later at Gad's Hill, until adulthood.

Chapter 16

On 12 June 1858 Charles Dickens published an article in *Household Words* under the heading 'Personal', in which he commented upon his domestic situation. *The Times* also printed the same article. When Dickens's own publishers refused to print the article in *Punch,* on the grounds that they did not think it suitable for a humorous journal, Dickens ended his relationship with them.

The hiatus in Dickens's friendship with the writer, William Thackeray, was caused when Thackeray tried to clarify the innocent position of Georgina Hogarth in the break up of Dickens's marriage. His well-meaning comments, made at The Garrick Club, inadvertently caused Dickens to become the subject of gossip and in order to preserve Dickens's reputation Georgina Hogarth agreed to submit to a doctor's examination which certified her as *virgin intacto*.

Chapter 17

A number of biographical sources record an occasion when an item of jewellery intended for Ellen Ternan fell into the hands of Catherine Dickens by error. The Association for Promoting the General Welfare for the Blind was founded in 1854 by Miss Elizabeth Gilbert. Although Dickens was involved in many charitable acts both public and private, the incident concerning the blind beggar is fictional.

Chapter 18

Edward Bulwer Lytton Dickens, known to his family as Plorn, was privately educated at a small school in Tunbridge Wells, unlike his other brothers who had been schooled overseas. He was considered to be of a cautious disposition and the phantom of his imagination was indeed an asthmatic sheep residing in the fields at Gad's Hill.

Chapter 19

By the end of 1858, Charles Dickens had given more than one hundred readings across England, Scotland and Ireland over a twelve-month period. This was to yield huge financial returns. At this time Ellen Ternan was still pursuing her own career as an actress.

Chapter 20

Charles Allston Collins, the younger brother of Wilkie Collins, was influenced by the Pre-Raphaelite movement and his work, *Convent Thoughts*, was exhibited at The Royal Academy. Charles Collins abandoned art in favour of a literary career in which he experienced nominal success.

Chapter 21

By 1859 Caroline Graves and her daughter, Elizabeth, were installed at 124 Albany Street. Wilkie Collins continued to reside with his mother at Hanover Terrace. *The Woman in White*, written by Wilkie Collins, was published in serial form in 1860.

Chapters 22 and 23

In March 1859, Catherine Dickens wrote to Angela Burdett-Coutts and asked her to appeal to Dickens to end the separation. Dickens refused in the strongest terms.

While Ellen Ternan and her sister, Maria, were residing at 31 Berners Street, a man describing himself as a policeman enquired about the domestic arrangements of the household. Why he did this was unclear, it is possible that he was paid by a man with unscrupulous intentions toward the Ternan girls. Whatever the true explanation, Dickens was outraged.

Chapter 24

Dickens, who suffered from insomnia, often took lengthy night walks. His observations from such occasions form the basis of articles under the title of *The Uncommercial Traveller* and were published in Dickens's own journal *All The Year Round.*

Chapter 25

Catherine Dickens was not present at the marriage of her daughter Katie to Charles Collins. The incident where Dickens weeps into Katie's gown after she had gone is well documented.

Chapter 26

The painting by John Everett Millais, which features Katie Dickens as a model is entitled *The Black Brunswicker.* During his time with Katie in Paris, Charles Collins began the notes which would form his first novel *A Cruise upon Wheels.* There were no children from the marriage.

Upon learning of the death of his brother, Alfred, Charles Dickens made all the necessary funeral arrangements and found accommodation for his sister-in-law and her children close to Gad's Hill.

Chapter 27

The London General Mourning Warehouse was situated in Regent Street. Dickens's dislike of the funereal customs of his time were well known to his family.

Suicide rates among young women living in London were very high. A report, written for *Uncommercial Traveller* articles, records an account concerning a young woman found dead on the canal path. During the years that Urania Cottage was open, four women by the name of Sarah are recorded as living there. None of these are directly connected with the individual of whom Dickens wrote.

Chapter 28

During the estrangement between William Thackeray and Charles Dickens, a strong friendship sprang up between Katie and Thackeray. Katie also re-established her friendship with the Thackeray girls.

Chapter 29

During the month of December, Dickens gave ten readings across Scotland, the north of England and Birmingham. Biographical accounts differ as to whether Dickens was obliged to cancel his reading upon the death of Prince Albert or whether he offered to do so as a mark of respect. He did not, however, view Prince Albert highly.

Chapter 30

Charles Dickens Junior married Bessie Evans, the daughter of his father's publisher Frederick Evans, despite his father's disapproval. They had eight children. From the month of June 1862, Dickens's whereabouts became increasingly vague.

Chapter 31

Walter Dickens died on 31 December 1863. The account of Dickens having an uncomfortable premonition is based on fact.

He was not to learn of his son's death for another six weeks.

Chapter 32

The crash at Staplehurst occurred on 9 June 1865. Dickens was very anxious that the existence of Ellen Ternan as his companion on the trip remain anonymous. His physical and mental health was not the same thereafter and he died five years to the day of the rail accident.

Chapter 33

The painter Valentine Prinsep was a British artist who had significant friendships with members of the Pre-Raphaelite Brotherhood. The exact nature of his relationship with Katie Dickens remains unclear.

Chapters 34 and 35

Wilkie Collins witnessed Caroline Graves's marriage to Mr Joseph Clow in October 1868. It is thought that Collins met Martha Rudd in 1864 and that by 1868 she was living at an address in Bolsover Street. Between the years 1869 and 1874 Martha Rudd bore

Collins three children. By April 1871 Caroline Graves returned to live with Wilkie Collins at Gloucester Place. He never married either woman.

Chapter 36

Despite his reluctance to part from Ellen Ternan, Dickens recognized that there was a huge financial reward to be earned from reading in America. He made elaborate plans for a coded message to reach Ellen by telegram to instruct her as to whether she would be able to join him.

Chapter 37

A pocket diary belonging to Charles Dickens was lost during his trip to America. It currently belongs to the Berg Collection of English and American Literature.

Ellen Ternan's sister, Fanny, married the writer Thomas Trollope, brother of the author, Anthony Trollope. Ellen stayed frequently with her sister and brother-in-law at their home in Italy and did so during Dickens's visit to America. The character of Giancarlo is fictitious.

Chapters 38 and 39

Alfred D'Orsay Tennyson Dickens owned farming land in New South Wales, Australia where he lived for forty five years. He later went into business with his younger brother Edward 'Plon' Dickens in Melbourne. Alfred's wife, Jessie, died when she was thrown from a horse in 1878. Whilst touring America in 1912 giving lectures about his father's work, Alfred died suddenly. He is buried in Manhattan.

Chapters 40 and 41

The Swiss Chalet was a gift from Charles Fechter and can be seen in the gardens of Eastgate House in Rochester. Dickens's 'Farewell Tour' spanned the final two years of his life and encompassed up to eighty readings in England, Scotland and Ireland. His eldest daughter, Mamie Dickens, never married.

Dickens gave his final reading on 15 March 1870 at St James's Hall, Piccadilly. He read from *A Christmas Carol,* and the trial scene from *Oliver Twist.* He performed the 'Sikes and Nancy' scene taken from *Oliver Twist* for the last time on 8 March 1870.

Epilogue

Catherine Dickens outlived her husband by nine years. Ellen Ternan married George Wharton Robinson in 1877. She gave her age at the time as twenty three rather then thirty-seven, effectively making her two years her husband's junior. When her son, Geoffrey, discovered his mother's connection with Dickens he destroyed any remaining correspondence of evidence with the relationship. Katie Dickens was married to Carlo Perugini less than one year after the death of Charles Collins in 1873. The artist Valentine Prinsep remained single until 1884.